PRAISE FOR *BROUGHT TO*

"*A profound analysis of complicated family dynamics that should appeal to caregivers seeking inspiration and solace in their own lives. Wheeler's gripping novel is ambitious in the way it tackles the heavy subject matter of losing a parent to Alzheimer's disease ... another layer of complexity is added to the saga through the family's back story ...*"

—**Kirkus Reviews**

"Brought to Our Senses *is one of the most true-to-life, gripping accounts on the complexities of interconnected family relationships that has appeared in recent years ... Very highly recommended as a striking jewel that is a glowing standout from the growing stack of dementia fiction sagas.*"

—**D. Donovan, Senior Reviewer,** *Midwest Book Review*

"*A vivid painting by a true storyteller using broad brush strokes to illustrate the complexity of Alzheimer's caregiving on families in conflict. You'll find hope in relationships mended by the most tragic of life's circumstances.*"

—**Dr. Daniel C. Potts, Neurologist, President of Cognitive Dynamics, Coauthor of** *A Pocket Guide for the Alzheimer's Caregiver*

BROUGHT
to our
SENSES

BROUGHT
to our
SENSES

A NOVEL

KATHLEEN H. WHEELER

ATTUNEMENT
PUBLISHING
Illinois

8 ATTUNEMENT
  PUBLISHING
Illinois
www.AttunementPublishing.com

This book is a work of fiction. Any references to historical events, real people, or real places are used fictitiously. Other names, characters, places, and events are products of the author's imagination, and any resemblance to actual events or places or persons, living or dead, is entirely coincidental.

For information about special discounts for bulk purchases, please contact Attunement Publishing at PO Box 7003, Springfield, Illinois 62791 or info@AttunementPublishing.com.

Publisher's Cataloging-in-Publication
    Wheeler, Kathleen H., author.
      Brought to our senses : a novel / Kathleen H.
    Wheeler. -- First edition.
      pages cm
      LCCN 2016930589
      ISBN 978-0-9965555-3-1
      ISBN 978-0-9965555-1-7
      ISBN 978-0-9965555-2-4

      1. Adult children of aging parents--Fiction.
    2. Alzheimer's disease--Patients--Fiction. 3. Mothers and daughters--Fiction. 4. Illinois--Fiction. 5. Domestic fiction.   I. Title.

    PS3623.H4299B76 2016   813'.6

First Edition
Manufactured in the United States of America

In memory of my mother
With love to Paul, Sarah, and Annie

For each copy of this book sold,
a donation will be made to
organizations that support dementia
patients, family caregivers, or
research to find a cure.

And inside every turning leaf
Is the pattern of an older tree
The shape of our future
The shape of all our history

—Sting

CONTENTS

Chapter titles in this book are identical to titles of certain Sting songs as his music has been instrumental in helping the author write this story. But notwithstanding the author's gratitude for this inspiration, please understand that Sting did not participate in or authorize this book, and it has not been endorsed by him and no such affiliation or endorsement is intended or should be inferred.

FAMILY TREE

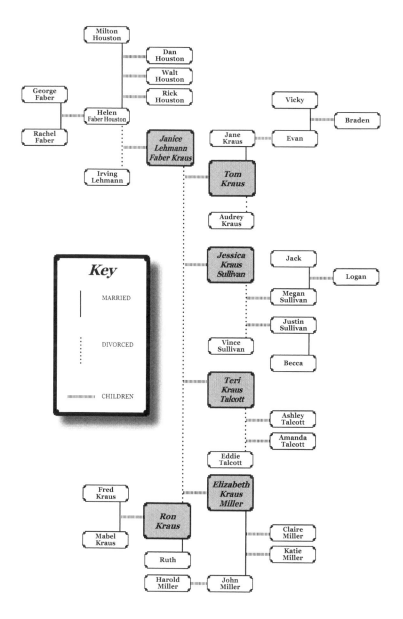

I

Ghost Story

May 22, 2009

I watch the western sky
The sun is sinking
The geese are flying south
It sets me thinking
I did not miss you much
I did not suffer
What did not kill me
Just made me tougher

—Sting

---

lizabeth had known for over a decade what would eventually claim the life of her mother. Now that the time had come, the funeral was playing out like an old movie on cable TV that she'd watched a thousand times. She'd known it would take place right here in Smithburg, Illinois, the small town where all but one of the Kraus siblings had grown up. She'd known which funeral home would host the service and what music would be played. The details had all been decided in advance, before Janice had declined too much. The only thing Elizabeth couldn't possibly have predicted was how her mother's death would forever change the lives of the surviving members of her family, her own most of all.

"Frankly, I'm glad it's over," she said to a dear friend as they hugged.

"I know, I know, but it's still hard. My prayers are with you and your family."

"Thank you, Darla, so kind of you to stop by." Elizabeth excused everyone from this awkward situation with the same reply. No one wanted to linger and discuss the killer by name.

"I'm so sorry for your loss," one of Janice's neighbors said to Elizabeth with a pat on the arm. "But at least she's not suffering anymore." Elizabeth tried to count how often the same condolence had been uttered in the past few hours from a trickle of friends. No more than twenty guests had paid their respects, although it seemed like she'd heard the same expression from them all.

"Yes, thanks for coming to see us," she said, as graciously as possible. The final visitor worked his way down the receiving line to her three older siblings.

Taking advantage of her chance to slip away, Elizabeth threw open the French doors to the parlor and invited grief into the mourning room she had prepared for the occasion at hand. She dusted off the memories, cleared the cobwebs of denial and anger, and readied the cushions of acceptance for a belated retreat. Grief, however, declined her hospitality and sent a distant relative named relief for a visit. The unwelcome guest took a seat and could not be persuaded to leave.

Elizabeth had once thought of herself as a good daughter. She knew that, in her mother's eyes, she was the best of three daughters. The Kraus siblings all knew it, unfortunately. Their dysfunction as a family had been built upon that fact, though it was only recently that Elizabeth had begun to understand and try to make amends. But how good a person could she be if she couldn't muster even a moment of grief? Her mother deserved that, didn't she?

Elizabeth was jolted from her thoughts by the sight of her father-in-law Harold entering the foyer—the *only* person forbidden to attend this gathering. "What are you doing here, Dad?" she asked. "I told you not to come."

"Well, I don't think that's fair," Harold said. "I want to pay my respects, just like everyone else."

"No, you don't understand. You have to go, please," Elizabeth said, motioning toward the door.

"I'm an old man now, Elizabeth," Harold said, his deep voice carrying into the parlor. "Can't we let bygones be bygones? Just let me stay for the service."

"It's not me—you know that," Elizabeth said as she glanced over her shoulder, but it was too late.

"What the hell?" Teri shouted as she broke free of the receiving line. In the previously quiet room, heads turned toward the commotion. "Why is he here, Elizabeth? You promised he wouldn't come!"

"He wasn't supposed to be—"

"Teri, keep your voice down," Tom said, catching up to her and reaching out to pull her back, with Jessica trailing close behind.

"I will not, damn it," Teri said. "You are not welcome here, Harold, so get out now!"

"All right, Teri," Jessica said. "You've said what you needed to say. Can you come back into the parlor now?"

"This is not the time or the place," Elizabeth said, holding Harold's arm firmly, her eyes searching for her husband. "John, there you are. Could you help, please? Get your dad out of here."

"Dad, come on," John said as he grabbed his father's arm. "Let's go—now. I told you not to do this. How could you?"

"'Cause he's an asshole!" Teri said over her shoulder as Jessica guided her back to the funeral parlor. "I wonder if his wife knows he's here."

"Just let it go," Tom said.

"Are you kidding me? She's still sore after all these years? I never understood—" Harold shook his head and continued to mutter as John escorted him out.

Elizabeth was just about to turn away when she saw another man in the parking lot. It was her father Ron. He was leaning against his car with his hands in his pockets, making no motion to come in. When he saw his youngest child had spotted him, he gave a slight nod. Elizabeth returned the gesture and headed back to the parlor.

The four Kraus children sat in the front row in birth order: Tom on the center aisle, then Jessica and Teri, and finally Elizabeth on the outer aisle. Spouses and children sat behind them. The funeral director came over and bent toward Tom.

"Sorry about the disturbance," Tom said. "Could you tell Reverend Wentworth we're ready now? Thank you." Turning to his sisters, he added, "Let's just get through this, shall we?"

"If we must," Jessica said.

"If *we* must?" Tom asked quietly. "I'm the one who has to get up and speak."

"Don't be nervous, you'll be great. And besides, there's nobody here but family anyway, thank goodness. It's not like anyone here doesn't already know most of our secrets."

Elizabeth leaned toward her sister Teri. "You'll never guess who's in the parking lot," she said in a hush.

"Has Harold still not got the message?" Teri demanded.

"No, shhh," Elizabeth said. "It's Dad. Our dad."

"Dad?" Teri said.

"Dad's here?" Tom and Jessica asked in unison.

"Yes, but he's just standing outside," Elizabeth said. "I can't imagine him coming in."

"Well, he's more welcome here than Harold, that's for sure," said Teri.

"And I thought this funeral was going to be boring!" Teri's twenty-year-old daughter, Ashley, joked from her seat in the third row.

Teri smirked, but Elizabeth remained stone-faced. "Oh, come on, Lizzie. That was funny, and you know it." Teri jabbed her elbow into her sister's side.

"Like mother, like daughter, I guess," Elizabeth said with a faint smile.

"And we're starting fresh, right?" Teri said.

"Right." Elizabeth took a deep breath. "Starting fresh."

Behind them, people shifted in their seats uncomfortably.

"Could we just get on with this?" Tom said.

"Good idea, if that's all right with you girls," Jessica said, looking pointedly at her younger sisters.

"All right, all right," Teri said.

The Kraus family sat quietly, listening to the final refrain of their mother's favorite hymn, "In the Garden." At the front of the room a flattering eight-by-ten portrait of Janice Kraus sat on a table surrounded by flowers, mostly red carnations and roses. In the photograph Janice was wearing a red suit and laughing. It was just a snapshot taken at a party about fifteen years earlier. Always an attractive and vivacious woman, she would have wanted to be remembered exactly that way. She'd used her beauty to her advantage, keeping her appearance immaculate and posing whenever there was a camera around.

Janice hadn't begun to look her age until the disease caught up with her. Alzheimer's had a way of doing that to people, as all the Kraus siblings had seen at the nursing home. They'd watched one patient after another come in, waste away, and leave for more advanced care, if death hadn't caught up with them first. Janice had outlived most of them. It was hard to say whether that longevity had been a blessing or a curse.

Reverend Wentworth stepped forward. "We're here to celebrate the life of Janice Kraus," he said, "and we're here to see what God has to say to us because God is a God of grace and comfort. But first, Janice's son would like to speak."

Tom reached the podium in two strides. He took a sheet of paper from his jacket pocket and stared at it. He looked at the congregation, at each of his sisters in turn, and behind them to his wife. Glancing back, Elizabeth saw her smile at her husband in encouragement. Tom folded the speech and stuffed it back in his pocket.

"Hmmm," Teri whispered. "Maybe he's not going to sugarcoat it after all."

"You think honesty would be better?" Elizabeth asked.

"Would you two be quiet already?" Jessica said.

The room fell silent as Tom cleared his throat and tried to speak.

2

Consider Me Gone

1996–1998

Roses have thorns
Shining water's mud
And cancer lurks deep
In the sweetest bud
Clouds and eclipses
Stain the moon and the sun
And history reeks
Of the wrongs we have done

—Sting

Early 1996 was a time of beginnings and endings in the Kraus family.

For Elizabeth, who gave birth to her first child on a snowy January morning, a baby girl felt like a fresh start.

When Tom announced on a dismal day in March that he and

Audrey, his wife of fifteen years, were calling it quits, life as he knew it seemed to be over.

For Teri, who'd finally had enough of her husband, Eddie, and fled her nine-year marriage in April, the need to move herself and two children back in with Janice was humiliating. She could practically hear everyone thinking, "*How predictable*," even if no one was saying it.

Janice hinted at problems of her own on a sunny day in May, though that wasn't the reason she called her daughter.

Elizabeth was staring into the cupboard at jars of baby food when the phone rang. "Hello?" she said.

"The most dreadful thing has happened," Janice said.

"Mom—are you all right?" Elizabeth put the strained applesauce back on the shelf and closed the pantry.

"No, I'm not, as a matter of fact. Teri and I got into it this morning, and I kicked her out. She's gone."

"Wait. What are you talking about? What happened? Where would she go? She can't go back to Eddie. Where are the kids?"

"I don't know where she went, and frankly I don't care. There's no way she could stay here with me, not after what she did. And the kids are her problem, not mine."

"What? Slow down, Mom. You're gonna have to explain because I don't know what you're talking about. What did Teri do?"

"Oh, you know how she is, same old thing. I just couldn't tolerate her using me. She'll have to find another way, and it won't be me doing her dirty work. She has some nerve, I'll tell you that!"

"Mom, what is going on? And where are Ashley and Amanda?"

"Have you heard from Teri today? I want to know what she said and how she tried to make this look like it's my fault."

"Mom, no one has called me, so you're gonna have to fill me in."

"No, I don't want to talk about it ever again. That's the end of it. They can blame me all they want, but it's not my problem. As far as I'm concerned, they aren't even my children anymore. Let's see how they like that!"

"Who is 'they', Mom? Who are you talking about?"

"Well, your sisters, of course! Have they called you about this? What did they tell you?"

"I've already told you, no one has said anything to me, Mom. Calm down before you hurt yourself."

This argument made no sense. It wasn't any more unusual for Teri to do things that upset their mother than it was for Jessica to bail her out. So that was the answer! Teri must have packed up her kids and gone to Jessica's house. That's where her mother got the ridiculous idea that her two older sisters were plotting against her. But with Janice still ranting on the other end of the phone, now was clearly not the time to convince her of the error of her ways. All Elizabeth could do for the moment was listen and come back to the discussion the next day when Janice's thinking wasn't clouded by anger. In the meantime, she needed to talk to Teri—and Jessica.

Elizabeth did revisit the disagreement with Janice the next day, and the day after that, and several times the following week. Every conversation was identical. Janice repeated the same details and asked the same questions, though as the days wore on she seemed to alternate more and more between rage and paranoia.

"I'm so angry at Teri," she'd say in one discussion. "Do you understand that, Elizabeth? Does Jessica?" But during another talk she'd say, "You don't hate me for telling Teri to leave, do you? Please don't hate me. Does Tom know about this? Does he hate me?"

"Mom, stop. Nobody hates you," Elizabeth said, again and again. "We're all just concerned. None of us really understands what happened, what Teri did wrong."

"Oh, so now you're going to start siding with Teri!" Janice would lash out. "Of all my four children, you're the one I thought I could still count on. No one knows better than you what your sister is like, and now you're taking her word over mine? How could you?"

"No, Mom, no, I just want to know—Mom?" The phone was dead.

"Mom? Mom, are you there?" Stunned, Elizabeth would try to phone Jessica to see if she had any better idea what was going on. But time after time, she got nothing but a busy signal.

"Hello," Elizabeth said when Jessica finally picked up. "I can hardly believe I got through. I've been dialing for a week."

"Sorry about that," Jessica said. "Teri's been using the phone a lot. You should see it around here. There are folded-up pages of classified ads everywhere, with big red circles and asterisks and scribbles. Teri's either making calls, or running out the door to a job interview, or checking out an apartment."

"I'm amazed at your patience," Elizabeth said.

"What was I supposed to do? Let Teri and her kids be homeless? What kind of sister would that make me? What kind of aunt?"

"Did it ever occur to you that if we were more like a normal family, you wouldn't need to be Teri's surrogate mother every time there's a crisis?"

There was a long pause before Jessica said, "Is that what you called to tell me?"

"No. Maybe a little bit. But I'm really just trying to figure out what happened between Mom and Teri, because Mom—"

"Geez, hold on a sec, Elizabeth. The kids are fighting again." Jessica covered the phone, but Elizabeth still heard her yelling. "Megan, Justin, please, just give the girls a break, okay?"

"What's the problem?"

"Well, you know, my two are your basic self-centered teenagers. They don't want anyone messing with their stuff, and they certainly don't want to entertain a toddler or a grade-schooler."

"That must be hard," said Elizabeth. "Ashley and Amanda must be confused—and scared about what's going on."

"Hey, look," Jessica said. "Teri's walking up the front steps now. Why don't you ask her what happened with Mom? I need to go referee the kids." Elizabeth could hear the sisters talking as Jessica tried to hand the phone over, though she couldn't make out the words.

"Okay," Jessica said into the phone, sighing deeply. "Teri is apparently just dropping by from checking a few apartments and has to get ready for a job interview, so she doesn't have time to talk now. But she says she'll meet you at the coffee shop on Jefferson tomorrow at eleven because she'll be in that area and has a big break between appointments. I, of course, will be left with the children…again."

"You know, you could just say no."

"I love you too," Jessica said.

─◦◦◦─

Elizabeth arrived at the coffee shop five minutes early the next morning, and Teri showed up ten minutes late. "Don't say it," said Teri a little breathlessly as she hurried in and sat down.

"I wasn't planning to," Elizabeth said, thinking of John at home watching the baby. "What would the point be?"

"You just can't resist, can you?"

Elizabeth felt her jaw clenching. "I just want to know what's up with you and Mom."

"Believe it or not, a credit card application set Mom off," said Teri. "I needed to get credit established in my own name, but the bank insisted on a co-signer because I don't have a job yet."

"Makes sense," Elizabeth said.

"Mom agreed to help, and she signed the form. When the bank processed the paperwork, they called her to confirm."

"So?"

"Mom told the bank she had no idea what they were talking about and that the signature must be a fake," Teri said, anger raising her voice. "So no credit card for me—a real bitch in my current position."

"That's ridiculous! Why would she do that?"

"Exactly what I asked. And she went nuts, like foaming-at-the-mouth, rabies kind of crazy, denying she agreed to sign. She kicked us out and said she was writing me out of the will."

"Well, that's not the first time she's played the inheritance card. Since there's no money, it's no biggie," said Elizabeth. "But Teri—"

"What?"

Elizabeth paused before saying, "No, it's nothing."

"Don't do that," Teri said. "I hate when you do that."

"What?"

"When you make it obvious you've got something on your mind, but then you don't tell me because—because you don't think I'm smart enough, or you assume I'll screw things up."

"I don't do that!" Elizabeth said.

Teri cocked her head.

"All right," Elizabeth said, taking a deep breath. "Maybe I do that occasionally."

"Yep, occasionally," Teri said. "So, you were about to say something about Mom."

"Actually, it's about Mom and Claire," Elizabeth said. Born in January, Claire was now five months old. She was Janice's fifth grandchild, so the newness of grandparenting had worn off, but something was wrong. "This is all still new to me. I've been struggling to balance motherhood with full-time work. I thought Mom would help, the way she did with you and Jessica—"

"So that's it," Teri said. "You figure because you were Mom's favorite, you deserve her time more than I do now that my jerk husband has kicked me and his kids out."

"You're unbelievable," Elizabeth said. "Am I hurt? Yes. But this is not just about me or Claire. It's about Mom." She looked at her sister for a minute, and then stood up to leave. "Forget it. I should have known better than to think you'd listen."

Teri watched Elizabeth gather her purse and jacket, and then

said, "Wait, Lizzie—I mean, Elizabeth. Sit back down. I'm sorry.
You're beating around the bush, and it's making me cranky. I've
got a lot going on right now, and my patience is already thin, not
that I ever had a lot to begin with. There, I criticized myself and
saved you the trouble. Now will you just spit it out?"

Elizabeth put her bag on the table and sat back down. "Teri,
Mom hasn't taken care of Claire once since she was born."

Teri stared at her sister for a moment. "Oh, come on, you're
exaggerating. You're her favorite—the apple of her eye. She should
be obsessing over your baby's every breath."

"Teri, how often did Mom come over to visit after Ashley and
Amanda were born?"

"Are you kidding me? I couldn't keep her away! I had to set
ground rules because she was driving me nuts, dropping by unannounced, always giving me advice I didn't want."

Elizabeth bit her tongue to avoid saying Teri could use all the
parenting advice she could get. "Right," she said instead. "And she
was exactly the same when Megan and Justin were born."

"Wait—what? You mean she really hasn't helped you out with
Claire even once?"

"Not once," Elizabeth said. "She doesn't even visit."

"Okay, *that* doesn't sound like Mom," Teri said. "Have you
tried just talking to her about it, asking her to come over?"

"Of course," Elizabeth said. "You know how close we've always
been. Don't look at me that way. I'm not trying to rub it in and
start an argument here. But you said it yourself. She should be
doting on Claire. And yes, I've invited her over plenty of times.
She's agreed to take Claire three times, and then cancelled every
time. But not even cancelled. She's just forgotten."

"Like how?"

"The first two times, I wanted her to come over and watch
Claire for a few hours so I could have a nap or get some housework

done. She just didn't show up. When I called to check, she acted like she didn't know what I was talking about."

"And the third time?" Teri asked.

"That was when I stopped trying," Elizabeth said.

—∽∽—

Elizabeth had given up one afternoon about three months earlier, around the end of March. She and John had planned their first night out, and Janice was finally going to babysit her newest grandchild.

"Hey, Mom, sorry we're late," Elizabeth had said, hauling Claire in her carrier and dropping a diaper bag on Janice's kitchen counter.

"Oh, hi," Janice had said after a long pause, eyeing the baby. "What are you doing here?" She'd been parked in front of a mound of paperwork spread across the table.

"You agreed to watch Claire tonight, remember? John and I are looking forward to an evening out—finally."

"What? No. I can't possibly do that, not tonight. I've already made other plans and was just getting ready to leave." She'd grabbed her purse and rifled around for her keys.

"I called you last week about this, Mom," Elizabeth had said to jog her memory. "I even had you write it on your calendar, see?"

"I'm sorry," Janice had said, heading toward the garage. "How about another day? I really do need to get moving." Her mother always seemed to be shooing her away these days.

"Where? Just where are you going this time?" Elizabeth had demanded.

"Well, I—I'd rather not say." Janice had stepped into the garage and held the door open for her daughter to leave. "It's none of your business."

"Okay then." Elizabeth had gathered her child and belongings in silence and followed her mother out. She and John would have to aim for a different night out with a more reliable babysitter.

—⟳⟲—

Janice's forgetfulness, her disinterest in her new granddaughter, and her decision to kick Teri and her kids out of her house were just the beginning. After their coffee shop chat, Elizabeth and Teri had decided they should sit down for a talk with their older sister. But before that happened, Jessica saw for herself that something was wrong. It was a Sunday in July, and Jessica was on her front porch watering a hanging flower basket when her mother drove up. She could tell the minute her mother stepped out of the car that something was wrong.

"Jessica, I have the most terrible news," Janice said in tears from the doorstep.

"Mom, are you driving like this? You're a mess! Come—sit down and tell me what's wrong!"

"It's Duke."

"Your boss? What about him?"

"Duke is dead. I just heard this morning."

While watching *Wheel of Fortune* in his recliner, Duke had suffered a massive coronary and died without a sound while his wife prepared pork chops in the next room.

"Oh, Mom, I'm so sorry," Jessica said. Duke had been a friend to the whole family, and to her mother in particular.

"I can't believe he's gone, just like that."

"I know he was much more than just your boss." Jessica chose her words carefully.

"He never followed doctor's orders after the first one. I was on him constantly to take that seriously, stick to his diet and exercise. But he didn't and now—"

"You need some time for this to sink in. Stay here with me awhile, okay?"

"Not even a chance to say goodbye," Janice said to herself.

Janice had been Duke's secretary for twenty years, and they had established a close relationship in that time. Nevertheless, her reaction to his death surpassed what any of her children could have expected. At the age of sixty-two she started forgetting days and times for engagements. She could talk at length about events long past but couldn't remember a detail discussed ten minutes earlier. She repeated herself often, asking the same question four or five times in a few minutes and forgetting what she was going on about in the middle of a sentence.

Two months after Duke's death in September the company appointed a new CEO. His first major decision was to close the Springfield office. Rather than offering Janice a position back at headquarters, he handed her a pink slip and said, "I wish I had more time to spend with my grandchildren. I envy you. You've been of great service to this company, and now you deserve to enjoy your retirement."

The loss of her job weighed almost as heavily on Janice as the passing of her boss. She'd always bragged about never retiring because she enjoyed working so much. A strong-willed woman vocal in her wishes, she suddenly became incompetent with the simplest tasks. How did she transfer money from her savings account again? Who was she supposed to call when the clothes dryer stopped running? And for heaven's sake, why didn't this key open the sliding door any longer? As if 1996 wasn't bad enough already, Elizabeth realized her mother was starting to imagine things too.

"Hi Mom, it's Elizabeth. How's it going today?"

"What are *you* doing calling me?" Janice said.

"Just wanted to see what you're up to," said Elizabeth.

"Well that's funny, seeing how you just told me you never wanted to speak to me again for as long as you live."

"What are you talking about, Mom? That's crazy."

"No, it isn't. That's exactly what you said, word for word!"

It took a minute for Elizabeth to realize what her mother meant.

"Mom, this is Elizabeth, not Teri." By the pause at the other end of the phone, Elizabeth assumed her mother had mistaken her voice. Although Teri had moved out of Jessica's and was renting her own apartment, she and Janice were still not on good terms after their falling out earlier in the year.

"Mom? Are you there? Are you crying? Mom, it's me, Elizabeth. What's wrong?"

"I know exactly who this is," Janice said. "Whatever I've done, I'm so sorry, Elizabeth. Please, please forgive me."

"Mom, calm down. I'm not mad, and everything's fine. You're just confused, that's all."

More phone calls were placed to all three of her daughters. And then visits. Janice started dropping in on her children and friends at strange hours of the day and night. She came to Elizabeth's house early in the morning expecting to go see a movie, and she arrived at Jessica's around lunchtime planning to be a guest for supper. She stopped by her friend Susan's long after dark to go shopping when all the stores were already closed.

―⁂―

Without a job Janice had too much time on her hands. Her memory problems became more pronounced as she idled away the hours, forcing a family discussion about shared concerns regarding her health.

Elizabeth organized the debate three months after Claire's first birthday. "Okay, Tom, it's Elizabeth. I'm at Jessica's, and she and Teri are on the line so we can all talk."

"I'm headed out on a date in about an hour," said Tom glancing at his Rolex, "but I'm all yours until then."

"Wow, back on the market already?" said Teri. "I'm not ready for the dating scene yet. I'm still trying to scrape by working as a single mother."

"It's been over a year since Audrey left for that lover of hers," said Tom, as surprised by the passage of time as his sisters. "Unlike our mother, I won't let bitterness keep me from finding happiness again. I've gone out with a number of women already."

"Good riddance to Audrey," Teri said. "She was a cold fish who thought she was better than everyone else. And what kind of woman doesn't want to have children, anyway?"

"Put your claws away, Teri," said Jessica. "Good for you, Tom. I'm glad you've moved on. That's hard to do. I should know since I'm still single nine years after my divorce."

"Yeah, well this one's special. Her name's Jane, and she's an interior decorator. Kind of funny, we met while I was picking out furniture for my new condo. I let it slip why I needed so much new stuff. We've been together over five months now, and things are getting serious."

"That's great, Tom," Elizabeth said. "I want to hear more about her, but for now we better stick to Mom."

"Okay, what's the latest then?" said Tom, sitting down to concentrate.

"Look, she's getting worse, no doubt in my mind," said Teri without pause. "She repeats the same questions over and over because she forgets the minute you answer her."

"Last year was rough—Duke's death, getting laid off, the family squabble—ahem," said Elizabeth. "But she swears once she finds another job, everything will be okay."

"She's got to be depressed. Maybe that explains her behavior?" asked Tom.

"I'm telling you, there's no way she could land a job," Teri said. "She may be able to keep herself up, dress sharp, slap on some makeup, dye her hair to hide the fact she's sixty-three. But listen to her for a few minutes, and it's obvious the lights are on but nobody's home."

"She's made no attempt to find work either—zero," said Jessica. "That's downright odd if, as she claims, a job will solve all her problems."

"Exactly," said Elizabeth. "That independent spitfire who raised three kids all by herself can't figure out how to apply for a position after working for twenty years?"

"Maybe she just needs more time to adjust to all these setbacks," Tom said. "I don't know. Are we jumping to conclusions?"

"Right, like she's gonna magically snap out of this?" Teri huffed into the receiver. "Come on, she's losing it. She needs a doctor or some kind of professional help!"

"Maybe Tom's right. We just watch and wait a while?" said Jessica.

"Tom hasn't been around to see what's really going on with Mom," said Teri. "And you know better, Jess. Get some guts and say what you really think!"

"But I don't know—"

"You're certainly not helping by yelling, Teri," Elizabeth said with a shudder, the tone bringing back the ugliness of their childhood together.

"Okay, stop. Let's all just voice our concerns with Mom—one on one," said Tom, knowing they'd never all agree. "If she hears from all of us, maybe we can convince her to talk with her doctor."

"Sounds like a good starting point, but that might be difficult since she's gotten so sneaky," said Jessica.

"What do you mean?" asked Tom.

"She's trying to avoid us now to hide what's going on," said Elizabeth.

"That's true," said Teri. "I've noticed she's not answering the phone, or she picks up and then makes pathetic excuses to end the call right away—sorry, gotta be someplace or do something—blah, blah, blah."

"Well, somehow we've got to get through to her," said Tom. "What else can we do?"

~~~

While Janice's children were arguing about her well-being, Janice herself knew something was wrong. She just didn't know what, and didn't want to discuss it with her family. She ended each heart-to-heart the same way. "I'm a tough old broad and can take care of myself—always have, always will. I don't need you or anyone else to worry about me, so mind your own business."

She started buying self-help books and natural remedies to improve her memory, always explaining to the staff in the stores that these products were for a friend, but she kept forgetting what she'd bought and purchase more. Several different brands of Gingko Biloba and books by different authors—or sometimes more than one copy of the same book—were scattered all over the house.

She transformed her kitchen cabinets into a super-sized message board with post-it notes stuck everywhere she could reach. The reminders ranged from the mundane "dentist appointment on Tuesday" with no note of time or date, to the more cryptic "don't call Tom," or the disturbing "your brother Dan died." But she never took the notes down. Instead, every few days she rearranged them in random order, even posting new scribbles on top of old ones.

~~~

"Now, when is Tom's wedding?" Janice asked Jessica.

"Mom, we leave this Wednesday," Jessica said, wondering whether this was the twentieth time her mother had asked, or the fiftieth. "Look at the cupboard above your coffee pot. You posted the trip itinerary right there."

"Wednesday," Janice said, "the fifth?"

Jessica glanced at the calendar. Tom and Jane's wedding was

clearly marked on Saturday, April 25, 1998. But these days Janice only kept a calendar on the wall for the pictures. One of her daughters always had to flip the page to the right month, but only when she was out of the room.

"No, Mom," Jessica said, knowing better than to try to explain the date. "This Wednesday, in three days."

"You won't go without me, will you? I don't want to miss his wedding."

"No, Mom," Jessica said. "We won't go without you."

—⚘—

Elizabeth stayed overnight before the flight to make sure Janice was ready on time, and she got through the boarding procedure without fuss. The chaos began the moment they lifted off and didn't stop until they got home.

"Mom, sit down, will ya?" Teri said from her seat on the plane. A friend was watching her girls so she could make the trip, but she felt like she was still babysitting another child. "You are worse than a toddler on a sugar high!"

"Come on, Mom." Jessica guided Janice back to her seat.

"Note to self," Teri said. "Demented mother does not do well in aisle seat."

"Teri!" snapped Elizabeth.

"What?" said Teri. "It's not like she'll remember what I said in three minutes."

"I'm tired of sitting," Janice said. "What's taking so long? Where are we going?"

"Same place as we were going the last time you asked, and the time before that," Teri said.

"Teri, that doesn't help," Jessica said.

"Like I said, she'll forget in a few minutes."

"I don't understand," Janice said. "Where are we going?"

"Florida. For the wedding. Remember?" Elizabeth said, squeezing the last of her patience from the armrest.

"So you're not exactly the model of patience either, are you, Lizzie?"

"Don't call me Lizzie, and don't give me that look. It may have worked when we were teenagers, but it doesn't now."

"This wedding trip will go more smoothly if you both call a truce," Jessica said.

"Wedding? Whose wedding?" asked Janice.

"Tom's!" the sisters said in unison.

Two long hours later the plane landed. "Oh, here it is," Janice said, standing up and opening an overhead bin.

"Mom, the plane hasn't stopped. You need to sit down," Jessica said.

"But we're here, and I need my bag."

"No, Mom. We checked ours at the airport. That one's not yours."

"This is mine," Janice said a minute later as they pressed up the aisle. She stretched for luggage in the overhead bin that looked nothing like hers.

"Pardon me, but that's mine," said the woman in front of her.

"Mom, *no*. Leave it!" Teri swatted her hand away.

"Why? It's mine!"

"No, it isn't. We checked ours, Mom! And your bag is blue, not black."

"Good, almost missed it." Janice grabbed one last bag near the exit.

"For goodness sake, Mom, let's go get your suitcase inside, okay?" Elizabeth took Janice's hand to lead her off the plane.

Things didn't improve at the baggage carousel. Nor when Tom tried to hug his mother and she pushed him away until Jessica introduced her to her son. Nor when they checked into the oceanfront hotel and she wandered off until Elizabeth noticed and pursued her. When she was finally asleep, the three sisters slouched on the couch in the main room of the suite, their feet on the coffee table.

"Claire is less work than Mom, and she just turned two," Elizabeth said. John had stayed home with their daughter so she could make the wedding. Now she wondered which of them was charged with the more difficult task.

In a restaurant the next day Tom and Jane stopped eating as Janice poured salsa atop coleslaw, plopped potato salad in a sandwich, and shook salt on chocolate cake.

"Starting to get the picture, big bro'?" asked Teri.

"Just let it go, Tom," said Jessica. "Of all the things she does now, odd food choices are not the ones I choose to fuss over."

"You're right," he said, returning to his own sandwich.

An hour later as the family headed out to the beach for a walk, Janice said, "I'm hungry."

"Mom, we just ate," Tom said. "You had a potato salad sandwich, coleslaw with salsa, and salted chocolate cake an hour ago. Those are pretty memorable lunch choices."

"Oh, okay." But two minutes later Janice said, "Listen, I really need some food. When do we eat?"

"Her appetite these days seems to rival yours during one of your teenage growth spurts," Jessica said, "and each meal starts the vicious cycle all over again."

"Wow," Tom said.

"Yeah, wow," said Teri. "It's easy to leave it at 'wow' when you have your great engineering career and a brand new bride in Florida, a thousand-plus miles away."

"Teri," Jessica said. "We've all made our choices. This is Tom's. Let it be."

"Yeah, Teri," said Elizabeth. "It's not like all your choices have been flawless."

"Easy for you to say, little princess," Teri shot back.

"Girls!" Tom said. "Could we just have a nice walk and try to enjoy our time together? Please?"

"Tom's right," Jessica said.

"Okay, fine," Teri said.

Tom picked up his pace and walked ahead of his sisters, his head down. His fiancée, usually quiet, spoke up. "You ladies do remember the reason you're all here is for our wedding, right?" She hurried to catch up with Tom and slipped her hand in his. The family walked on in silence for a few minutes before Janice voiced her displeasure.

"I'm ready to leave," she said.

"But we just got out here, Mom, and it's such a beautiful day," Jessica said.

"She means we just stopped fighting," said Teri.

"That too, if I'm being honest," Jessica murmured. "Mom, let's stay out here a little while longer."

"No. I don't like the wind, and I want to go *now*."

Ignoring Janice proved easier than arguing, so nobody replied and the family walked on in silence, each lost in their own thoughts, studying the sand at their feet. It was Teri who looked up a few minutes later and realized Janice was no longer with them. "Damn it, where'd Mom go?"

"She was right here," Elizabeth said.

"How'd she get away so fast?" said Jessica. "For an old lady, she can scoot."

"Let's head back," Elizabeth said as she combed the shoreline. "She couldn't have gone far yet." They quickened their pace, all eyes scanning in every direction.

"There she is," Tom said as they approached the hotel. "Who is she talking to?"

"The parking lot attendant, of course," Teri said. "Who else would an old woman without a car talk to?"

"Not helpful, Teri," Tom said, speeding up to a jog.

"I'm sure I parked it right here," Janice said. "Someone must have stolen it."

"Did you lock your car, ma'am?" the attendant asked.

"Well, of course, I always do!"

"Okay, let's step inside then, and I'll get some information to file a report—"

"Wait, wait," Tom said as he caught his breath. Looking at the attendant's name tag, he said, "Jay, is it? My mother's car couldn't have been stolen because she didn't drive it here."

"What?" Jay said.

"I did too," said Janice. "I always drive."

"Mom, we *flew* here," Jessica said. "Your car is back home in Illinois."

"Where are we again?" Janice looked around at the ocean and palm trees.

"Are those Tom's keys?" Elizabeth asked, grabbing the set Janice was waving around. "He's been looking for these since yesterday!"

"They're mine," Janice said.

"Right," Teri said. "And my missing makeup is yours, and Jane's glasses, and Elizabeth's shirt—they're all really yours."

"I don't know what you're talking about," Janice said. "And I'm hungry."

"How are we going to survive your wedding tonight, Tom?" asked Elizabeth, shaking her head at the thought of what their mother might do.

Janice surprised them all by getting through the wedding without incident. She understood exactly what was going on and beamed with pride as the mother of the groom. Delighted by the nuptials, she chatted with the other wedding guests after the ceremony, shaking the hands of well-wishers and accepting congratulations with grace.

"See, we didn't need to worry after all," said Jessica as she watched her mother from a distance. "Everything went off perfectly."

"Unbelievable how she can pull herself together like that," Teri said. "Let's hope it continues."

Janice saved the worst for last instead. "I'm tired and want to go to bed," she said from the reception later. Surf and turf had just been served, but she paced the banquet room parquet, unwilling to sit or mingle.

"Mom, we just got here, and it's only seven o'clock," Jessica said to divert her attention. "You don't want to miss all the fun, and the cake hasn't even been cut yet!" If anything could convince her to stay, it was dessert.

"Take me home, I've had enough. I do *not* want to stay here." Three rounds of rock-paper-scissors later, Teri resigned herself to driving Janice back to the hotel.

"I'll be back just as soon as she's asleep," Teri said.

But it didn't work out that way. Teri got her back to their room, off to bed, and apparently asleep. Just as she tiptoed toward the door, she heard a voice behind her. "Aha, caught you! Get back in here, young lady!"

"Mom, what are you doing back up? I thought you were sleeping."

"I'm not as stupid as you think, and you are not sneaking out again."

"Sneaking out—what?"

"You heard me. It's past your curfew, and you are not going anywhere."

"Curfew?" Teri laughed.

"There's nothing funny, so you can cut that out right now."

"I'm going back to the wedding, Mom. Thanks to you I've already missed over an hour, and how many more times do you think my only brother is gonna get married? Go back to bed, go to sleep. I'll see you in the morning."

"I'm warning you," Janice said, waving her finger at Teri. "If you leave, you're grounded."

Teri stood in the doorway, mouth agape. "Mom, I'm thirty-three years old, and I'll do as I damn well please. My teen years were ugly enough. I have no desire to revisit them. And I'm not staying here with you just because you want to skip your son's wedding!"

"Wedding? What wedding?" Teri took another step, wanting only to escape another explanation. "Get back in here, young lady. I mean it! If you think you're going to get away with this one more time, you're in for a big surprise."

Teri turned to look at her mother, so angry and frustrated she was ready to explode. But then she saw her mother's face—eyes wide, jaw set, cheeks flushed. Her mother was right about one thing. They'd been through too much of this when Teri was young. Even she couldn't put a confused old woman through that pain all over again.

"Okay, okay, Mom," Teri said, "Forget it, I'll stay here. Don't get yourself all worked up."

"Yes, you will stay here. I'm your mother and don't you ever forget it!"

"No, I'd never do that. Go to bed now, Mom. I promise I won't go anywhere."

—ᴦᴕᴕ—

"Kraus, party of eight," Tom said the next morning when they all met up to say their goodbyes before heading home.

"Yes, Mr. Kraus, I see your reservation right here," said the hostess. "So nice to see you again, and congratulations on your wedding."

"Thanks, Lori," said Tom. "It was a lovely ceremony."

A tanned blonde in an elegant black dress and heels led the Kraus family past the potted palms, through a maze of tables set with bright white linens, sparkling stemware, and china emblazoned with the club's blue and gold insignia. White-collared wait staff smiled politely and stepped out of their way, the smell of Eggs Benedict and cinnamon rolls wafting from their trays. As their party reached the large table reserved in the center windows facing the marina, a waiter appeared beside a shining ice bucket where two bottles of champagne were already chilling. He pulled out a chair for the guest of honor.

"Mrs. Kraus," he said with a smile revealing teeth as white as the tablecloth. "You look even more radiant than usual today, ma'am. Clearly marriage agrees with you."

"What a view," Elizabeth said, admiring the boats bobbing gently in the water a stone's throw from their table. "You get membership here just for being an employee at your company?"

"My membership is part of my executive package, which is a reward for years of long hours, hard work, and grueling travel around the world," Tom said.

The feast began with the popping of corks and the clinking of crystal in a toast to the newlyweds. While they dined, Tom and Jane directed conversation towards safe topics—favorite moments from the wedding, travel arrangements for later in the day, details about their honeymoon to St. Martin. Janice tried to keep up but failed, and then busied herself returning to the buffet so many times the others lost count.

Tom had no intention of sharing how disappointed he was that his mother had left before the reception got going. Her early exit left him riddled with guilt. He felt horrible for asking his father *not* to attend the wedding for his mother's sake, so his presence wouldn't set her off in her altered state. With the chance of a family scene so high, like at Teri and Elizabeth's ceremonies over a decade ago, he had thought it was the right move. Even though Ron had agreed, now the decision just seemed like such a waste.

"Megan and Justin, will you take your grandmother for a tour of the grounds out back?" Tom asked once the plates were

cleared. "I'm sure she'd enjoy the landscaping, and the view of the
Intracoastal Waterway is spectacular."

"I'll do it," said Teri, pushing her chair back in a rush. Still ticked she had missed all the fun, she wanted to grab a smoke and escape the stares of the rich snobs.

"No, you stay here," said Tom with a look that glued her to the seat.

"Um, sure," Megan said after an awkward pause. "Come on, Grandma, let's check out the flowers and boats." Justin tagged behind without a word, glancing back on the way out.

"I'll join them to help keep her occupied," said Jane, placing her hand on Tom's shoulder as she got up. When the coast was clear, she added, "Look, I went through some tough times with my folks too. It's hard, but you four need to get your act together."

"Do we have to do this now?" said Jessica with her fingers pressed against her temple. "I'm kinda regretting my decision to hang around the bar all night."

"Aw, sorry you're not feeling your best, Jess," said Elizabeth. "Indulge a little too much maybe?" She already knew the answer because she hadn't touched a drop of alcohol. She'd given up drinking since she was trying to get pregnant again, although she was hiding the news from her siblings. This trip had given her doubts anyway. Wasn't it crazy to want another baby considering this mess with her mother? But at thirty-two, she felt like it was now or never.

"You don't sound sorry," said Jessica, "but I sure am. I can't believe Megan drove me home in the rental car last night, and Justin lugged me through the lobby up to our hotel room. What was I thinking?" While she'd sworn never to make the same parenting mistakes as her mother, she'd certainly made enough of her own.

"Ahem. We don't have a lot of time, and Jane's right," Tom said to focus their discussion. "Mom's worse off than I imagined, and nothing's been done in what, a year? She continues to decline, and we just can't ignore this any longer."

"*We?*" said Teri. "Don't make me laugh! What you really mean is *us*, right? Jessica, Elizabeth and I need to take care of this while you relax down here at your fancy-schmancy yacht club!"

"Keep it down, Teri," said Jessica, darting glances at the other tables nearby. "It's not Tom's fault he lives so far away and can't help out."

"It certainly is his fault," said Teri. "He moved as far away as he could to avoid all of this!"

"Now hold on," said Tom, "You know—"

"How nice for you to make long distance demands without having to lift a finger to do a damn thing," said Teri. "It's not that simple, but you wouldn't know because you're not around to take the heat."

"Okay, this isn't getting us anywhere," said Elizabeth. "Don't be so hateful, Teri."

"Ignoring things, my ass!" Teri was on a roll. "We've all tried to reason with Mom. Explained the problems we've seen, begged her to go see a doctor."

"That's true," said Jessica. "She won't listen to any of us, won't admit anything's wrong."

"Then she starts with the threats," said Teri, imitating her mother unkindly. "Stay out of my business. I'll cut you off, don't think I won't! And I'll pack my bags and move back to Nebraska if you don't leave me alone."

"It's beyond frustrating to get shut out every single time you try to talk some sense into her," said Elizabeth.

"I've had those same conversations too, you know," said Tom, waving off a waiter who approached to refill the water goblets.

"Then how can you sit there and command us to do something?" asked Teri. "She's in denial, and that's not going to change no matter what you want."

"Damn it, my head is about to explode. I cannot take this one more second," said Jessica. "I'm outta here—gotta get some fresh air."

"Me too, I need a cigarette." Teri disappeared right behind Jessica.

The oldest and youngest siblings were left facing six empty chairs. "I'd expect Teri to blow up, but that's not like Jessica," said Tom. "What's up with that?"

"Honestly, we're totally fed up with Mom—the outbursts, the defiance, the spiteful things that come out of her mouth, all of it," said Elizabeth. "These last two years she's put up a wall we can't break through."

"We haven't even figured out where to start, and we're already at each others' throats," said Tom, his voice trailing off as he looked out the window into the harbor.

Elizabeth ran her hands through her hair and leaned back in her chair. "You know, we're not like these other families," she said with a nod to the diners around them, "privileged and perfect in their blue blazers and obnoxious jewelry. And we're never gonna sail off into the sunset."

"Yeah, I know, I don't expect a miracle. But we should be able to sit down and talk without someone going off, for crying out loud."

"Face it, Tom, we're pretty much screwed."

3

Synchronicity

1934–1951

A connecting principle
Linked to the invisible
Almost imperceptible
Something inexpressible
Science insusceptible
Logic so inflexible
Causally connectible
Yet nothing is invincible

–Sting

A scandal the size of the Cornhusker State rocked the village of Maxwell, Nebraska during the Great Depression. In a quandary, the church council called an emergency meeting to determine the proper course of action, naming their spiritual leader as the sole defendant.

"Reverend, thank you for joining us here tonight," said Barney

Henderson, the elder in charge. "We need to address the rumors, and we appreciate your cooperation."

"I understand, Barney," said Reverend George Faber, the minister of the only Christian church within hundreds of miles. "Ask what you must."

"Is it true then, what we've heard?" Barney asked, too embarrassed to spell out the charges. The news blew through the county like the merciless wind across the sand dunes and low-lying grasslands.

"Yes, I'm afraid so," the Reverend said. "My daughter has recently given birth."

Janice Mae Lehmann was born on the first day of spring near the edge of the Nebraska Sandhills in 1934. The newborn's unmarried parents, Helen Faber and Irving Lehmann, christened their child in honor of her grandfather; Janice meant "God's gracious gift."

"Reverend, with all due respect, our congregation does not take this sort of offense lightly," the elder said. "You've taught us that yourself."

"I've also preached about forgiveness, Barney," the Reverend said. "Regardless of my daughter's error in judgment, my granddaughter is a blessing from God. I accept this child into my home. She's going to need love and support more than most."

"Our parishioners are deeply troubled, George. I'm sorry to have to say it, but this mistake, as you call it, brings into question your authority to lead the flock on the Christian path."

"I see. Then I suppose I must resign my position to another more worthy of your regard," Reverend Faber said. "Effective immediately."

⁓⚬⚭⚬~

Things weren't just falling apart for the minister alone.

Irving tried to explain his own dilemma to Helen. "I need to go and make money for you and Janice. There's no work here."

"Stick around awhile, things have to get better," Helen said, fearful of being left to fend for herself and a child.

"Please try to understand, darling. If I could, I would. You'll both be in my thoughts constantly, and I'll write to let you know how things are going."

"Don't do this to me!" Helen said. "I need you to stay with us."

"I'm doing this *for* you," Irving said. "I have to leave and find a way to support you two, and I've heard things are better off out west in the big cities. You and Janice will be safe with your parents for now."

—✦—

Reverend Faber dabbled as a cattle farmer at a ranch not far from town. His wife Rachel, a homemaker with a hair bun twisted too tight, was reluctant to welcome a grandchild after raising six children of her own, of which Helen was the youngest and only one still living at home.

"Helen says Irving's headed west to search for work," George said from the rocking chairs on the front porch one evening.

"That darn fool couldn't find his way out of a boxcar," said Rachel without looking up from her darning. "I told Helen as much, but she had to go and fall for him anyway. And now she's cost us your ministry."

"Helen and her child will live here for as long as they need a roof over their heads. Do you understand me, Rachel?"

Rachel dropped her sewing on her lap and looked her husband in the eye. "There's no reason to raise your voice, George."

"Have I made myself clear, Rachel?" George said, lowering his volume a notch. "They stay with us, and you are not to go against my wishes. Helen needs our help to get by now, and we *will* provide it."

"Yes, of course. As you wish," Rachel said, returning to her sewing. Her husband had a blind spot for their only daughter, she thought, and that illegitimate baby of hers might just be the downfall of them all.

The townsfolk were less accommodating, refusing to release the Fabers from scrutiny, and Rachel's fears were borne out. The stares and whispers wore down their spirits, while George proved himself to be a better cleric than a farmer. Long before Janice's first birthday they relocated to the city of Lexington in a neighboring county, where George found a new parish. Life returned to normal, but because of the sacrifices on behalf of their daughter, the minister and his wife cared little about Irving's plight and were content allowing him to wander the plains without a steady job or a paycheck.

"Evening, Ma," George said to his wife after returning home one night.

"Supper's nearly ready," Rachel said, handing the mail over with a glass of iced tea. "And you'll find another one of them letters arrived today."

"When is that slacker going to give up?" George asked, flipping through the envelopes and plucking out the offensive one with his nose crinkled, like he smelled something rotten.

"You ever read any of those?" Rachel asked.

"I've burned every one without reading a line," George said. "I check for money, of course, but there's never a penny. There's nothing more Helen needs to know. And I forbid you to tell her he continues to write."

"Yes, sir, as you wish," Rachel said.

As time went by, Helen found herself too busy raising a daughter and working odd jobs to think much about Irving. She assumed he had given up on her, a familiar story for farmers at the time, when drought on the prairies buried everyone's dreams in the dust. But whatever Janice lacked in a father, she had many times over in her grandfather as she grew from an infant to a little girl under his protective eye.

"—and God bless Mama, and Grampa, and Gramma," Janice said with folded hands, kneeling beside her bed.

"Okay, Punkin, hop in," Helen said, pulling back the pink patchwork quilt, the same one that had covered the bed in her room as a child.

"Oh, come on, honey," Helen said as she tousled her daughter's hair. "Don't be silly."

"How come she never talks to me then?" Janice said, her voice nothing but a whisper. "She shoves my plate at me. And when she does my hair, she brushes it so hard it feels like she'll yank it right out."

"Grandma is busy, that's all," Helen said as she pulled her daughter close. "Besides, Grandpa is lots more fun, isn't he?"

"I love Grampa, he plays with me—a lot. And he smiles."

"Stick with Grandpa when you can, Janice. He's your best bet," said Helen with a sigh. She knew her mother bore little more than resentment for her daughter and felt guilty that her child carried the burden of her own sins.

Janice followed her mother's advice and spent much of her time with her grandfather at work, fascinated by the church. She loved choir practice and hid in the nooks and crannies of the Lord's house, listening to hymns she memorized word for word. She attended all the Bible studies and learned the passages nearly as well as the minister himself. Joining him on his rounds tending to his congregation, she became the familiar ragamuffin clutching his hand as they walked the beat on dusty streets. Janice developed a deep respect for God, and her devotion made Reverend Faber proud. She loved her days with her Grandpa, but it was always a bad day when Mama had to work and she had to stay at home to help Grandma with the chores.

Sometime after Janice's fifth birthday, the winds of change

blew a twister named Milton Houston into Helen's life. Much older than Helen, Milton was not a bachelor by choice but because a vile and violent temper had scared a short list of prospects away. He was the meanest junkyard dog in Dawson County and sunk his teeth in when he drank, which was more often than not.

"Today's our three-month anniversary," Helen said to Milton as they settled into the rockers on the Fabers' porch one evening. "I'm glad I had the night off work to celebrate with you."

"Is that so—three months?" said Milton, distracted as he fiddled with his pocket.

"Pardon my manners, would you like a lemonade?" Helen stood to go inside.

"No," Milton said and pointed to her seat. "I'd rather talk now."

"Well, okay then," Helen said as she sat back down. "Talk about what?"

"Helen, I've been thinking. Well, it seems like the right thing—your parents agree."

"What are you getting on about, Milton?"

"Oh, I'll just spit it out then. I'm no good at this sort of thing. Will you marry me, Helen?"

"Oh my, what a surprise, Milt!"

"Here," he said and pulled a ring from his pocket. "This was my mother's, now it's yours if you'll have me."

"Yes—yes, of course," said Helen. "I'm just surprised, it's so soon." Her voice trailed off as she squinted at the stone.

Helen was desperate to wed. Her reputation was shot, and she was unlikely to find a better candidate than Milton. He made a meager living as a carpenter and lived in a gloomy concrete home built entirely underground; a failed experiment in energy efficiency made the house a bargain to buy. It suited his dismal nature perfectly. She jumped at his proposal for fear nothing better would come along.

"There is one matter to be settled though," Milton said.

"What's that?" Helen said, admiring the ring on her finger.

"Your daughter is not welcome in my home," he said.

"Oh, I see," said Helen, pulling the ring to the tip of her finger without quite taking it off.

"That's not my child, and you know how I feel about her. There's no room for negotiation on this. If we marry, she'll have to stay with your parents."

Helen thought for a moment. *Irving is long gone, without even a letter to say goodbye. Suitors have not exactly been lining up at my door. And my father loves Janice. Maybe if I marry Milton, with all his faults, God, and my father will be able to forgive my sins. Lord knows this man needs someone to love him and give him children, and no one else is going to do it.*

The summer wedding was simple, with Reverend Faber officiating. Helen wore her Sunday dress, and Milton put on his only suit. Janice picked a bouquet of wildflowers for her mother. Afterward there was a small reception, just family, at the Faber's home. After a short time Helen disappeared upstairs with her daughter and explained that she felt Janice would be much better off with her grandfather. When Helen descended the stairs carrying a tattered suitcase held together by an old belt and walked out the door with her new husband, Janice clung to her grandfather's leg. That fall of 1939, when her grandmother registered her for kindergarten, she gave her name as Janice Faber.

It was well into September when news of Helen's marriage reached Irving, now drifting from county to county and state to state, wherever he could find work as a ranch hand. He'd written faithfully for a while, but had never received a single reply, so he'd finally given up. He'd always hoped his luck would change, and he'd be able to go back for his child and her mother, but he wasn't about to turn up a minute before he could prove his worth to her father. Reverend Faber may have been a man of God, but Irving didn't relish the thought of landing on his doorstep without something to show for himself.

On hearing this wedding news, however, he quit his job and made his way to Lexington, where he turned up on the Fabers' porch one night to inquire about Helen. He prayed the Reverend would have mercy and hear him out. All he wanted was to talk to Helen one last time, find out why she'd never written him back, and maybe get a look at his little girl.

It was long after dark, and Janice was fast asleep when Reverend Faber caught sight of Irving and wasted no time persuading him, at the muzzle end of a shotgun, to leave and never return. With no reason left to stay in Nebraska, Irving made his way to the train tracks and hopped the next freight car full of lost men dreaming of better days out west. Going to sleep in the straw to the sound of clacking wheels, Janice's father listened to the train whistle wail for a daughter he'd never know.

⁓ ❧ ⁓

Within six years of Helen's marriage to Milton, she bore him three sons. Though they were Janice's half-brothers and lived only blocks away, the bunker they called home was off limits to her, which was probably for the best. Milton's favorite entertainment after a night on the town with his buddies was to beat his wife and sons. People might have shaken their heads and whispered to each other about the cuts and bruises Helen and her boys almost always wore, but they didn't say anything. Over time Janice agreed that her mother had been right to leave her with her grandparents. She stayed with them until the day of her thirteenth birthday. That was the day her Grandpa died.

"Ma, look at me," Helen said to Rachel, who was staring blankly out the kitchen window. "Everything will be okay."

Rachel made no reply.

"Ma, snap out of it." Helen squared her mother's shoulders to look in her eyes. "We've got decisions to make, a funeral to plan, and I need your help."

"Nothing will ever be the same," Rachel said without emotion. She'd discovered her husband's body earlier that day when she'd taken him a roast beef sandwich and an apple for lunch. He'd been slumped over his desk at the church, where he'd suffered a massive heart attack while writing his next sermon.

"I know, I know. It was unexpected—so sudden."

"I can't do it anymore," Rachel said, shaking her head.

"Can't do what?" Helen said. "Can't plan the funeral?"

"Not the funeral. I can't keep Janice here with me any longer." Rachel buried her face in her hands as she bent over to weep. "She reminds me too much of—" Her voice trailed off. Helen wrapped her arms around her mother's shoulders and sighed as she watched the strongest woman she'd ever known fall apart.

At home later, she realized there was no point putting off the discussion with Milton. "She's just a girl," Helen said. "She needs to be with family."

"I'm *not* her father, remember?" Milton said. "And she's thirteen, for God's sake. By that age I was out workin' the fields. She can take care of herself."

"I cannot turn her away to fend for herself!" For perhaps the only time in her marriage, Helen stood up to her husband, hands on her hips, and looked him in the eye. "She is *my* responsibility. I've got to provide for her to get through school, and I can't do it alone."

Milton knew there would be no living with Helen if he refused. She could be a nuisance, but he needed her to care for his boys, so he agreed to let Janice move into the shack next door. He'd bought it years before with hopes of leasing it out but had never gotten around to fixing it up. As usual, there were conditions.

"She can join us for supper every night, but that's all. She can eat with us, and she can help you clean up. I don't want to see her in my home at any other time. I'll increase your food budget enough to keep her kitchen stocked for her other meals. If she wants anything else, she can get a job and buy it for herself."

"Whatever you say, Milt. Thanks." Helen knew not to push her luck with her husband's generosity. These arrangements were the best offer she'd get.

"Here are some boxes for your clothes and books," Helen said the next morning after she'd stayed up all night scrubbing and tidying the rental. "Let's strip your bed first and get the frame and mattress loaded in Milt's pickup."

"You look tired, Ma, let me do that," said Janice, still trying to process the news she had to move.

"This will get done quicker if we work together."

"I should tell Grandma goodbye," said Janice once the last of her belongings were loaded on the flatbed.

"No, honey, best to leave her be for now. She needs some time alone, that's all." *There's a reason she's shut up in her room anyway,* Helen thought to herself, *and it's the guilt of kicking out a grand-child in need.*

"She's not even going to see me off?" Janice said to herself as she walked away from the only home she'd ever known.

"Now, I need to warn you," said Helen as they drove less than a mile to unload, "the place is as clean as I could get it, but still pretty bare. I'll work on Milt to borrow some of our older furni-ture—a little bit at a time."

Janice remained silent until her mother cut the engine, never paying attention to the house next to Milton's before. "Leans quite a bit," she said, cocking her head to correct for the tilt.

"It's not much to look at, I'll admit," said Helen as she side-stepped the holes up the front porch with a box in her hands. "But it's built solid, probably withstand a tornado I bet."

The rotted gray clapboards had fallen off in chunks and exposed the frame beneath. Still concerned about the exterior façade, Janice walked inside to find exposed lathe and wire on the walls where large sections of plaster were missing. She moved through the rooms on the first floor with her mouth agape, unable to form words, let alone sentences.

"Let's set up your bed and dresser in here," Helen said, pointing to a room in the back. "We don't want to push our luck with this old house, so I think it's best if you stay on the first floor."

"Is that why there's a bed sheet hung over the stairs?"

"Yes, the second floor is off limits, stay downstairs." *I couldn't bear for her to see how bad it is up there*, Helen thought. "And I'll replace the tablecloth over the front windows with curtains as soon as I can sew some. You can even help me pick out the fabric if you like."

Janice had made it to the kitchen and saw a flash of motion— something, who knows what, had scurried under the blackened stove. She froze and crossed her arms to assess the room. A single light bulb dangled from a cord above a card table and folding chairs. The curled linoleum was the dingiest flooring she'd ever seen.

"Don't look like that, Janice. It's the best I could do on short notice. We'll fix the place up, I promise. It's just going to take a little time, that's all. And I'll be right next door if you need me."

"I'm gonna go unpack my room." Janice turned away and bit her lip to stop the tears. *If I need her*, she thought. *What a joke.*

Janice fashioned a life for herself from the ramshackle property, minding her own business and keeping friends at a safe distance. She lied about her age to get a job at the soda fountain downtown, and played cello in the school band to get lost in the music. She stole time with her mother while Milton was away at work, helping to care for her brothers. All the while she wondered why and how her mother tolerated such a man.

Only Betty knew the truth and was allowed inside the shanty Janice called home. The two had been inseparable since second grade when Betty offered to share her sandwich after Janice's lunch was stolen. Years later, Janice could still count on her best friend.

"Thanks for inviting me to dinner again tonight," said Janice, painting her toenails while sprawled across a purple rug.

"No problem," Betty said, brushing her hair atop unmade bedcovers. "You know my parents love having you over, and my little brother adores you, even if he is annoying. It's not a good start to the weekend unless you spend the night."

"I don't want to overstay my welcome here. But . . . well, you know . . . I like it a whole lot better at your house. You're so lucky. Your family seems so . . . normal, you know?"

"Any time, Janice, I mean it. No need to explain."

In spite of her living conditions, Janice proved as normal as any other teen. "There you are. Here's the boy I wanted you to meet," said Betty one evening after finding Janice behind the counter at the soda fountain. "Can you take a break?" She nodded her head toward two young men standing nearby. "That one's Nick; he's mine. The other one is Ronald."

"Ronald looks pretty good," Janice said, eyeing the lanky, handsome young man. "Just a sec, let me check with my boss."

"Janice, this is Ronald," Betty said a few minutes later. "Ronald, I'm pleased for you to meet Janice."

"How do you do?" Janice said, tucking her hair behind her ears. He was even more handsome up close, she thought.

"Nice to finally meet you, Janice," said Ronald, clearly at ease with himself and everyone else. "Betty has been talking about you for weeks now."

"Oh, I hope she wasn't a pest!" Janice's cheeks flushed the color of the cherries on the sundaes.

"Not at all," Ronald said with a grin, already smitten by the pretty brunette with the big smile and the infectious laugh.

The young couple hit it off and began double-dating with Nick and Betty. If they could afford it, they caught the latest film from their favorite seats in the balcony of the Majestic. If money was scarce, they cheered on their high school football and basketball teams for free. When all else failed, they hung out playing euchre at one of their parents' homes. But they never went to Janice's place.

Ronald was three years older than Janice and a senior at another high school. Confident and whip smart, he seemed more promising than the infantile boys in her freshman class. Ronald found Janice mature for her years. She didn't talk much about her life, so at one point he sat Betty down for the details. Knowing Janice's situation made him love her all the more, but he never asked her about her family. Clearly, she preferred to keep her circumstances a secret, and he respected that. For her part, Janice soon found Ronald filled the void her grandfather's death had left in her life. He was strong, but tender. She felt safe with him. They dated steadily all through her high school years while he pursued a teaching degree at a college nearby.

"I'm sorry, Janice," Ron said one spring day from the porch swing at his parent's bungalow. "I know I should have told you this sooner, but I've realized teaching just isn't for me."

"Oh! That's a surprise," she said. "What's happened?"

"I've tried, really I have. And I've tried to stick it out here while you finish high school."

"But?" The color drained out of Janice's face.

"But I'm not meant to be a teacher. I see that clearly now. And I'm frustrated because there's a whole world out there calling to me."

"What exactly is the world saying then?" she asked, hearing a tremble in her voice and wondering why her father and her mother and her grandfather all suddenly came to mind.

"I want to join the Army with Nick. It will give me a chance to see the world and time to figure out what I really want to do."

Janice stopped the swing with her foot and leaned back, unable to speak.

"It's just two years of service, Janice," Ronald said and grabbed her hand. "I wouldn't dream of going away unless I knew you'd be waiting for me when I came back."

"What—what do you mean wait?" She fought to hold off tears.

"I mean I want to get married, Janice, *before* I go. And after two years we'll be able to start our life together. The military will pay for my education then, whatever I want."

"A wedding?" She laughed suddenly.

"I love you, Janice. Will you marry me before I head out?"

"Yes—yes, of course I will!" She threw her arms around him and sent the swing back in motion with a jerk.

After finishing her junior year of high school, Janice dropped out and married Private Ronald Lee Kraus. The small ceremony was held at her grandfather's church, just Nick and Betty as their best man and maid of honor, with Helen, Rachel, and Ron's parents in witness. Milt refused to attend or let Janice's brothers go. No father to give away the bride, who wore a simple ivory suit and pillbox hat to say "I do" to her groom in his khaki service uniform.

It was June 1951 and Ron was on a short leave from basic training. Soon after he would deploy to Seoul as a clerk in a personnel office coordinating the transport of vehicles throughout Korea. Before leaving he helped Janice move out of Milton's rental and get situated in the home of her new in-laws.

Helen put on a happy face while she helped her daughter pack her things into two of the nice suitcases her in-laws had loaned her for the purpose. Ron and his father were sitting outside in the car waiting to drive her to her new home.

"I'll miss you," Helen said.

"Well, I won't miss this place," Janice said with a kick to the door frame, avoiding a direct response to her mother's comment. "But I'll only be a few miles away."

"You know Milt won't let me visit."

"You gonna walk me to the car then?" Janice asked to change the subject. She didn't want to talk about her stepfather ever again, and she'd never understand why Helen chose him over her.

"No," Helen said, looking out the front window to the waiting car. "I'll see you off from here. I don't want anyone to see me in my house dress."

"Okay," Janice said. "Well, bye then. See you round." She kissed her mother on the cheek and bounced down the overgrown front walk.

"Mrs. Kraus?" The elder Mr. Kraus held the door as his new daughter-in-law climbed into the back seat with his son, loaded her suitcases in the trunk, and then turned to give a polite wave to Helen. As he drove away, he wondered how any mother could allow her own daughter to live that way.

—⁓⁓—

Fred and Mabel Kraus had been blessed with a child late, after ten years of marriage, and thereafter devoted themselves to his care and upbringing. They adopted Janice as the daughter they'd always wanted and welcomed her into their home during Ron's absence overseas. Married for thirty years, the couple was comfortable in their relationship and content with their brick bungalow on the south side of town. By no means rich, they were happy to share what little they had with their daughter-in-law. Fred punched the time clock every weekday as a watch repairman for Montgomery Ward while Mabel was a homemaker passionate about preparing meals for the enjoyment of others.

"Wanna know one of Ron's favorite dishes?" Mabel asked Janice one afternoon not long after the wedding.

"Sure, what is it?" said Janice.

"Meatloaf! Oh, how he loves a good meatloaf."

"I had no idea."

"That's what I'm planning for supper tonight," Mabel said as she pulled ingredients from the fridge. "Would you like to help out?"

"I'd love to." Janice clapped her hands together. "Then I can make it for him when he comes home!" She had never learned to cook from either her mother or grandmother, and the soda fountain didn't help much, unless it came to ice cream treats.

"Exactly," Mabel said as she squeezed Janice's hand lightly. "All right then, grab an apron first, over there behind the door."

Fred entered the kitchen to grab a glass from the cupboard. "Evening, ladies. I worked up a thirst out in the yard." Janice greeted him with a grin, and he asked, "So what are you two up to?"

"Making meatloaf, Fred," said Mabel. "Now skedaddle unless you plan to be of some use."

"Oh, meatloaf tonight? Great," said Fred as he filled his glass at the tap. "Janice, I did have a question for you though."

"What is it?"

"Well, I just found out my company has an opening for a clerk in the clothing department."

"Really?" Mabel said while she cracked eggs in a bowl.

"I thought you'd be perfect for it, Janice. And I wondered if you'd have any interest?"

"Are you kidding?" said Janice. "That sounds like a huge step up from root beer floats. I'd love a job at Ward's!"

"Okay, I'll put a good word in for you then," said Fred. "And now I'll leave you ladies to cook."

Soon Janice worked alongside her father-in-law at the department store, saving every nickel for a promising future with her new husband. Unlike her father whom she'd never known, her mother who'd abandoned her, her grandfather who'd died, her grandmother who'd resented her, and her stepfather who could barely stand the sight of her, Ron and his parents were people she could count on, the way all of Nebraska counted on the corn at harvest time.

With a deep faith in God and strength forged in hardship, Janice looked ahead with great expectations. She'd wait for her husband faithfully, work to support him while he finished college, and follow him wherever his career called. They'd build a lifetime of memories, leave her sad Nebraska childhood far behind, and never look back.

4
Every Breath You Take
1999

———— ⠿ ————

Every breath you take
Every move you make
Every bond you break
Every step you take
I'll be watching you

—Sting

———— ⠿ ————

Bang . . . bang . . . BANG!

As Jessica readied for the workday, she was interrupted by the pounding on the door. She ambled to the foyer, exhaled as she prepared her response, and eased the door open, already knowing who waited to greet her at this ungrateful hour.

"Hi, Jessica, sorry I'm late," Janice said with a grin. "But I'm all ready to go, and it looks like a great day for a drive." The sun woke the tulips in the spring of 1999 while the cardinals chirped a happy tune.

"Oh yeah, right. Well, come in for a minute, will ya?" Jessica said from her doorstep in robe and slippers, a mug in her hand.

"The gas tank is full, and I've got the directions from Illinois to Nebraska in the car," Janice said as she followed Jessica inside. "If we hit the road soon, we should reach Omaha before nightfall."

"How 'bout a cup of coffee first, Mom?" Jessica yawned as she moved towards the kitchen. Janice followed like a puppy eager to please.

"Well, okay, sure, but it will slow us down a bit."

"I'm not quite ready yet—have a seat." Jessica had learned the best way to distract her mother was good coffee, so she poured a fresh cup and added just the right amount of milk and sugar.

"I'll finish dressing and be right back." She disappeared and left Janice to her scattered thoughts.

In the eight months since Tom's wedding in Florida, it was becoming commonplace for Janice to drop by Jessica's house—not Teri's or Elizabeth's—in the early hours of the day expecting to drive to Nebraska. With Megan away for her freshman year of college, just she and her son were at home now. Luckily, she was already up this morning, but not Justin. A senior in high school, he'd roll out of bed thirty minutes before the first bell and make a mad dash to beat it. Often Janice came on the weekend, awakening them both on one of those precious days when they should have been able to sleep in late.

Janice was obsessed with Nebraska. She wanted nothing more than to drive to Omaha and Grand Island to visit distant brothers who had not extended an invitation. Although her short-term memory was spotty at best, her early memories were still intact and she longed for her birthplace as she would for a childhood friend.

Jessica was a good sport about these early morning interruptions, feeling she had been cast in a poor remake of the movie *Groundhog Day*, in which a man relives the same day of his life over and over until he learns some lessons and gets it right. *I'm just not sure what lessons I'm supposed to be learning,* she thought. *But I guess maybe that's the point.*

Her response to her mother varied depending on the circumstances of each visit. On a work morning like this one, once she had Janice settled in with a cup of coffee, she would finish getting ready for work. On her way through the kitchen she'd take her mother's arm and say, "All right, Mom, I'm dressed now and need to get to work. It's getting late. I'll walk you out to your car, okay?"

"What?" Janice would say. "Oh, all right then. I've taken up too much of your time already."

"I'll see you again soon," Jessica would say as she closed her mother's car door on the problem for another day.

Janice would then drive home, certain she had forgotten something important. Eventually she would find the suitcase in the backseat and take it inside for closer inspection. The bag would remind her of what she'd set out to do, and the neurotic Nebraska cycle would start all over again.

She needed a companion though. She'd been having difficulties getting around town and wouldn't dream of traveling a long distance alone. When local driving problems arose, Elizabeth dealt with them.

"Hi, Elizabeth, this is Mike with State Farm—again."

"Hello, Mike, how are you?"

"Don't sound so enthusiastic," Mike said.

"I'm sorry, Mike, you know it's nothing personal. Is this about Mom's most recent adventure?"

"So you already know about the accident."

"Well, I know there was one. Mom told me she pulled up behind an elderly woman stranded on Route 47, who then backed up and rammed her car before speeding off."

"That's not what happened."

"I bet you hear that excuse all the time, right?"

Mike diplomatically ignored Elizabeth's sarcasm. "She was

upset that the trash collector skipped her pickup," Mike said. "She jumped in her car to tell them about their mistake. They didn't realize she was behind them, and they backed up. They smashed the front of her car pretty good."

"You're kidding me. She almost got taken out by a garbage truck?" Elizabeth knew it was no laughing matter, but at this point she had to either laugh or cry. The amount Mike knew about her family was embarrassing enough. She didn't need to add sobbing on the phone with the family's insurance agent to the list.

"No joke. Turns out her trash wasn't being picked up because she quit paying her bill some time ago."

"That's not surprising. She can't keep up with her bills now."

"She doesn't understand our claims process anymore."

What do you expect me to do about it, Elizabeth thought, but didn't say anything. Her silence was Mike's cue to continue.

"She's been to my office the last two days, stomped in and insisted she wasn't reimbursed for her latest car repairs. Even after I helped her track the check through her bank, she came back *again* this morning demanding payment. I had to repeat yesterday's conversation all over again!"

"Mike, I'm really sorry for the trouble she's caused you." How could she explain to him that this was a minor glitch in the scheme of things, Elizabeth thought. Her mother was forgetting more important details, like the fact Elizabeth was expecting her second child on May 25, 1999, which was just a few days away. Each mention of the baby's arrival was like announcing her pregnancy for the first time.

"I think it would be best if one of you kids handled her insurance matters," Mike said as if he were not stating the obvious. "And as a friend concerned for her safety, not as an insurance agent, I think it would be a good idea to check up on her—make sure she's still a safe driver."

No kidding, Elizabeth thought. "We'd take over in a heartbeat if she'd let us, Mike. But she won't admit she has a problem and insists on keeping all her business private." She hesitated before adding, "She thinks we're out to steal her money and lock her up someplace." *Why am I sharing this with a stranger,* she wondered.

"Well, I see—that's too bad."

"We're keeping tabs on her driving, just so you know. My brother Tom was home recently and rode as a passenger in her car for several days. She still obeys all the rules of the road, and he felt perfectly safe."

"I guess that's good." He didn't sound convinced.

"I know it's difficult to deal with her. We've heard the same complaints—everyone from the dentist to the bank. She's a handful. We're watching and will take over when necessary. Until then, we appreciate all you've done to help her along."

—⁓⁓—

Meanwhile, Janice had stepped up her Nebraska campaign.

"Mom came by *three* times last week," Jessica said to Teri one afternoon when she stopped by her sister's duplex.

Teri had settled into a nice place to enroll her girls in a better school district. Ashley was now ten, and Amanda was five and starting kindergarten in the fall. Teri had a fenced-in backyard and got a cute little mutt, trying her best to provide for her kids on her own. She and her ex didn't agree on much, but at least Eddie pitched in with child support. He had become a long distance father after moving to Peoria for a better job.

"Three times, really?" Teri plopped down on the sofa, holding a Furby she had picked up from her living room carpet.

"Yeah, it's making me crazy."

"Well, maybe it's time to give her what she wants to stop this nonsense," Teri said.

Jessica stared at her, jaw dropped.

"What?" Teri asked. "She's telling us loud and clear what she wants most, right?"

"Yes, but—Nebraska? Do you really want to go back there?"

"I know—it will suck. But we could make it happen for her. And if we're going to, we should do it now, before it's too late."

"I can't believe you're suggesting it, Teri. You, of all people!"

"Yeah, well, there are benefits to her illness, ya know?"

"Like what?"

"She doesn't remember my teen years anymore." Her head was cocked and eyebrow arched in one of Teri's classic facial expressions. No mistaking that attitude. But the look disappeared as Teri lowered her head and stared down at the furry robot in her hands.

Sitting on the sofa beside her sister, Jessica squeezed her hand. "What's wrong?" she asked.

"My past has been erased—it's like a 'get out of jail free' card. She's not mad anymore, so it's easier to do things for her now. It feels wrong to be enjoying it."

"I know what you mean, same for me."

"Yeah, but you didn't . . . you weren't . . ."

"Teri, you were a teenager," Jessica said. "All teenagers act out in one way or another."

"You and Tom didn't. And Elizabeth—she was little Miss Perfect."

"Okay, first, Elizabeth was never perfect, and you know that. Look at her now. She couldn't fix a decent meal to save her life."

"Huh, you got that right," said Teri. "She's pretty much a disaster in the kitchen."

"Listen, Mom was really unfair to you. I mean, the way she played favorites with Elizabeth was unfair to all of us, but it didn't affect Tom and me like it did you. Tom was already out of the house by the time Mom and Dad divorced. And we had more time with Dad, more time when life seemed normal."

"Yeah, I suppose," Teri said. She dabbed the inside corners of her eyes. No way would anyone ever catch her with runny mascara because of her screwed-up family, she thought.

"Besides, Tom and I acted out in different ways," Jessica said, remembering how it all went down.

Tom had left and never come back, acting like some kind of jet-setting millionaire with his great career and his exotic vacations. Jessica never had the opportunity to live that kind of life, but she had managed to settle only a short distance away and avoid her siblings while raising her kids. She knew her mother was blowing it as a parent and her younger sisters needed her. Maybe if she and Tom had both paid more attention, or maybe if they'd worked harder at encouraging their father to get involved, things wouldn't have spiraled so far out of control. But Jessica wasn't prepared to say any of that out loud.

"I guess I've got the vacation time to go," she said instead, wondering if anything she did now could make up for her past mistakes.

"Great," Teri said. "We can split the driving, and we can bring Ash along as a distraction! She's always up for a road trip, and she loves the Grandma she remembers when she was little. School's out next week, so Amanda can go stay with her dad. He'll agree if I ask nicely."

"That's a great idea!" Jessica said. "Let's do it. Megan will be home for the summer, but she and Justin will be fine on their own a few days. I'd ask their father to check in on them, but he's probably too busy with that child bride and toddler of his."

"That good-for-nothin' skirt chaser. Vince will never grow up, so don't waste your time."

*

The trip was ill fated from the start. In June the four travelers started off early on a Saturday morning in high spirits. Ashley wanted to play cards with Grandma, and at first Janice was game.

But she soon lost interest in Go Fish. Looking for license plates from different states lasted less than five minutes. They hadn't been on the road for half an hour yet when Janice asked, for the first of five-hundred times that day, "Are we there yet?" Soon the day seemed as endless as the infinite rows of corn pointing the way to Nebraska.

Jessica, Teri, and Ashley were relieved to make it to the Holiday Inn. They requested a single room on the second floor with two double beds to save money and keep close tabs on Janice. She pulled herself together when Walt picked them up for a late dinner, chatting nonstop during the short drive to catch up with her favorite brother. With a Jekyll and Hyde duality, she turned from a monster to a mouse when distracted by an agreeable diversion.

"Here you go," said a waitress after leading them to a tiled table in a side room.

"Oh, I love this place," Janice said, pulling up her wooden chair. Walt had picked her favorite Italian restaurant, a familiar chain to make things easy on her. Above the bustle of kitchen staff clanking dishes, Dean Martin was crooning the classic "That's Amore."

"What sounds good tonight, Janice?" asked Walt.

"Oh, I always get the same thing here," said Janice, waving away a menu. "The chicken parmigiana, delicious!"

After the group ordered, Janice devoured breadsticks and followed Walt's stories, asking sensible questions at all the right times. Dinner was served, and she ate without mixing food together strangely. Jessica and Teri exchanged bewildered glances, waiting for their mother to slip up and do something peculiar. It never happened though, and everyone enjoyed a pleasant meal.

"No, thank you," Janice said to the waitress who returned with a dessert menu. "But can you tell me where the restroom is, please?"

"Sure, head straight through here, then take a left," she said, pointing the way. "It's all the way to the back on the other side."

"Excuse me for a minute," Janice said.

"I'm glad to see her doing so well," Walt said after Janice left. "From what you've passed along, I was really worried about tonight, but she seems fine."

"Yes, she's got her wits about her tonight," said Teri. "It's baffling how sometimes she comes across completely normal."

"We've had a long day too," Jessica said. "So it's surprising to see her this way tonight. But I'm glad—for you."

"Just wait," said Teri, a scowl darkening her face. "We're gonna pay for this later, I just know it."

"Do you have to be such a killjoy, Teri?" asked Jessica.

"Will she be able to find her way back from the restroom?" asked Ashley to change the topic, straining her neck in the direction Janice had disappeared.

"Good question, hon," said Teri. "We'll send out a search party in a few minutes if she doesn't come back."

Janice returned to the table on her own without incident, ending the evening on a happy note. After Walt dropped them back at the hotel, the sisters got their mother and Ashley to bed and turned in themselves. Not much later, Janice, who could only sleep for thirty to forty-five minutes at a time, woke up and began prowling the hotel room: rifling through suitcases, scrounging for food, rearranging furniture, and attempting to leave. This happened numerous times during the night.

"Your turn," Teri would say to Jessica.

"Are you sure it's not your turn?" Jessica would plead.

"I'm sure. I'll get the next one."

At breakfast Janice and Ashley looked bright and cheery while Teri and Jessica hunched over their coffee. Janice once again hid her problems while visiting her youngest brother Rick in Grand Island. For Teri and Jessica, the day was a lot like riding the roller coaster of Janice's split personality.

By the time they made the three-hour drive back to the hotel, even Ashley's patience was wearing thin. "Grandma, we'll be there when we get there!" she snapped. "Asking every ten minutes won't make it any faster."

Hearing Ashley say the same words the two mothers had each spoken to their own children many times made both of them stifle a laugh.

"What are you two laughing about?" asked Ashley until a smile crept over her face, too. "All right, all right, you two, enough with your giggles. Now just get us back to the hotel, will ya?"

"What are you all laughing about?" Janice asked, quickly followed by, "Are we there yet?" The three exploded into laughter, releasing enough of the day's tension to allow them to get through the night.

They'd only been on the road for two hours the next morning when all hell broke loose.

"Where are you taking me?" Janice demanded. "I don't know where we are, but you better just turn this car around and get me home. *Right now!*"

"Settle down, Mom," Jessica said. "That's exactly what we're doing, but it's going to take awhile. So just sit back, relax, and take a nap."

"You are *not* taking me home. I know what you're up to—don't think I don't! You're going through my house right now, and I won't stand for it! *Take me home!*"

"*Who* is going through your house?" said Teri. "What are you talking about, Mom?"

"Well—the others—"

"Hmmm, Elizabeth is the only one who's left at home," said Teri. "Are you charging your darling baby with a crime?"

"I don't know—where are we?"

"We are smack-dab in the middle of Missouri and took time off from work and our families to take you to Nebraska. And this is how you thank us?" Knocked off guard by Teri's blast, Janice sat quietly. But the impact of Teri's words didn't last long.

"*Take me home right now!*" Janice said fifteen minutes later, startling Jessica so much she nearly veered into oncoming traffic. Teri could not hold back any longer.

"Shut up, Mom, *right now!* Do you hear me?" Teri jabbed her mother's shoulder to deliver the message. "I don't want to hear one more word out of you until we get home, and that will not be for *three more hours!*"

"Teri, stop—" Jessica pleaded.

"No, I won't stop. I can't take it one more minute! We did exactly what she wanted and took her to Nebraska! Now she's yelling at us every five minutes and can't understand we *are* taking her home! It's unbearable, really!"

"We did *not* go to Nebraska—" Janice said.

"Not another word, Mom, I mean it. Shut your mouth until we get home!" Teri spit the words out while Jessica's knuckles went white on the steering wheel. Ashley cowered in the back seat, willing herself to disappear.

Teri's lashing worked for a good hour, until Janice forgot she was offended and started up again. As a last resort they all ignored her, and it worked. When they heard snoring from Janice's side of the back seat, they all sighed and relaxed a bit. Reaching her house, they made sure Janice had her house keys, then they left her on the doorstep and fled.

"Can we agree never to do that again?" Jessica asked.

"Deal," said Teri. "Sorry I suggested it, and sorry for—"

"Let's skip the apologies, Teri. It's not your fault. I went along with it. I guess we just didn't realize she's already past the point of no return."

"Ya think?" said Ashley with a yawn.

—◦◦◦—

The trip to Nebraska had not solved any problems. Janice could no longer form new memories, so for her it was as if it had never happened. But it wasn't a total waste of time and money because it forced the Kraus siblings to face what was coming. The day after their return Jessica phoned Teri, Elizabeth, and Tom. They were all in agreement, which was not something that had happened often in their family. Together the three daughters researched attorneys specializing in elder law and found three good candidates.

One attorney stood out above the rest. Alex Hartmann was a senior partner in one of the most respected law firms in Springfield. His practice occupied an entire floor of the Richter building, the epicenter of law downtown. He wore enormous wire-rimmed glasses that made him look wise. More importantly, his own mother had died after a long battle with Alzheimer's, and he now specialized in legal issues surrounding elder care. When Jessica phoned to update Tom, he agreed Mr. Hartmann sounded like the best man for the job, even though he was the most expensive. "You'd never catch me saying money is no object," Tom said, "but we'll figure it out."

The following Tuesday morning in July, a month after the trip to Nebraska, the Kraus daughters gathered around a conference table in Mr. Hartmann's impeccably appointed offices for their first planning meeting. A secretary hovered, dialing Tom in by phone.

"Okay, now that everyone's here, I'll go get Mr. Hartmann." Moments later he strode in.

"Let's get started then, shall we?" he said.

"Straight to business then," Elizabeth said to Teri out one side of her mouth.

"I like him," Teri whispered back. "He's not wasting one minute of billable time."

"Yeah, I like that, too," Elizabeth said. "Wait—did we just agree on something?"

Teri smirked. "Mom's illness seems to have a few upsides."

"All right," said Jessica. "Where do we begin?"

"Durable power of attorney," Mr. Hartmann said, tapping his finger on the conference table.

"Excuse me?" Teri said after several seconds of silence.

"The first step is to draw up a durable power of attorney," the lawyer said. "And it must be done quickly. Are you familiar with this?"

"I've heard the term," Elizabeth said. "But honestly, I'm not sure exactly what it covers."

"It's a binding agreement that authorizes a designated person to act on behalf of someone else if or when that individual becomes disabled or incapacitated." He had gotten up from his chair at the head of the conference table and was now strolling its length. He spoke with authority and confidence, as if he had given this speech a million times. "It can be written to cover both the person and their property, which is what I would recommend to handle your mother's finances and make healthcare decisions for her when the time comes."

"That sounds like exactly what we need," Tom said from the speakerphone. "How long will it take to set that up?"

"Well, that depends. Your mother is the variable we cannot control."

"You've got that right," Jessica said.

"She has to agree to sign the document to make it legal."

"Let's just kiss that option goodbye then," said Teri. "Because hell will freeze over before that happens."

"Geez, Teri, we won't get anywhere with an attitude like that." Elizabeth looked at her sister with squinted eyes and a sneer.

"Well, excuse me for calling it like I see it. But I'm right, Lizzie, and you know it!"

Teri had a point, Elizabeth thought, though she was reluctant to agree out loud. Convincing Janice to skip naked through a crowd of people and toss hundred-dollar bills like confetti would be easier than persuading her to give up her freedom to children she felt were out to steal her money and lock her up.

"It's true," Elizabeth said finally, noting Teri's satisfaction out of the corner of her eye. She just hated to admit when Teri was right about anything. "Are there any alternatives?"

"No, I'm afraid not at this point in your mother's progression," said Mr. Hartmann. "For the document to be valid, the grantor – that's your mother – must be in her right mind at the time the durable power of attorney is executed."

The three sisters stared at the attorney, brows crinkled in concentration.

Mr. Hartmann was always surprised to see siblings who were so different showing the same facial expressions. Some families were more comfortable with their similarities than others. "This is an important detail I need you to understand." He sat down and folded his hands on the table. "Your mother's mental health is uncertain. If anything happens to bring her sanity into question in the eyes of the law, it will be too late for a durable power of attorney."

"So we need to convince her to sign right away?" Tom's voice said through the phone.

"Time is of the essence, yes." Mr. Hartmann wondered briefly how the absent older brother fit into the family portrait.

"But how in the world are we going to do that?" Jessica said. "She fights us on *everything* and gets so nasty. I can't even get her to take her blood pressure medicine. She slaps the pills out of my hand."

"Can you enlist the help of anyone outside the family?" Mr. Hartmann asked. The siblings grew silent for a moment. Mr. Hartmann was familiar with this process and knew they were going through the list of friends their mother had alienated in the past few years.

"What about her lawyer?" Elizabeth said. "She trusts him."

"And because it's a professional relationship, she hasn't pushed him away yet, as she seems to have done with most of her friends," Tom said. "You know, all those phone calls from her worried friends you girls were telling me about."

"Are you suggesting you could have dealt with them better, Tom?" Teri asked.

"Teri, he didn't say that," Jessica said. "Can we just stick with the matter at hand?"

There was an awkward silence in the room. "I think her lawyer's our best bet," Elizabeth said. Shoulders shrugged around the room. "Tom, what do you think?"

"You're the ones in the thick of it," Tom said. "I trust your decisions. Let's start there."

Interesting, Mr. Hartmann thought as the Kraus daughters shook his hand and headed toward the elevator. *I could have sworn this would be one of those families that would fall apart in a crisis and never recover.*

William Stevenson had served as Janice's legal counsel for twenty-five years, during and since her divorce. She kept him busy revising her will every few months, whenever she disinherited whoever had offended her last. Even Elizabeth had heard the all-too-familiar threat, "Leave me alone, or I'm gonna cut you off and move back to Nebraska!" Teri loved it when that happened.

Tom traveled home to lead the appeal along with Elizabeth in hopes of persuading Mr. Stevenson to join forces with them. They met in his office on North Eighth Street, which amounted to a room rented from the second floor of a turn-of-the-century Victorian, once grand but now in disrepair. The stately old homes had been partitioned for commercial tenants when the downtown business district expanded into the neighborhood.

Elizabeth had never met Mr. Stevenson before, but he looked just like she had imagined after she'd heard him described in passing. In his short-sleeve polo and khakis, he appeared more like the manager of a discount store than a lawyer, missing only a nametag. In fact, he charged bottom-of-the-barrel rates, so in a way he was running a discount business. That was probably why Janice had been able to manage his fees back when she was an unemployed mother of four seeking representation in a divorce.

"Thank you for seeing us on short notice," Tom said as soon as they were seated. "I'm only in town a few days, and we wanted to speak to you about an urgent matter with our mother."

"Yes, please continue," Stevenson said as he shuffled papers across a desk littered with cigarette ashes.

"Certainly you've noticed her condition declining?" Tom said.

"Her condition?" Stevenson fidgeted in his chair. "What exactly do you mean?"

"Her memory problems and odd behavior?"

"No—" Stevenson leaned back and raised his hand to his chin, as if he was trying to imitate *The Thinker*. "No, I don't know what you're talking about."

"Really?" Tom was thrown off. "Well, we've noticed. She cannot retain any new information and has become paranoid and aggressive. She's been declining at an alarming rate the last couple of years."

"Hmmmm," said Stevenson.

"Since she refuses to admit a problem or seek medical help, we feel it's time for a durable power of attorney. We've hired legal counsel to take care of the matter."

"And who would that be?" Stevenson asked, doing his best to maintain a poker face.

"Alex Hartmann," said Tom. "We'd like your assistance to convince our mother that a durable power of attorney is in her best interest—so we can step in and help out, if and when it becomes necessary."

"I see." Stevenson swiveled his chair to look out the window behind his desk, tapping his fingers together.

"Can we count on your help then?"

"Well, thank you for bringing this to my attention," Stevenson said as he stood to open the door. "I'll have to discuss this with my client and get back with you."

"Wait, don't you want to discuss some of the problems she's having right now?" Elizabeth asked.

"You've told me you feel she's having problems. Client confidentiality prevents me from sharing anything with you. But thank you for your visit. I'll be in touch with you if I need to."

"What was that all about?" Elizabeth asked as they stepped over weeds growing through cracks in the front walkway of the crumbling mansion. "Did he just kick us out?"

"Yes, he did," said Tom.

"He wouldn't even look us in the eye. He has no intention of helping, does he?"

"Tipping him off was a mistake. This is going to be harder than we thought."

Tom, Jessica, Teri, and Elizabeth kept their appointment with Mr. Hartmann the next day, though Janice and Mr. Stevenson did not join them as they'd hoped.

"Stevenson won't help," Mr. Hartmann said.

"How'd you know that?" Teri asked.

"Because he called me first thing this morning, and I wouldn't describe the conversation as friendly."

"Sounds about the same as our meeting," said Elizabeth.

"He denied your mother has any health issues whatsoever."

"That's a flat-out lie," Jessica said.

"Not only did he warn her against a durable power of attorney, he also pointed out— loudly I might add—that Janice is *his* client and not in need of counsel from any other attorney at this time."

"So he was telling you to back off?" Teri said.

"Yes, indeed." Mr. Hartmann's chuckle hinted of prior dealings with Mr. Stevenson.

"How could he say a durable power of attorney isn't in her best interest?" Jessica said.

"Who does he think will take care of her when things get out of hand? There's no one else but us."

"Either he's unwilling to admit her illness in his own self-interest, or your mother is doing an excellent job of covering her symptoms when she's around him."

"Well, I took a big hit," said Tom. "Mr. Stevenson worked Mom into a frenzy. She remembered long enough to kick me out of her house several times yesterday."

"Luckily, Tom has a knack for handling her," Elizabeth said.

"She forgets so quickly. I just walked out of the room to let her cool off. Then I took her out to dinner, and the incident was forgotten."

"There are some blessings to her condition, aren't there?" Mr. Hartmann said. "I remember the double bind with my mother very well. No problem. Time for Plan B."

"We have a Plan B?" Jessica said. "How cool is that?"

"It's too late for your mother to select any one of you to help out. Your only option will be to proceed with guardianship through the court once you feel certain she's become incapacitated."

"And now is *not* that time?" Tom asked.

"At this point, from what you've told me and considering the position her lawyer has taken, her competency will not be easy to determine. The success of a petition for guardianship is difficult to predict. And I don't like to lose, so I'll be counting on you to wait, watch, and monitor her closely."

"Guardianship?" Teri said. "Are you saying we're gonna have to sue our own mother?"

"Well, that's a hard way to put it, but yes, I'm afraid you are," Mr. Hartmann said. "But you don't need to worry, because you'll be ready when the time comes. Right now you need to watch for signs. Her ability to drive is crucial, as well as her ability to handle money."

"She's already having problems with the bank and she's having regular car accidents—small ones," Jessica said. "All the people she deals with—insurance agent, dentist, bank, post office—are constantly begging us to straighten things out."

"Yet she muddles through on her own, a key point in determining competency. In my experience, the signal to seal the deal for guardianship has to be a big one."

"Like what?" Teri asked.

"I'm not talking about a bounced check or even a fender bender, but a debacle of such magnitude as to make it impossible for you *not* to proceed through the courts."

"Could you be a little more specific, then?" Tom said.

"Certainly. There has to be a trauma that will put Janice's life in jeopardy, or the lives of others. No judge will dismiss proof of that significance."

"Oh my God," said Teri. "Does it really have to get that bad before we're legally allowed to act?"

"You will know without a doubt, whatever the catastrophe might be, that the time has come to intercede on your mother's behalf. Failing to respond, you would be considered negligent for her protection as well as the safety of others."

"It seems to me," Elizabeth said, "that it makes more sense to step in *before* something terrible happens, so no one gets hurt."

"I can understand why you'd see it that way," said the lawyer. "But if you ever find your own sanity in question, I guarantee you'll appreciate the strict guidelines for guardianship."

"Great, so all we need is a suicide or murder then," said Tom.

5

Forget About The Future

January–May 2000

⎯⎯⎯⎯⎯ ◌◌◌ ⎯⎯⎯⎯⎯

We'd best consult our horoscope
In case this feeling wasn't meant to last
Let's just forget about the future
And get on with the past

—Sting

⎯⎯⎯⎯⎯ ◌◌◌ ⎯⎯⎯⎯⎯

"Claire, can you ring the doorbell, honey?" Elizabeth asked her four-year-old daughter. Her hands were full at the moment, one holding a seven-layer salad getting heavier by the minute and the other guiding her toddler Katie up the steps.

"Okay, Mommy!" Claire said.

"Happy Easter, so glad you could all make it," said John's sister Nancy. "Come on in and let me take your coats and things. I'll put everything in the first bedroom for you. My, your Easter dresses sparkle, girls!"

"Thanks, Sis," John brought up the rear with a diaper bag and an armload of toys to keep the girls busy. "Sorry we're late."

"No worries, I remember how these things go with two little ones in tow," said Nancy. "I think you know everyone here, so please make yourselves at home."

"It's so nice to see you again, Stuart," Elizabeth said. "Pardon us while we squeeze by."

"Hi, Noreen, Happy Easter to you too," said John. "Claire, watch out, don't step on her feet."

"Do we finally get to meet your new little one?" asked Eleanor.

"Oh yes, this is the baby. Her name is Katie," said Elizabeth as she picked her youngest up to move through the room.

John heard his name called, and nothing more. "It's so hard to talk with all the chatter, Ralph," he said with Claire glued to his leg. "I'll catch up with you a bit later."

"Hi, Mom," Elizabeth said over the din when she saw Janice tucked into the farthest corner on a love seat with Harold, John's father. "I see you made it before us." Janice made no reply.

A quizzical look around the room returned awkward glances. *I'm used to her ignoring my children,* Elizabeth thought to herself, *but why isn't she paying any attention to me? After all, she's invited here because of her relationship with me.*

As Elizabeth watched, Janice patted Harold's knee with a giggle. "Oh, I tell you what—" she said and whispered the rest in his ear confidentially, then planted a kiss on his cheek.

"Let me get this salad to the fridge," Elizabeth said, escaping with her children at her heels. "John, can you help me with this?"

"Did you see what I just saw?" John asked from the safety of the kitchen.

"What, Daddy?" Claire said with a tug on his sleeve. "What did you see?"

"Oh, I think Daddy got a look at the dessert table," Elizabeth said, wincing from the white lie. "But dinner first, no sweets 'til later! Now go find your uncle to say hello."

"Liz—" John said, his face turning red. "What is going on? When did this—? Did you know anything about this?"

"I'm just as surprised as you are, John. But now is not the time. Let's not make matters worse by drawing attention to—them."

"Oh, so you think no one else noticed that?"

Elizabeth peeked into the living room. Everyone seemed to be making a point of *not* looking at Janice and Harold. She heard bits of discussion—about the weather, the level of the water in the pond—anything to avoid acknowledging what was happening in the corner. "No, John, I think everyone has noticed and is trying hard to ignore it and keep this meal pleasant. And we should do the same. We'll talk about this later."

"Right, later then." He bounded back into the action. "Hey, Francine, did you see Claire's Easter bonnet?"

At home later, with the kids tucked in bed, John stood in the bathroom doorway in his pajamas watching Elizabeth brush her teeth.

"What was going on tonight?" John asked. "What could my father be thinking? I can't believe what I saw. They were acting like hormonal teens who couldn't keep their hands off each other!"

"I know, I know," Elizabeth said. "From the way they were carrying on I'd say this has been going on for a while."

"You're not saying they're a couple?"

"Well, I'm sorry, John. What else would you call that? They were cuddled up all evening, ignoring everyone around them!"

"How could my father date *your* mother, who just happens to be suffering from severe memory problems?"

"It doesn't make any sense," Elizabeth said, shaking her head. "It just doesn't add up."

"Unless he doesn't fully understand her illness," John said.

"Regardless of what he does or doesn't know, she is still my mother!"

"Oh man, this is too strange. I don't even want to talk about it with the rest of my family."

Bizarre was the best word for it. No one would ever accuse Harold of being erratic or rash. Born and raised on the poor side of town, he was a devout Catholic, a World War II veteran, and an engineer retired after working decades at a factory. He had been married for fifty-four years before his wife's death three years ago. Devoted to her and their five children, he'd been more of a father to Elizabeth in the twelve years she'd been married to his son than her own dad had been in her entire life.

Harold was still an attractive man, too. Even at seventy-six, he stood straight up to his full six feet in height and carried his athletic frame proudly, crowned with an impressive full head of thick, gray hair. Any woman over the age of sixty, and even a few younger ones, would have considered him a good catch. Until now though, he'd spurned the advances of several women.

The sudden romantic interest was all the more surprising because Janice and Harold had known each other for years as in-laws. Because her mother was single, Elizabeth always invited her to gatherings with John's family. She had even dined with both of John's parents at their house from time to time. But there had never been a hint of anything more.

"How could this have happened?" John said as they lay in bed staring at the ceiling. "It's obviously been going on for a while now, but how have they managed to keep it a secret?"

"And why did they decide to share the news by pawing each other at a holiday dinner?" Elizabeth asked. "I think you better have a word with your father. Let him know exactly how serious Mom's health issues are now."

"Yeah, I'll do that." John reached to switch off the light. He was not looking forward to that discussion.

"The sooner the better," Elizabeth said in the dark, her words carrying them both into a fitful night's sleep.

—⁓⁓—

John stopped by his father's house the next weekend. "Hi, Dad," he said after finding his father on the back porch, finishing up a sandwich while watching "SportsCenter" on the television.

"Oh, hi. Didn't expect to see you today," Harold said from his seat on the glider. "Join me here for a swing. It's shaping up to be a nice day outside."

"I'm here for a reason," John said as he sat in a chair for a better view of his father's face. "I'm concerned about you and Janice, and I need to make sure you know what's going on with her."

"What do you mean—going on with her?" Harold stopped rocking.

"She's ill, you know, Dad? I'm sure I've mentioned her memory problems before. And it's getting worse—much worse. It's not a good idea for you to get involved with her now."

"Memory problems? Oh, come on! She's no different than me or anyone else our age," Harold said. "She's healthy as a horse. Take it from me, someone who knows all about it."

"Liz has been watching her the last couple of years, Dad. There's more to it—she hallucinates and is completely paranoid her kids are out to get her. They're all convinced it's serious."

"Listen, I'm an old man, John," Harold said, his voice turning to a growl. "And I enjoy her company, she makes me happy. It's just a natural part of getting older to forget things sometimes and repeat stuff. You're just too young to understand, that's all."

"No, that's not it."

"She's not sick, that's nonsense. I don't want to hear another word of this—we're finished here. I'll do what I please."

John left defeated, feeling like a ten-year-old still afraid of his pop.

Janice continued her relationship with Harold into the spring; it grew out of control like the weeds. They began spending all their time together and took bicycle rides on the country trails, packing a picnic lunch to share during rest breaks. Their cars became permanent fixtures in each others' driveways, tipping everyone off to their whereabouts. Members of both sides of the family began contacting Elizabeth and John to ask questions. John's family was more tolerant because they didn't know the full extent of Janice's illness. The loudest opposing voice in the mix came from the Kraus side, of course.

"What the hell is Harold up to?" Teri asked Elizabeth over the phone. "They're still at it—lovey-dovey and all—and Mom is cuckoo for Cocoa Puffs. He's taking advantage of her, Lizzie!"

"And what am I supposed to do about it, Teri?"

"Make them stop—duh! Mom shouldn't be seeing anyone in her state, you know that."

"They're adults, Teri, not kids who can be grounded or have the keys to the car taken away. They can do whatever they please, and they don't care what anyone thinks."

"You're not taking this seriously, and you have to do something, damn it!"

"Look, John has already tried, and his father won't listen. We're just gonna have to wait and see how this all plays out."

Oblivious to the family's complaints, Harold and Janice enjoyed a mutually beneficial relationship. She could no longer cook for herself and had stopped trying; he'd become a decent chef as a widower. Like Pavlov's dog she was conditioned to stop by his house every night around suppertime. He was happy to have a woman's undivided attention in exchange for a meal, although conversation with her wore on his patience.

"You're such a good cooker," Janice said one night.

"Glad to share a fine pot roast," Harold said. "I'd never finish this on my own."

"Hey, I was thinking about driving to Nebraska." Janice changed the subject like her hair color. "I really need to get back to see my brothers and their families."

"I know, it must be important since this is the third time you've brought it up tonight."

"Third time? Oh, aren't you funny?" Janice stopped to ponder for just a moment. "Not one of my daughters will take the time to go with me, can you believe that? After all I've done for them."

"Well, they are kinda busy working and raising kids, you know? Maybe in a few months one of them will be able to swing it?"

"Hey, this is so good. Is there any more? You are such a good cooker! Did you know that?"

"I've been told that before."

Janice wore Harold down with her repeated requests, and he agreed to drive with her to Nebraska. Elizabeth learned of their plans not from her mother, but from her father-in-law.

"Hi, Elizabeth, this is Dad," he said over the phone. "I thought you should know that your mother and I are leaving in the morning for Nebraska, and we'll—"

"What? Are you crazy?" Elizabeth said.

"She wants to go really bad. I've agreed to drive so she doesn't have any problems getting there or back. I've put our schedule in the mail so you know where we'll be and when we'll be back."

"Dad, this is a really bad idea," Elizabeth said after recovering her composure. "My sisters took her last summer, and it was a complete disaster. You need to cancel this trip."

"That's funny, she told me she hasn't gone in ages. But it's no problem, trust me. I'm going to make sure everything goes smoothly."

"It will be too much for her, and strange places make her worse than usual. Please don't go. Really, I mean it!"

"You know, you really worry too much about your mother,

Elizabeth," Harold said like he was an expert on the subject. "She's not as bad as you say, and I'll be with her the whole time. We'll be home safe and sound before you know it. See you when we get back."

They left for Nebraska one morning in May of 2000. Janice drove her car and Harold navigated from the passenger seat, equipped with maps and snacks. With his directions, she headed westward towards her Promised Land, the endless cornfields leading the way. They made it to the hotel in Omaha shortly after sunset. As soon as they unpacked, she phoned her brother Walt and invited him to join them for a late-night drink. Harold had brought everything required to make Old Fashioneds, his favorite cocktail.

Walt stayed until the early hours of the morning. His sister seemed happy enough, he thought, and he could manage her repetitive conversation for a few hours, no problem. He wasn't quite sure who this Harold person was though or why he kept refilling his sister's cocktail glass. She'd never been much of a drinker, and Walt knew alcohol didn't mix well with her health issues. After insisting he had to leave around one-thirty a.m., despite Harold urging him to stay for just one more, he decided he'd find a time to speak with Janice alone the next day to voice his concerns.

"It's late, and I'm bushed," Janice said to Harold after locking the door. "I think I'll go straight to bed."

"Okay, I'm gonna take a quick shower then," said Harold. "You go ahead and get comfortable." He planted a quick peck on her cheek before disappearing into the bathroom.

Janice stumbled towards the bed with a giggle, too tipsy to worry about changing her clothes. She fumbled with the alarm clock for only moments before she gave up, turned off the light, and dozed off.

After his bath Harold found his way to the bed using his hands to feel along the wall in the dark room. He jammed his toe into the television stand as he turned a corner and let out a stifled cry, "Argh—darn it, that hurt!"

"What the—," Janice said, woken by his outburst. "Wait, who's there?" she said after realizing someone was sitting down on the bed.

"It's me, Janice," said Harold with a scowl. "Just stubbed my toe, that's all. Sorry I woke you."

Janice shot straight up and flipped on the light, knocking the clock to the floor. She looked around the room to get her bearings, and then eyed the man sitting at the end of the bed, rubbing his foot and muttering under his breath. He looked up to apologize again and was taken aback by the fear that distorted her face.

"Janice?"

"Get out of my room!" she shouted. "How did you get in here? What do you want?" She bolted for the door.

"Janice, what on earth? Pipe down right now! You'll wake the entire hotel!"

"Get away from me! How did you get in here?" Janice demanded as she struggled to unlock the door. "I mean it, get out, get out—get out of here right now!"

"For God's sake, Janice, what is wrong with you?" Harold said as Janice finally got the door open and he followed her into the hallway. "Get back in here and stop this nonsense at once."

"No, no—stay out of my room!"

"You're just confused, that's all. Remember, we're in Omaha visiting your family—we're staying at the Holiday Inn."

The night manager and a blue-shirted security guard arrived on the scene less than three minutes after the switchboard had begun lighting up with calls from adjacent rooms. But their efforts to calm Janice and usher the two back into their room proved futile. Bewildered and lacking an explanation, Harold checked into a separate room in the early hours of the morning, embarrassed by all the commotion.

After Harold vacated her room, Janice dumped all her belongings in her suitcase and checked out.

"Ma'am," the night attendant asked, "are you sure you want to go without your friend? The man who got the other room?"

"I don't know what you're talking about," Janice said. "I am traveling by myself!"

"Okay then."

"I could use some help with directions though," she said. "Can you tell me how to get to Springfield, Illinois from here?"

"Sure, no problem," the night attendant said. "It's easy—just get on Interstate 80 heading east. Turn right out of our parking lot and the exit is a mile down the road on the right." Janice looked confused by the simple directions, so another employee agreed to lead the way and wave her on at the entrance ramp.

Harold awoke later that morning and rushed to check on Janice, still shocked about the ruckus overnight. When there was no answer to his knocking, he hurried to the front desk, where he learned Janice had left soon after he switched rooms. Realizing she had been on the road for nearly four hours, he recognized the emergency at hand. Swallowing his pride, he called home to pass along the details.

Elizabeth knew something was wrong the moment the phone rang at six forty-five a.m. and only got "hello" in before Harold proved her right. *This is my mother*, she thought, as panic spread from the pit of her stomach. *I cannot stand to hear all the sordid details of them sharing a hotel room. As much as I want to yell at him, I have to focus now because Mom's in danger. There's no way she'll find her way home on her own—none whatsoever.*

"So how am I going to get home, Elizabeth?" Harold asked after telling her everything straight up. "Janice left me here without a car."

"You're smart enough to figure out public transportation," she said and hung up, not wasting another minute and dreading her next move.

"Oh my God, can you believe that pervert? Taking advantage of our mother like that," said Teri. "Loading her up with liquor when she doesn't even drink and then wondering why she got so confused. Lizzie, I don't care what you say. He's a horrible man! Oh, and by the way, I told you so!"

"Yes, you told me so. But can we just focus on what we need to do now, please?"

"Wait till I get my hands on that bastard," Teri said. "How could he leave her like that? Didn't he say he was gonna keep her safe—didn't he? How could he let her check out on her own? What the hell is wrong with him? He's as mentally unstable as Mom if you ask me!"

"Teri, enough! Tom has made a plan and we each have things to do. He's called the police, who are issuing bulletins in Nebraska, Iowa, Illinois, and Missouri. Jessica has made a list of every relative, friend, and acquaintance we should call in case Mom checks in with any of them. Get a pen and paper so you can write down your portion of the list."

The longest day of the year became the longest day any of the Kraus siblings had ever lived through. At seven p.m., sixteen hours after Janice had left the hotel in Omaha, Jessica's phone rang.

"Hello," she said, grabbing the receiver on the first ring.

"Yes, hello, is this Jessica Sullivan?"

"Yes it is."

"My name is Monica, and I'm calling from the Davenport Police Department about a woman we believe to be your mother," she said. "You are one of the children who reported Janice Kraus missing, right?"

"Yes—is she okay?"

"Oh yes, she's perfectly fine, don't worry about that. She's here with us now. One of our guys found her pulled to the side of the road a few miles out. Once she calmed down, she let him look through her purse. That's when we figured out her identity."

"Thank goodness she's all right!"

"She wasn't making much sense, so they brought her to head-quarters. She was so confused—couldn't even tell us her full name, poor thing."

"Thank you so much." Jessica brushed tears away before they had a chance to fall. Struggling to keep her voice level, she asked, "Can she stay with you till we can get over there to pick her up?"

"That would be best," Monica said. "We don't feel it's safe for her to be driving. I'll personally see to it that she gets something to eat and stay with her until you arrive."

Jessica, Teri, and Elizabeth made the three-hour drive north in Jessica's Explorer. "Why did we have to take my SUV anyway?" said Jessica. "This thing's a gas guzzler."

"Cause you're the oldest," Teri said. "Why else?"

"Oh great, gotta rub it in, don't ya?"

"I'll help pay for gas, Jess," said Elizabeth.

"Ha, like that will get you off the hook." Teri pushed herself between the two front seats. "It's your fault we're out here in the boondocks."

"Cut the crap and sit back, Teri. I'm not to blame for Harold's—"

"All right you two, no more finger pointing," said Jessica. "If you can't be nice, just be quiet."

Elizabeth leaned back with a sigh, crossed her arms, and stared out at the farmland blanketed in moonlight.

"Okay, great weather we're having, huh?" Teri said after five minutes of uncomfortable silence that felt like an eternity to her.

"Really?" asked Jessica, catching her smirk in the rear view mirror. "Oh, and by the way, I call dibs on driving Mom's car back home—alone. You guys can bring her home in this car together. Won't that be fun?"

"Oh, damn it," said Teri. "Why didn't I think of that?"

THUMP. Elizabeth smacked her own forehead against the side window, just hard enough for her sisters to hear.

Further discussion focused on directions to Davenport, and they arrived at the police station around midnight, nervous about what awaited them.

"This could have turned out much worse," the on-duty officer said. "You realize that, right?"

His question was answered by bobble-heads all around.

"You must take whatever precautions are necessary to make sure this kind of incident *never* happens again. Your mother should not be behind the wheel."

Elizabeth stifled the rage that rose like bile in her throat. She could not tolerate being scolded like a schoolchild who failed to do the homework. How were they supposed to take care of this, she thought. Until now the lawyers hadn't helped them out. She wanted to scream about the legal system that refused to let them take over and shout at the cop ignorant to their struggles over the last four years. Most of all, she wanted her father-in-law to be held responsible for getting them into this mess. She sulked in silence instead, nodding in agreement to appease the policeman.

After the lecture the sisters joined their mother in the break room. They found Janice slouched in a chair and clutching her purse tightly against her chest. Gratitude replaced exhaustion on her face when she spotted her children, and she spoke gibberish as they prepared to leave. They quickly escorted her out before anyone changed their mind, feeling lucky their mother's actions hadn't caused more serious consequences for them all.

"I was working on the books here, but now I'm ready to go. Where are my library books anyway?" Janice asked and then pointed out the car window at the dark stretch of cornfields.

"We're heading home now, Mom," Teri said from the back seat while Elizabeth drove.

"Ha, did you see that teddy bear? That was funny, my norisay is here somewhere."

"Just relax, it's gonna take awhile," Elizabeth said.

"And I ate fillebriz for lunch! Is Duke coming?"

Elizabeth glanced back at Teri, her eyebrows raised. Duke had been dead for years.

They pulled into Janice's driveway as dawn broke. "I'm exhausted," Elizabeth said. "I can't remember the last time I pulled an all-nighter."

"Didn't you take turns and get some sleep?" Jessica asked.

"Sleep?" Teri said. "Mom flapped her jaw the entire way. And now look at her." Janice, from whose memory the entire episode had already disappeared, was humming to herself while pulling her trash cans to the curb as if she knew it was pick up day.

"You still have her car keys, right?" Elizabeth asked Jessica.

"Oh, yeah. I'm taking them home with me."

"I'm going to have some breakfast now, girls," Janice said cheerily. "Anyone care to join me?"

"No thanks, Mom," said Jessica. "I think we're all going to head home."

Janice disappeared into her house, and the siblings got into Jessica's car.

"Here you are, Elizabeth," Jessica said, pulling up in front of her sister's house. "Liz, you okay, sweetie?"

Elizabeth took a deep breath and wiped the tear that had escaped down her cheek. "It's just . . . all the things . . . that could have happened . . . and I did try to talk to Harold . . . John did too . . . he wouldn't listen . . . you can't blame this all on us."

"I know that, Lizzie," Teri said. "I was just angry. You know me." The sisters were silent for a moment. "There's one good thing to come out of this, though," said Teri.

"What could that possibly be?" asked Jessica.

"I think Mom just handed us the life-threatening catastrophe Mr. Hartmann told us to watch out for."

6
Demolition Man
1974–1978

─────── ∞ ───────

I'm a walking nightmare
An arsenal of doom
I can kill a conversation
As I walk into the room
I'm a three-line whip
I'm the sort of thing they ban
I'm a walking disaster
I'm a demolition man

—Sting

─────── ∞ ───────

"**M**ax is dead," Janice said to her three youngest children, whom she'd gathered around the kitchen table.

"What? Max? Noooooo!" said eight-year-old Elizabeth, bursting into tears. "I knew it. This place did him in! Why did we have to come here?" Her biggest concern with their move had been for the safety of their black cat, a prowler by trade.

"Are you sure, Mom?" Jessica asked as she wrapped her arms around Elizabeth and pulled her in close. At fourteen she was the eldest child in the house now that her brother was away at college. "He's only been missing a few days. Maybe he'll still turn up."

"He turned up, all right," said Janice. "I found him on the shoulder of Route 47 this morning."

"Can we see him?" Teri said with the morbid curiosity of a nine-year-old.

"Teri, stop it," Jessica said as Elizabeth started crying louder.

"What?" Teri said, wondering why she was always the one being scolded these days.

"That's enough out of you, young lady," Janice said. "Trust me. You don't want to see Max—it was a pretty bad hit. He didn't suffer though, it was over in an instant."

"Can we bury Max?" Elizabeth said. "Please, Mom?"

"Yes, of course we can. We'll give Max a proper send off. What a good idea, honey."

"Whatever," Teri said.

In the summer of 1974 the Kraus family moved from Fort Wayne, Indiana, to the suburban community of Smithburg for Ron to start a new job in the nearby capital city of Springfield. It was an uncertain time, not only for the family, but for the entire nation as well. Richard Nixon had just resigned the presidency only days before they packed up for the neighboring state of Illinois.

This would be Elizabeth's third move, but the oldest two children had been through many more. After Ron had returned from the Army, he'd gone back to school, choosing the field of accounting because he excelled in mathematics. Tom had come along in 1954 while Ron was still working on his degree, and he and Janice had lived in campus housing designed for married couples. The position he'd landed after graduation was not the job of his dreams, but it did provide stability and room for advancement. With that security Janice was eager to grow their family, and Jessica was born in 1960.

The frequent transfers that followed with two young children were stressful. By 1964 Ron and Janice were arguing often. In a rash moment after one of their fights, Janice got the idea another baby would bring them back to the way they'd felt when Tom and Jessica were little. Less than a year later in April of 1965, they'd added Teri to their family.

Elizabeth's arrival was accidental in March of 1966, and the timing, when Teri was just eleven months old, fostered fierce competition between the sisters. Friends constantly joked about how little Teri looked or acted like her siblings, with her bright red hair and forceful personality. Elizabeth, on the other hand, was a pleasant, undemanding baby, much easier to deal with as the youngest of four. As the years passed, stress in the family grew.

Between Ron's work pressures and Janice's parenting issues, the cracks in their marriage deepened. But the move to Illinois had nothing to do with Ron's career. Janice had discovered a love letter scrawled on a scrap of paper in Ron's trousers on laundry day. The news travelled quickly around the office and throughout town. So just as the Faber family, years earlier, had moved from Maxwell to Lexington to escape the repercussions of Helen Faber's "mistake," Janice and Ron fled to Smithburg, where no one knew their names or secrets.

Although Ron and Janice made the move with the best of intentions, the ups and downs of their relationship didn't improve. Shortly after their arrival Max's broken body, laid to rest in a shoebox where the Kraus family's back yard butted up against the cornfields of the Tate farm, seemed like an omen of things to come.

Not long after Max's burial, the children had been woken in the middle of the night by another of their parents' fights. "It's after two in the morning, why even bother coming home now?" Janice had demanded, her voice a high-pitched frenzy.

"It's none of your business. I'll do as I damn well please," Ron said. "Cut it out, Janice. You'll wake the kids."

"Cut it out?" Janice nearly screamed. "I certainly will not cut it out! You have a responsibility to me and your children, and I need you here to help out. So you had better find a way to get home, whether you like it or not."

"Yeah—or what? I pay the bills around here. I slave away at a job I hate—the one you *made* me take. That gives me the right to do as I please without being harassed. End of discussion."

The girls' dreams were interrupted by fighting almost every night. Burying their heads beneath their pillows and blankets, they tried to shut out the sounds of their parents' marriage falling apart. By the time they got up in the morning, Ron would be gone. Some days Janice would serve breakfast with her jaw clenched and her face set in stone. Other days she'd force a smile and crack jokes that weren't funny and laugh hysterically. One way or another, the girls learned the best strategy was to play along with whatever mood she presented.

The marriage came to an abrupt end a few months later. One night after Jessica, Teri, and Elizabeth had all gone to bed, Janice gathered up all Ron's possessions and dumped them in the driveway. In the accompanying note she instructed him to remove his belongings and never again to step foot in the house. "I'm getting rid of you and your baggage," she wrote, pleased with her turn of phrase.

Janice gave the kids no warning. She simply summoned them to the table, much as she had to announce Max's death. "Your father is gone," she said. "We have separated and will be divorcing. He will not be living here any longer."

"Gone where?" asked Jessica.

"I have no idea," said Janice. "I don't know if he's figured that out yet."

"Can we see him?" Teri asked. Wrong question, she realized instantly. Why was she always saying the wrong thing? Why couldn't she ever get it right like Elizabeth?

"Not for now. He's going to be busy looking for a new job and a place to live."

"Why does he need a new job?" Jessica asked.

"Apparently he doesn't like his old one," Janice said. "He feels it ties him down. And he feels we tie him down, too."

"When can we see him?" Teri knew her father liked her better than her mother did.

"Listen, I can't tell you. This is too new, and I don't have the answers. I have no idea how this is all going to work." Janice slumped into her chair. "But I need you to know this was *his* doing, not mine."

"He wanted the divorce?" Jessica said.

"No, I want it because your father cheated on me." Her shoulders sagged. She fought back tears and bit her lip. The girls sat motionless and silent.

"Elizabeth, do you have any questions?" Janice said, concerned her candor was too much for her youngest, who had not spoken a word.

"No."

"Are you okay, honey?"

Teri rolled her eyes. Her mother would never ask her that kind of question.

"Yes." Elizabeth kept her eyes fixed on her shoes and picked at her cuticles. She was too ashamed to tell her mother she was relieved the fighting would be over. She had been raised in a single-parent family for as long as she could remember. Her father was gone before she woke and didn't get home until after she went to sleep. All she knew about him was the fights that woke her up in the middle of the night, and the angry breakfasts without him the next morning. She couldn't understand why her older sisters cared at all where he was going or when they might see him again.

—∞—

Ron left his job in Springfield, while the rest of the family remained in Smithburg to adjust to their surroundings. Tom was already out on his own attending college in Indiana. Jessica began her freshman year of high school, Teri entered the fourth grade, and Elizabeth started her third-grade year. After being a home-maker for the last twenty years, Janice was forced to earn a living for the first time since her children were born.

"Mom, I didn't know things were so bad," Tom said to Janice over the phone when she broke the news. Away for the last two years, he had no idea what was going on with his family.

"I know, it must be a shock, and I'm sorry you had to hear this way," said Janice.

"I wish you would have told me sooner. Maybe I could have helped, or at least been there for you."

"I didn't want you to worry or mess up your grades," Janice said. "Just graduate. Whatever else happens, I want to make sure you get your degree. Promise me."

"That hardly seems like the most important thing right now, Mom."

"No—it is. Promise me you'll graduate and build a life for yourself, Tom."

"Okay, Mom, I will. I promise you." Tom knew what his mother wanted for him, and from him. She wanted him to say the right things, like the dependable eldest, so that she could then free him of his responsibilities. He was happy to oblige. While it was business as usual for him, Janice bombarded Jessica with duties back at home.

"Jessica, now that I'll be working, I need you to help out more around the house," Janice said to her eldest daughter in private.

"Like how?" Jessica asked. Wasn't it bad enough she had left all her friends back in Fort Wayne, she thought. Now what did her mother want from her?

"I need you to watch Teri and Elizabeth after school until I get home."

"But Mom, I want to join some clubs to make new friends—just like you told me to. And those all meet after school."

"I'm sorry, but you have to be here every day. The girls are too young to be left alone."

"Well, how am I supposed to fit in around here then, huh? You said high school should be the best time of my life."

"And I need you to start dinner every night."

"What? Are you kidding me?" Jessica asked.

"I'll finish up when I get home, but it will be getting late, so you'll need to get things started."

"Mom, that's not fair!" I'm not their mother."

"Fair? Ha! Is it fair that we're in this position now?"

Jessica glared at her mother.

"No, life is not fair, Jessica. So get that notion out of your head right now. It'll save you more misery later, trust me."

"I want my old friends back, and my old life!" Jessica stormed off to her bedroom and slammed the door.

Janice had suspected her circumstances might change. Several years before the move after Elizabeth started kindergarten, she had gone back to school for her general equivalency diploma. While her kids were away learning, she had done the same by attending adult education classes and studying in secret. At the age of thirty-nine she had accomplished her goal without fanfare. Tucking her certificate away in a box for safekeeping, she had wondered when she might need to put it to use in support of her family. That time arrived sooner than expected.

Luckily, Janice found employment quickly, thanks to good timing and a man named Duke Simpson. He had struck it rich by the low standards of his southern Illinois region when he was named the CEO of a booming corporation headquartered in Belleville. He'd ordered the establishment of a bureau in the state capital for business purposes. Because Janice's application hit his desk at the moment of need, he hired her as a bookkeeper for the satellite office in Springfield. The two hit it off immediately.

Duke played the part of commander-in-chief to perfection in both his professional and personal life. While average in stature, his authority made it seem like he towered over those around him; he was right in all matters and unquestionable in his actions. His staff jumped at his command and cowered at his temper. While he recognized and rewarded excellence, he was quicker to notice mistakes and punish his employees. Living in luxury with his wife and kids, he dominated his family in the same manner as his staff. Nobody messed with him.

One day after school the girls were sprawled on the family room floor watching *Gilligan's Island* when Janice entered with a man they'd never met. "Girls, I'd like you to meet my boss, Mr. Simpson. He's in town for a few days and has offered to help paint the living room."

"Hi, I'm Jessica," she said, standing up and extending her hand politely. "That's nice of you to help us paint." Jessica had no way of knowing Duke's subordinates would find this suspiciously out of character for their boss.

"Well, your mom sounded like she could use some help around the house," Duke said. "And I actually like to paint. It's better than a lot of other chores I can think of."

"Hi," Teri said with a wave, not budging from her spot on the floor as she returned her attention to the television.

"Nice to meet you," Duke said.

"And this is my youngest, Elizabeth," Janice said. "She's a bit shy."

"Hi there," Duke said warmly.

"Hi." Elizabeth couldn't think of anything else to say and looked away.

"So show me this room to be painted then," Duke said.

After the painting was done, Duke offered to help out quite often. The kids got used to seeing him and welcomed him as a trusted ally of the family.

Another companion turned up closer to home. Her name was Susan, and she was one of the first people Janice met after moving to Smithburg because she often frequented the grocery store where Susan worked. Susan had children of similar age, and together they shared a passion for shopping, antiques, gossiping, and silliness. Susan made Janice feel more like a teenager than a middle-aged woman—the teenager she'd never had a chance to be. And after years of moving all over the country with Ron, she valued her first long-term adult friendship.

Susan became a valued confidante, the only person Janice really talked to about her struggles as a single parent. Ron had moved to Milwaukee soon after the separation, and she was monitoring his contact with the children. With limited education and work experience, Janice worried constantly about money and struggled to pay the bills. Her patience wore thin with all her daughters, but particularly the middle one.

─⟊⟊⟊⟋─

"Thank you for joining me on such short notice, Mrs. Kraus," said Mrs. Kennedy, Teri's sixth grade school teacher. She pointed towards the chair beside her desk, and Janice sat like a youngster awaiting punishment.

"Yes, of course," said Janice as she glanced at the clock on the wall, worried because she'd had to leave work an hour early. "What's this about?"

"I'm concerned about Teri and felt you should know what's going on," said Mrs. Kennedy. "She's acting up in class and disrupting lessons, and her grades have dropped drastically. I'm sure you've noticed that already."

"Yes, I'm well aware that she is the class clown. She craves attention for some reason. And we've already discussed her grades and the need to study harder."

"There's more though," Mrs. Kennedy said with a pained look on her face. "She's been stealing lunch money from some of the children."

"What?" Janice said as she shifted position in her chair. "I don't know anything about that!"

"Well, we just caught her in the act yesterday after a student tipped us off that it had been going on for some time. Teri spent the afternoon in the principal's office, and we told her that we would be talking with you."

"She didn't say anything to me last night. Not a word."

"Your daughter has developed a mean streak that raises a red flag," Mrs. Kennedy said matter-of-factly. "Is there anything going on at home that would cause such a change in behavior? Anything we should know about?"

"We're working through some issues right now," said Janice. "But it's under control, and she knows everything will be fine." *There's no way I'll tell her about the divorce,* Janice thought. *No one will understand, and I have no intention of being the latest gossip in this little town.*

"All right then," said the teacher as she crossed her hands on her desk. "We'll let you handle discipline with your daughter. If the problems continue however, it may be wise to seek professional help. We can refer you to an excellent child psychologist, so please don't hesitate to call if you find you need to later."

"I'm sure that won't be necessary. I'll take care of this, and things will get back to normal. Thank you for your time."

Great, Janice thought as she left. *How can I handle this on top of everything else?* Teri was becoming a problem child, and not just at school either. Girls got nasty as teens, but Jessica had been easy compared to Teri, who'd become a shrew from the moment she woke until her head hit the pillow again. Everything set her off, and she spewed nothing but dirty words to tell the world she was angry. *Where did she pick up that foul language anyway,* Janice wondered.

Teri started smoking cigarettes, which was far worse than the cursing. She was caught red-handed puffing away in the backyard, and she was only eleven years old. No amount of punishment made a bit of difference, grounding her or taking away the television only spurred her on. She laughed right in her mother's face, saying "Like I care about that, you can't stop me!" Pretty soon she gave up trying to hide the filthy habit and came home reeking like a chimney.

Janice's biggest concern was that Teri was a loner. She didn't have any friends, and instead made enemies by picking fights and threatening her classmates. Like her grandparents and mother before her, Janice's instinct was to hide her daughter's issues to protect her family and their reputation, at least until she figured out what to do. But the threads in her loosely-woven cover up continued to unravel.

Teri wasn't Janice's only source of worry. One afternoon at work she took a call from school about another daughter.

"Is this Mrs. Kraus?"

"Yes, this is Mrs. Kraus speaking. Who's calling, please?"

"This is Bea Armstrong, the school nurse."

"Oh, hello Mrs. Armstrong," said Janice, bracing for the news. "Is there a problem?"

"I'm afraid so, it's Elizabeth again," the nurse said. "Same old thing—her tongue went numb, and she was complaining of blind spots in her vision. She just threw up before we could make it to the restroom."

"Oh, I'm so sorry!"

"Honestly, I should have known better. It's always the same symptoms in the exact same order."

"I'll leave right now to come get her."

"I've covered her eyes like you suggested, but the headache is already coming. I can't block the noise around us either. The poor thing—it's making matters worse, I'm afraid."

"I'll get her home to sleep it off," said Janice. "That's the only thing that works."

"Just remember, she cannot return for twenty-four hours since she vomited."

"Great—more time off work," Janice said to herself as she hung up. Thank goodness Duke was an understanding boss. Elizabeth's migraines were now coming monthly. *She's such a perceptive child,* Janice thought, *absorbing all the turmoil around her like a little sponge, but too afraid to speak up or act out.* If only she could soak up a bit of Teri's ferocity—and if only Teri could give some away.

While the kids suffered the effects, the long distance divorce dragged on with no resolution in sight. "Not again, Janice," said Ron with a deep exhale one night. "I already told you I can't send money right now."

"You don't understand," Janice said, panic making her shout. "The children have so many expenses, and the bills are piling up!"

"I can't send what I don't have, so it's pointless to keep yelling."

"Living with that girlfriend of yours in Chicago now and splitting the bills, you should have extra cash."

"Look, I haven't got this consulting thing figured out yet." Ron sat on the edge of the bed and checked to make sure the door was closed. "Drumming up my own business is hard work, and the last month has been slow. I'm damn lucky Ruth lets me stay here, or I'd be out on the street."

"Oh, boohoo, I don't wanna hear about your midlife crisis," said Janice with a snort. "You want the freedom to cherry pick work you think is worthy of your efforts, when what you need is a real job. You know, one where you work every day for eight hours."

"There are no full-time jobs out there at my skill level," said Ron. "We've been through this so many times."

"You're already neglecting your kids emotionally, which is becoming a real burden for me, by the way. I will not let you neglect them financially, so figure it out."

From the second floor of Ruth's suburban greystone Ron heard the swelling of sirens from the city as he made a snap decision. "That's it, Janice, I can't take it one more second. Go through my lawyer from now on because I'm not gonna let you badger me anymore."

"Oh great, let the lawyers have your money instead of me because you don't wanna talk—" She heard the click and slammed the receiver down with a groan.

All further conflicts and requests were funneled through lawyers, who charged outrageous fees for Ron and Janice's incessant squabbles. After a paper trail of accusations back and forth, the divorce was finalized over two years after their separation.

The agreement failed to make their problems disappear, and the Kraus household continued to struggle. Janice, Jessica, Teri and Elizabeth tried to settle into small-town life among the white-collar, middle-class residents of Smithburg, but circumstances threatened to expose their poverty. They scraped by without many of the usual conveniences while Janice constantly searched for new ways to save money. To keep the utilities down, she refused to run the air conditioning or water the lawn in the summer and set the thermostat unbearably low in the winter. She reduced her food bill by clipping coupons, shopping at the day-old bread store, and mixing powdered milk, which the kids refused to drink.

In middle school now, Elizabeth became a target for the school bullies, Betsy and Joanie. "Look at that, must be a flood coming,"

Betsy said to Joanie as they lounged on the hallway floor with their backs propped up to the wall.

"Ha, ha, you're right!" Joanie said. Taller and thinner than her sisters, Elizabeth was painfully aware that her hand-me-downs were always too large in the body and too short in the legs and arms. The poor fit made her the butt of jokes. "What's with those pants anyway? Looks like she can't afford a belt to keep 'em from falling right off."

"Mom, I need some new jeans," Elizabeth said to her mother after dinner that night.

"What? You don't need any clothes, Elizabeth. You've got a million things from your sisters!"

"Right, Mom, tons of stuff that doesn't fit because I tower over them!"

Janice started to speak and then stopped short to think about the best response. "Honey, you know I can't afford it right now. It's just not possible—" Her voice trailed off as she thought about the stack of bills already past due.

"Please, Mom," Elizabeth said. "The girls at school are making fun of me because my pants are too short."

Janice could see she was struggling to get the words out. "Okay, okay then. I know it must be hard." She pulled her daughter in for a hug. "I can't promise, but let me see what I can do."

Two days later Jessica took Elizabeth to J.C. Penney's and helped her shop for two pairs of jeans, armed with cash to pay for the purchase. Without any thought about how her mother could afford it, she picked out an ultra-hip pair of Chic stonewashed jeans and an off-brand pair of funky flare-bottoms, both of which dragged on the floor. It would take her years to outgrow these, and she would alternate between wearing the two, certain Betsy and Joanie could find no fault with her now.

The Kraus family could not get back on track, and Janice finally swallowed her pride and applied for aid through the school lunch program. Teri and Elizabeth began receiving midday meals free of charge in junior high. Delight quickly turned to horror when Elizabeth was given a different colored lunch token to be presented in the cafeteria. The plastic coins were fire-engine red instead of standard green, signaling disparity like a four-way stop sign. Unwilling to be singled out as poor, Elizabeth started skipping lunch by making excuses and avoiding the cafeteria completely.

While Elizabeth tried to hide her problems at school, Jessica was lucky enough to escape. She squeaked by with average grades and no extracurricular activities or awards to her name. As a latecomer to the scene, she was never accepted by the popular kids and fell in with the wrong crowd. Instead of smoking her homework and final exams, she smoked cigarettes and pot to dull the resentment of never fitting in and being forced to look after her younger sisters all the time. After an unsuccessful stint at the community college, she decided it was time to level with her mother.

"Mom, can we talk a few minutes?" Jessica asked late one night.

"What is it?" Janice said without looking up from the laundry she was folding.

"Well, for starters, I've dropped my classes—thought you might want to know that." She had enrolled in three courses and decided within a month that it just wasn't right for her.

"Why, Jessica? You haven't even given it a fair try yet!"

"It's not for me, Mom. I'm not a brain or anything like Elizabeth. I just need a job, ya know? A place to clock in and out like a normal person."

"You want to work for the state then? Like everyone else in this town?"

"I guess I do. What's wrong with that?"

"Those jobs are hard to come by," Janice said as she thought about it, wishing a better life for her dutiful daughter. "I guess I could ask Duke to put in a good word for you. He has lots of connections and could probably get you on board."

"Would you, Mom? That would be great!"

With Duke pulling the right political strings, Jessica got a secretarial job for a state agency in the fall of 1978. To her mother's dismay she promptly moved out of her family house and in with her boyfriend Vince, who rented his own apartment. But the real problem was not Janice's hurt feelings; it was that Jessica no longer served as after-school surrogate mother and referee to her two younger sisters at home. Without her there Teri and Elizabeth were at each other's throats.

"What are you doing?" Teri said after spotting Elizabeth at the kitchen counter for an after-school snack.

"It's called eating. You put food in your mouth, chew, and then swallow, see?" said Elizabeth with a smirk.

"Okay, smart ass. I'm hungry too, and those were mine," Teri said, her eyes narrowed to slits and her voice turned to a growl.

"Funny, I didn't see your name on the bag anywhere, and I know you didn't pay for these." Elizabeth finished off the last cookie and wiped the corners of her mouth.

"Why, you little bitch," Teri said as she shoved Elizabeth off her barstool. She hit the floor with a thud. *Finally, someone putting her in her place*, Teri thought.

"What the—what is wrong with you, Teri?" Stunned more than hurt, Elizabeth couldn't believe she had been attacked over the last Chips Ahoy. "Get a grip, will ya?"

"Oh, and everything belongs to you, doesn't it?" Teri was foaming at the mouth as she spit the words out. *It's not enough for her to be the one Mom loves most*, Teri thought. *She has to take everything for herself, food included. And there's no one left around here who gives a damn about me. At least Jessica used to take my side sometimes.*

Elizabeth picked herself up off the floor and walked away, realizing she had hurt her wrist while breaking her fall.

"And just where do you think you're going?" Teri asked and headed after her. "Huh? Answer me!"

Elizabeth broke into a run down the hall. There was no sense in calling for help because they were home alone. Teri followed suit by dashing after her, up for the chase. Rounding the corner and ducking into her bedroom, Elizabeth slammed and locked the door just as her sister rammed into it.

"Open up, you little chicken shit! I'm not finished with you yet, and Mommy isn't here to protect you." She pounded on the door between outbursts.

Elizabeth backed away to the farthest corner of the room and slid down the wall to a seated position on the shag carpet. She had been overjoyed to inherit Jessica's bedroom after sharing one with Teri her whole life, but right now she was most thankful for the lock Jessica had insisted on for privacy. Staring at the door, she wondered how long it would hold. The banging changed to kicking as Teri tired of the exertion.

"Ouch—God damn it!" Teri screamed after a sickening crack. "Here's another thing Mom will be mad at me about." Her foot had broken through the door and left a jagged hole the size of an apple. She retreated while muttering obscenities, and Elizabeth checked the clock to see how long it would be before her mother came home from work.

7
Truth Hits Everybody

May–August 2000

✾

Sleep lay behind me like a broken ocean
Strange waking dreams before my eyes unfold
You lay there sleeping like an open doorway
I stepped outside myself and felt so cold

—Sting

✾

Scott County Sheriff, Gary Newberry
05-12-00
Reference: Janice Kraus
Report by: Sergeant Tom Carter
On 05-06-00 at approximately 7:01 p.m. the Davenport Police Department dispatched Deputy Sorensen to 12499 105th Ave. for a subject reporting she was missing two children. Deputy Sorensen arrived at 7:15 p.m. Due to the nature of the call, I also responded, and I arrived at approximately 7:25 p.m. When I spoke to Janice she seemed very confused and somewhat upset. She stated she was

missing two children that were in second and third grade. She could not tell me their ages or names. At times she would refer to one of the missing children as Elizabeth. She could not tell me her name unless I would remind her, and she could not tell me her address. I sat and spoke to Janice for about fifteen minutes. She could tell me that she had a son, Tom, in Florida and two daughters that lived in the same area as her. Then the next second she would ask me what we were going to do about her missing children. She then told me of a daughter, Jessica, who also lived in Smithburg. When I asked her how old her children were, she told me they were in their thirties. She again asked me what we should do about her missing children. When I would remind her that her children were grown and we should call one, she stated she did not want to bother them. She could not remember any phone numbers for any relatives. I asked her to look in her purse for any numbers. At that time we located a number for her brother Walt in Omaha, NE. I had the police department contact him and he provided numbers for her daughters. The police department made contact with someone there, and they were going to be en route to pick her up. They also advised she had been traveling with a male companion, but she had left him at another location, and he had since returned home. When I asked her about that, she stated she was traveling alone. I then had the police department contact the hospital and the Women's Resource Center to see if they could care for Janice until someone arrived – they declined. I then had Deputy Sorensen transport Janice to the police department and asked that the staff in the jail look after her until her relatives arrived. I was worried that Janice could wander away and become lost again. When I spoke to Janice, at no time could she tell me where she was going and she had no idea where she was.

End of report.

"Well, we've got her now, don't we?" Mr. Hartmann said as he waved the evidence in his hand.

"The police report?" said Jessica.

"Quite incriminating," he said. "I've read it and am convinced any judge would grant guardianship now based on your mother's documented behavior and mental state." He scanned their faces for a response and continued when he saw only fear. "Don't worry. This is exactly what we've been waiting for, and luckily nobody got hurt."

"So what's next?" asked Elizabeth.

"We'll need to determine the best candidate to be named guardian, and I'd recommend that two of you share the task. That way no single person is burdened with the responsibility."

The siblings shifted their focus to each other. They hadn't thought this part through.

"I'll do it!" said Tom from the speakerphone. Jessica and Elizabeth shrugged their shoulders in unison.

"Could that work?" Jessica asked.

"I don't think you would be a wise choice," said their lawyer. "This job will likely require critical healthcare decisions to be made and paperwork to be signed on the spot. Unfortunately, you're just too far away for that, Tom."

"Nope, I don't want that pressure," Teri said. "I'll bet none of you want me to do it either. Count me out." She crossed her arms and leaned back in her chair.

"That leaves Jessica and me," said Elizabeth.

"Nothing else makes sense," Jessica agreed, "though I can't say I'm thrilled."

"I'm actually feeling a little bit like I have car sickness," Elizabeth agreed.

"Speaking of cars, does this mean we can take hers away now?" Jessica asked.

"And take over paying her bills?" Elizabeth added.

"That's what it will mean, and those are likely the two most pressing matters," said Mr. Hartmann. "But the next step is to take your petition for guardianship to a judge. You can't do anything without the court's seal of approval."

"How long will that take?" Tom asked.

"Well, justice moves at its own pace," Mr. Hartmann said, "but with this evidence of her incompetence I hope a judge will see this is a pressing matter and push it through quickly."

─❧─

Janice was oblivious to the court motion moving slowly forward. To her it was life as usual. Harold remained her love interest, although her illness weighed heavily on his mind now. Since the fiasco in Nebraska he had attempted to end their relationship several times as the strain of her behavior wore him down. She could not remember these break-ups and continued to show up at his house every afternoon expecting dinner. He was stuck and didn't have the heart to turn her away. Knowing that everyone disapproved of their involvement, he passed along only the most crucial information the family needed to know, like when Janice lost a crown on one of her teeth.

"Mom, let's call the dentist and set an appointment to fix that crown you lost the other night," Jessica said during a visit. "It should be in your purse wrapped up in foil."

"What are you talking about? My teeth are just fine," Janice said.

"No, Harold said you lost it during dinner the other night. He wrapped it up for you so you wouldn't lose it, remember?"

"That's not true. Everything's just fine."

"Come on, let's look for it together." Jessica grabbed her mother's purse.

"Get your hands off that," Janice said, snatching the bag from her daughter's hands. "I know what you're up to anyway. You want to lock me up and steal all my money!"

"What? Oh, come on, Mom! I just want to get your tooth fixed! Look in the mirror, and I'll show you which one it is."

"You aren't fooling me, not for a second. Get out of here and stay out of my business!" Every encounter with Janice was similar. In her eyes her children were the enemy, while to them she was now worse than a child because she would not listen to reason.

"Hi, Mom, how are you?" Elizabeth said as she entered Harold's kitchen. She had warned him beforehand she was stopping by and in need of his help. This was her fourth attempt to take care of an important matter, and so far her mother had stalled her efforts.

"Oh, what are you doing here?" Janice said from the dining room table.

"Well, I knew I'd catch you here, and we've got business to finish. It's the application to refinance your mortgage." Elizabeth glanced at Harold, hoping he'd chime in.

"What mortgage? I don't need another mortgage!"

"Not a new one, but your current mortgage, Mom. We discussed how it needs to be reworked at a lower interest rate to save you money. And this needs to be turned in right away."

"Harold, what's this all about?" Janice asked the only person in the room she trusted, and Elizabeth crossed her fingers behind her back.

"Well, you do need to sign these, Janice," Harold said, tossing a salad at the counter. "It's just routine stuff. Get it done so we can enjoy our dinner."

"I do need to take care of this?" She looked to him for assurance.

"Yes, it's important, so sign where she says."

Elizabeth placed the application, turned to the signature page, on the table along with a pen and backed up out of firing range.

"Hmmmmm," Janice said as she turned the pages without

reading. "No, I don't need this," she said and pushed the document away.

"Mom, please—just sign it!"

"No, I won't do it!" Janice started pacing the kitchen. "Why are you here? I won't let you steal my house and put me away!"

"Janice, really, there's no reason to—" said Harold.

"Accusations like that hurt, Mom, especially when I'm doing this for you," said Elizabeth.

"Go away," Janice said and pointed to the door. "I'll take care of this myself." She stormed off in a huff.

"Mom, we've got to get this in *now*. Please sign." Elizabeth turned to Harold, desperate for him to convince her.

"Damn it, Janice, get back here and sign the papers *now*," Harold said in a thunder that stopped her in her tracks. "This is to *help* you, and you're being ridiculous."

"Well, I'm sure it's not—"

"Do it!" Harold cut her short by shoving the paper and pen towards her. Hurt by his outburst, she sunk into the chair and signed where Elizabeth indicated.

"Thank you," Elizabeth said to Harold. She grabbed the application and fled to her car, where she sat banging her hands on the steering wheel and trying to stop the tears. She finally drew a deep breath, dabbed at her face with a tissue to avoid smudging her mascara, and drove away.

History books are filled with names and dates of battles and generals, territories won and lost, lives sacrificed. But in Elizabeth's mind no battle could compare with the daily skirmishes she and her sisters got into with their mother over trivial things like refilling prescriptions and throwing away spoiled food. After two months the court approved temporary guardianship status for Jessica and Elizabeth, giving them the authority to act until a permanent decision was delivered in the matter.

They thought the end was finally in sight. With legal credentials in hand they visited their mother's bank, opened a joint account, and ordered checks to pay bills and settle outstanding debts. They left her primary account untouched and transferred money to it so she could continue writing checks under their supervision. Then they visited the Smithburg Post Office and requested all of her mail to be forwarded to Elizabeth's address. That way she would know when bills arrived and due dates rolled around without worrying about her mother losing important papers or deliberately hiding them.

The last order of business was the most important and also most daunting task: confiscating Janice's car. Living on her own without transportation, she would need to be checked on daily and driven around for her personal needs. Because all three of her daughters had jobs and families of their own, they recruited Janice's best friend Susan to pitch in by visiting Janice every day of the week. Because she lived close by, Susan also agreed to take Janice to church and to continue their shopping excursions. Harold, on the other hand, remained in the dark; the sisters didn't trust him to keep their intentions from Janice.

On a rainy Saturday morning Elizabeth picked up Jessica and Teri and took Route 47 to their mother's house. The rain was falling so hard and fast Elizabeth almost pulled over to wait it out. But it was important they be there to deal with the inevitable fallout. When they arrived Janice was already up and dressed. She poured coffee and made small talk. She seemed unconcerned that her three daughters, two of whom could rarely sit in a room for five minutes without arguing, had shown up at the same time and were sitting quietly, sipping their coffee, listening to every word she said.

The doorbell rang promptly at ten o'clock and the color drained from everyone's face, except for Janice. She answered the front door, coffee mug in hand, and found a Sangamon County officer and a Smithburg policeman standing there.

"Well, hello," she said.

"Good morning, ma'am," said the officer in a smart brown uniform. "Are you Janice Kraus?"

"Yes, I am," she said. "Is there something I can do for you two? A cup of coffee on a rainy morning, perhaps?"

"No, ma'am, but thanks for the offer. This is for you," he said, placing a heavy manila envelope in her hands. "You have been officially served a summons by the Court of Sangamon County."

"What—what is this?" Janice said, studying the package.

"It's a legal document naming you in a court hearing, ma'am," said the nice looking policeman dressed all in navy. "You'll need to read this, and you may want to consult with an attorney."

"Legal document? What's this all about? Oh, I'm so rude. Come in out of the rain. Are you sure I can't get you some coffee?"

With her mother preoccupied, Teri ducked out through the garage door and drove away in Janice's car. While Janice spoke with the officers, Elizabeth slipped into another room and called Harold to fill him in and ask him to come out to her mother's house at once. Janice would need support from someone she trusted once she realized what was going on.

Soon the officers left, and Jessica and Elizabeth tried to explain to their mother that her own refusal to accept help had forced them to take legal action to protect her.

"Mom," Jessica said, "you've been having a lot of problems with your memory. We know you know this. We've seen all the books you have around your house, and the bottles of remedies."

"Well, what business is that of yours? Older people forget things sometimes."

"No, Mom," Elizabeth said, "it's gone way beyond that. You're forgetting to pay bills and you won't let us help you. You're getting into car accidents. So far they've all been minor, but one day you might hurt yourself, or someone else."

"Well, I don't remember anything like that," Janice said.

"Yes, Mom, that's the problem," Jessica said. "You don't even remember what happened in Nebraska."

"Nebraska! If only one of you girls had taken me there," Janice shouted, shaking her fists. "But no, you're just too busy with your own lives. Well, you have no right to do this. I can't believe the nerve of you treating your own mother this way." She was circling the room, stomping her feet, challenging all their claims. After a few minutes her frustration level peaked and she raced for the garage to escape.

"Oh no. Here we go," said Elizabeth.

"What? Where's my car? What have you done with my car? You've stolen it! How could you do that? I'm your mother. How could you steal from me? Shame on you!"

"Whoa, Mom, slow down," Jessica said with her hands raised.

"Did Teri do this? Where is she? That would be just like her. She was here, wasn't she? And now she's gone. She's taken my car, that little thief!"

"Mom, she hasn't stolen your car, but she's taken it for your own safety."

"She was always a little thief, that one!"

"No, Mom, it wasn't just her. We all planned this. We had to. You forced it by not cooperating."

"Cooperating? Cooperating with you ungrateful little thieves? Get out of my house now!" Janice shrieked. "I don't ever want to see either of you again. And I'm cutting you both—I'm cutting all three of you out of my will. Tom's the only good child I have left."

"Calm down, Mom," Jessica said. "Let us stay and help you."

"You can't steal my car! You can't just come in here and steal my car! Get out, and I mean it!" Janice ran into the bathroom and slammed the door shut, wailing and pounding on it, throwing everything she could get her hands on around the room.

"That will be a mess to clean up," said Elizabeth.

Jessica smiled weakly. "Yeah, like that's our biggest worry right now—cleaning up after Mom's tantrum."

"Too bad Teri's not here. She'd be proud of that one."

They almost didn't hear Harold's knock at the front door over the din their mother was making. Knowing he was better equipped to soothe Janice than they were, they left him there and drove away in silence. As Elizabeth pulled up to drop her sister off, Jessica asked, "That was the right thing to do, right? That was our only choice, wasn't it?"

"Yes, it was."

"Then why do I feel like such a criminal?"

"I don't know, Jess, but I do too. I didn't think it would be that bad. I thought once the summons was served she'd forget and be on her merry way."

"That's what I thought too," Jessica said with a sigh.

"I was feeling really proud of how we were all working together on this one. Not fighting like usual, you know?" Elizabeth said.

"Just go home, Liz," her sister said. "You look like you could use—I don't know—a cup of tea and a good cry on John's shoulder."

"What about you?" Elizabeth asked. "Are you gonna be okay?"

"Yeah," Jessica said. "I just think maybe, lacking the husband part of the equation, I'll go for something a little stronger than tea."

As hard as Harold tried, however, he found Janice beyond reason or consolation. She could not understand what had happened or recall anything she was told. All she remembered was that her car was gone, and the inability to come and go as she pleased gnawed away at her for days.

"Hello, is this the police?" Janice said while checking the number posted in three different places on her cabinets.

"Yes, you've reached the Smithburg Police Department. Is this an emergency?" asked the switchboard operator.

"Yes, it is! My car's been stolen! Please help me get it back!"

"Is this Ms. Kraus again?"

"Why, yes it is. I live at—"

"Ms. Kraus, this is Margie speaking. You just called an hour ago. I spoke with you then."

"What? Are you sure?"

"Yes, we've already talked about this, remember?" said Margie with as much patience as she could muster. "Your children have taken possession of your car. You need to speak with them about this, not us."

"My kids have my car?"

"Yes, ma'am. Please give them a call instead."

"Okay, I'll do that. Thank you." After hanging up she dialed another number.

"Hello," said Jessica.

"Jessica, do you have my car?"

"No, Mom," Jessica said with a sigh. "Did you call the police *again*?"

"My car is gone! And I need it back now!"

"Mom, we've been through this already—you cannot have your car back. It's not safe for you to be driving anymore."

"No, that's not true—I'm a good driver! Now give it back, I paid for it!"

"Mom, I'll come out and take you wherever you want to go. How about that?"

"No, I want my car back to go where I want, when I want!" She slammed the phone down in a panic.

"Teri, do you have my car?" Janice tried another daughter in desperation. "It's not right for you girls to take it. Bring it back right now, or I'll sue you for stealing it!"

Jessica, Teri, and Elizabeth put the visiting schedule into practice right away, but Janice refused to leave the safety of her house or go anywhere. Depression set in and stuck.

"Hey, Mom," Jessica said one afternoon when she checked on

her mother after work. "Let's go grocery shopping, looks like your fridge is pretty bare."

"What? Oh no, I don't want to go anywhere," said Janice from her spot on the sofa, staring off into space.

"Come on, let's get out for awhile." Jessica reached to pull her from the couch.

"No, I can't." Janice slapped her hands away. "I want to stay here, leave me alone!"

"Why not, Mom?"

"This is the worst day of my life, that's why. I just feel awful!"

"Why? I'm here to take you where you want to go. Everything's okay."

"No, it's not. Everything will never be okay. I can't stand it anymore. Duke's gone, and I don't know what to do!"

"Everything is fine." Jessica sat down next to her mother and wrapped her arm around her. "You'll see, just give it time."

"Time? I'm out of time! What should I do? Just kill myself?"

"Don't talk like that, Mom. We're all here for you, and we love you."

"I'm gonna burn this house down and get it over with," Janice said as she shook loose from Jessica's embrace.

"Come on, Mom, stop it. You're scaring me!" Taking a good look at her mother, Jessica thought, *how are we going to make this work?*

Four days after the summons was served, just after Elizabeth had put her daughters to bed, the phone rang. "This is Dad," Harold said.

"Yes?"

"Your mother is a mess, and I think it's wrong for you to keep her trapped in her house like an animal with no way to get around."

"We're trying to get her out and about but she won't budge," said Elizabeth. "And while I appreciate you coming to help her when I called the other day, you need to remember that her safety is not your job, it's ours."

"Well, you're making a big mistake!" he said and hung up.

While Harold's delivery was rude, his assessment was accurate. Elizabeth sat at her kitchen table feeling guilty. They hadn't thought through their approach enough. They should have anticipated Janice's reaction and prepared for the worst. She dialed the phone.

"Jessica," she said. "I think this has gone far enough. We need professional help. Medical help."

"You're right," Jessica said. "Mom's out of control."

—⚬⚬—

Dr. Kay Padrait was a geriatric psychiatrist accepting new patients. Elizabeth scheduled an emergency consultation and prepped the doctor before their appointment by providing the guardianship paperwork, the police report of the Nebraska incident, and a personal journal she had kept about the progression of her mother's illness over the last four years. Getting Janice to this physician involved trickery, so Elizabeth asked for Teri's help to take their mother out to lunch at her favorite restaurant. They were certain food was the only bait that would flush her out of hiding. While in some ways their mother's illness was tearing them apart, in others it was bringing them back together with a common cause.

After Elizabeth picked Janice up at her house, she stopped off to get Teri, and their plan was in motion. Janice clapped along to a Neil Diamond tune on the stereo. Teri had suggested that her favorite singer might be the ideal way to keep her distracted during the drive, and it worked. To get her into the medical clinic, Elizabeth explained she needed to make a quick stop before lunch. Janice bought the excuse and flipped through magazines in the waiting room. Teri stayed with her while Elizabeth spoke with

Dr. Padrait about her mother's condition. A few minutes later she returned to the waiting room.

"Mom, turns out I have a problem, and I need you to talk with my doctor so you know what's going on," Elizabeth said with a frown. Janice sprang from her chair and followed her daughter down a long corridor of doctors' offices.

"Hello, Janice," Dr. Padrait greeted her as she entered the office. Elizabeth closed the door behind them as instructed.

"Hi," said Janice blankly.

"Will you sit down and talk with me for a few minutes?" Dr. Padrait asked and gestured to an empty chair.

"Okay, I guess," Janice said. "What's going on?"

"Well, I understand you're having some difficulty with the loss of your car," the doctor said, wading carefully into a discussion. "I'd like to help you with that, so can you tell me a little more?"

Janice looked from the doctor, to Elizabeth, and back to the doctor. "Oh no, you don't," she said, bolting for the door. To her surprise there was a guard outside blocking her escape. Slamming the door, she began pacing the office.

"Let me out of here, I need to go," said Janice.

"Please sit back down. Let's talk about how you feel not being able to drive."

"I'm not telling you anything, and you can't make me stay here!"

"Please, Mom," said Elizabeth as she patted the empty chair, "just a few minutes."

"I shouldn't have to deal with this." Janice walked to the window and looked out to get her bearings. "You have some nerve. Who do you think you are?"

"I'm a doctor, and I'd like to help."

"Help? Ha, you can't help me. Nobody can."

"Are you feeling out of control with things going on right now?" the doctor asked. "Because I can help you deal with that."

"Help me deal?" said Janice with a snort. "What should I do then, kill myself?" At the mention of suicide, the exam came to a halt. A nurse summoned Teri to stay with Janice so Elizabeth could speak privately with the doctor, but she failed to see how anything useful could be done after such a disastrous introduction.

"Your mother is hostile and completely uncooperative," said Dr. Padrait.

"Well, yes, that's why we're having such a hard time dealing with her," said Elizabeth. "That's why we're here."

"Unfortunately, I cannot help her under these circumstances. Your mother needs to be hospitalized before we can proceed with any diagnosis or treatment."

"What do you mean? Right now—today?" Elizabeth stammered the words in shock.

"Yes, immediately."

"Are you sure that's the only way to help her?"

"I'm positive. She must be in a controlled setting and unable to flee, like she just attempted."

"Well," Elizabeth said with a pause, stalling for time as she thought. She didn't know whom to trust, where to go, or what else to do. Having her mother committed seemed like a drastic measure.

"You are her guardian, and I'll need your signature to admit her for emergency psychiatric care," Dr. Padrait said.

A secretary drafted the paperwork and helped Elizabeth set up a quick conference call with Jessica and Tom. They were all in shock over this unexpected detour, unsure where the road ahead would lead. They had reached an impasse, however, and could no longer handle their mother.

"Don't come near me," Janice cried out as two burly EMTs in matching blue uniforms closed in, one carrying a straitjacket. "No, no, I said stop. Get away from me!"

"Ma'am, please, settle down. We're not going to hurt you."

"Don't touch me . . . how dare you. Wait . . . what is that thing? Don't put that on me . . . stop it. No!"

Teri and Elizabeth heard their mother's screams from behind a closed office door. Her protests faded as she was subdued and escorted to the ambulance waiting outside.

"Help . . . help! Won't someone help me?"

8
Fragile

August 2000

―――――⚬⚬⚬―――――

Perhaps this final act was meant
To clinch a lifetime's argument
That nothing comes from violence
And nothing ever could
For all those born beneath an angry star
Lest we forget how fragile we are

—Sting

―――――⚬⚬⚬―――――

"Let me go—get your hands off of me!" Janice shrieked over the alarm she'd triggered trying to push open the door. She landed a knee to the orderly's groin and a slap to his face before he and another orderly got control of her.

"That poor woman," said the waif of a girl suffering from anorexia who watched from the activity room.

"Still, she's got spunk for such a tiny thing," said the middle-aged man nearby being treated for a gambling addiction.

"No, don't! Get that thing away from me. Help me, someone!" Janice saw the needle coming and fought against it, but her resistance was futile. Within seconds she'd gone as limp as a rag doll.

"She'll be out for hours—but make sure the restraints are secure," said the nurse with the spiky orange hair and flower-print scrubs. The two orderlies put her in a wheelchair and returned her to her room.

"This one's gonna be nothing but trouble," said the one with Janice's handprint on his cheek. "Do we get paid enough for this?"

"No, we don't. But we all gotta pay our dues on the fifth floor, so let's just do as we're told."

The Kraus siblings had no idea what they were getting into when they'd agreed, under duress, to have their mother committed to the psych ward against her will. What little progress they'd made moving past their own damaged relationships to work together in their mother's best interests had quickly evaporated. The stress of making split-second decisions, with scarce information and no time to research other options, pushed them back into the squabbling roles they'd assumed for most of their lives.

"Excuse me, we're here to see our mother, Janice Kraus," Jessica said into the intercom.

The nurse, the same one who'd wrestled with their mother earlier in her shift, buzzed the sisters into the unit. She was now completing paperwork before going home for the night after another long day. "Sign in," she said, without looking up. "Janice is in room 21 down the hall on the left."

"Hi, I'm Jessica, and these are my sisters Teri and Elizabeth. We'd like an update on our mother's status please," she said, making the effort to smile.

"Certainly," the nurse said, spinning her chair around to answer a phone. She glanced at them quickly but did not return Jessica's smile. "I'll check her file and come down to talk when I can. Oh, and I'm Barb."

"Nothing dismissive about her," Elizabeth commented as they walked away.

"She's probably just a no-nonsense type because she's so busy," Jessica said.

"Yeah," said Teri. "Like I'm sure that's her only problem."

The sisters were wary of more than the nurse's brusqueness. Some patients, dressed in hospital scrubs, leaned idly against walls and stared at them. Others shuffled by, their heads bent low, mumbling to themselves.

"You kind of expect that when TV shows depict these places, they're exaggerating for dramatic effect," said Jessica as they walked past door after door, checking room numbers. "But I guess maybe not."

Teri reached out and touched a wall. "You'd think once somebody called that shade of paint 'hospital green', hospitals would have gotten the message to stop using it," she said. The sisters might have giggled if they hadn't felt so ill at ease.

"Okay, here's room 21," Elizabeth said.

"Hi, Mom," Teri said, stopping just inside the door to the room and forcing herself to sound cheerful. Janice was lying sideways on her bed with her back to the door. "How are ya?"

"Wha?" Janice said and flopped over to look right through them. "Wha do ya wan?" She was glassy-eyed and tongue-tied.

"Mom, it's me, Jessica," she said, taking a gentler approach. "You okay?" She sat on the bed for a closer look. Without any makeup, the person staring back looked like an elderly woman wasting away in oversized garments.

"Fine." Janice blinked and her eyes watered up. "Can I go now?" Her hair was greasy and she reeked of body odor.

"You need to stay a while longer and get better first," Elizabeth said as she bent to kiss her mother on the cheek and crinkled her nose. "Do you know where you are?"

"Well, of course," said Janice.

"Oh, good," said Teri from her post at the door. "And where is that?"

"We're at the bank," Janice said, "but I'm done now." She paused and closed her eyes to concentrate. "Will you take me home?"

Behind them Barb cleared her throat. "Could I speak with you? Out here, please."

"We'll be right back," Jessica said to her mother.

"What exactly is going on here?" Elizabeth said to the nurse in the hall. "She's obviously been overmedicated."

"Actually, she's doing much better than she was earlier," Barb said. "It's a good thing you didn't come in this morning. She set off an alarm trying to leave and put up so much fuss she had to be heavily sedated. We were just able to remove the restraints around the time dinner was served."

"Restraints?" Elizabeth said.

"It's for her own safety, as well as the safety of the other patients," Barb continued. "When a patient has required heavy sedation, we don't know what state of mind they'll wake up in. Sometimes they can be very angry and violent."

"I'd be angry and violent if I woke up in restraints," Teri said, a little too loudly.

The nurse ignored Teri's remark. "You've approved all the drugs we're giving her: Ativan to calm her anxiety, Risperdal and Haldol to manage her psychosis."

"Yes, I approved all those," said Jessica. "But I had no idea they would affect her this way, and this is the first I've been able to see her since she was brought in here."

"And why does she stink?" Teri asked.

"Oh, well, that's another issue," said Barb. "Janice refuses to let any of us help her take a bath, and we're required to monitor all patients while bathing. It's for their own safety—particularly those who, like your mother, are on suicide watch."

"Suicide watch?" Teri said. "You mean because of what she said in Dr. Padrait's office? She didn't really mean that. She was just mad."

"I'm sure you know your mother better than we do, but can you imagine what would happen if a patient made a threat like that and we didn't take it seriously?" Barb asked. She looked at her watch. "Now, if you'll excuse me, my shift is over. If you have any other questions, you'll find Marie at the nurses' station."

"How the hell does someone like that sleep at night?" Teri said, a little too loudly. The nurse ignored her and continued walking away.

"She's just doing her job," Jessica said.

"For a change, I have to admit I agree with Teri," Elizabeth said. "I mean, Mom was getting to be a handful, but she was still coping until we agreed to this. Now look at her. She barely ever even takes an aspirin. They've got her so doped up, her system must be on overload."

"Look, I'm concerned too, but we talked this through," Jessica said. "What other choice did we have?"

"Seriously, Jessica," Elizabeth said and crossed her arms. "I can't believe you're saying that."

"I can't believe you're changing your tune," Jessica said. "Thanks a lot."

"Look, I don't like Carrot Top much, but I guess Jessica's right," Teri said. "Yes, I know that's funny coming from me, but my hair is red, not orange, thank you very much. Anyway, this might all be different if she'd been willing to cooperate—with us, or with Dr. Padrait, or with ol' Carrot Top—but you know Mom. She's so stubborn."

"Well, aren't you quick to forget how much that stubborn woman did for you, Teri," Elizabeth snapped. "If it weren't for her stubbornness you'd probably never have finished high school. And Jessica, without Mom you wouldn't have that nice cushy state job for the last—how long is it now since you thanked her for that career by moving out and abandoning us?"

"That really doesn't help the situation, Elizabeth," Jessica said.

"Oh, now the mothering tone comes out," Elizabeth responded.

"And what, you've never made a mistake in your life, Lizzie?" said Teri. "So that makes you right about everything? That's bullshit. Give me a break, geesh!"

The sisters stood in the hall, deliberately avoiding eye contact until finally Jessica said, "Look, Mom's almost asleep. Let's just give her a kiss goodnight and come at this again when we're not all exhausted and upset."

Over the next several days the siblings watched helplessly as the side effects from all the drugs worsened. Janice acted like a caged animal in a linoleum zoo, roaming the corridors of the psych wing day and night. Her walk turned into a shuffle with short, quick steps to the side instead of straight, full-length strides forward. By this time the girls recognized the unusual gait as a red flag for mental illness. When she did come to a standstill, she rocked back and forth on her feet; another warning. By her sixth day in the ward she started leaning to the left while she hobbled about.

"What's wrong with her?" Elizabeth asked the doctor on duty, a resident in blue scrubs who might have been good looking with some sleep and a shave. "Bending sideways like that is just so odd."

"It's caused by the medication," he said. "We can adjust to correct these minor gait problems, and it should all work itself out eventually."

"Minor gait problems?" Elizabeth said. "You call that *minor*? She looks insane, and it can't be good for her back."

"I assure you it will cause no permanent damage."

"Great," Elizabeth said. "That's really reassuring. Why did we ever agree to this? She wasn't this bad until we signed the papers to have her brought here."

The tired-looking doctor put down his chart. "Look, I see

this all the time. It's not unusual for families to second-guess their choices. But you made the right decision, and you have to trust we're doing the best we can for her."

"That's easy for you to say," Elizabeth said. "She's not your mother."

The doctor sighed, picked up his chart, and went on to his next patient.

Over Janice's first week on the psych ward the neurologists, psychiatrists, and gerontologists scheduled her for at least a dozen tests. But day after day they were abandoned because she refused to stay still, even when sedated. The technicians couldn't just put her out because some of the tests required her cooperation. Finally, after struggling to get through a physical exam, mental evaluation, blood tests, urinalysis, several chest x-rays, an EKG, MRI, and a CT scan, the doctors reached a diagnosis.

"Although Janice is in great health physically," Dr. Padrait said, "the MRI shows atrophy in her temporal lobe. In lay terms, that means her brain is shrinking." The siblings sat in the doctor's office, stunned into silence.

"Anything else?" Jessica asked finally.

"On the basis of the information from the MRI, we did a full dementia work-up," said Dr. Padrait. "Although there is no single test that can conclusively diagnose Alzheimer's, all the signs indicate that's what's behind your mother's problems."

She'd said the word the Kraus children had been whispering for four years. The room was silent for a moment.

"Although there is no drug that will cure Alzheimer's, or even halt its progress," the doctor continued, "a drug called Aricept sometimes slows it down a bit. So we've added that to her drug cocktail."

"Cocktail?" said Teri. "That's what you call it?"

"Perhaps an unfortunate expression, but yes," said the doctor. "I'm sorry, I know this is hard to take in, but I have other patients waiting. You're scheduled to see someone else who can help you with next steps."

"Thank you for meeting with me," Norman Craig said from his office right outside the psychiatric unit. "It's obvious your mother is severely ill, and we need to talk." He was the likable, grandfatherly type with a soothing voice and a gift for reading between the lines.

"Yeah, we all know that," Teri said. "So why exactly did we *have* to come discuss her with you?" Jessica and Elizabeth winced at her bluntness.

"Yes, I should explain that straight away, thank you," Mr. Craig said. "I am a social worker for this hospital, and it is my job to help you prepare for what lies ahead after your mother's diagnosis."

"After?" Teri asked. "I thought she'd been diagnosed."

"It's not conclusive," Jessica said. "It's never conclusive."

"It could be more conclusive than it is," Mr. Craig said. "There's just been one problem."

"Our mother isn't cooperating," Tom said through the speakerphone, wishing he could be present at these meetings instead of just listening.

"Yes, I guess you know your mother better than anyone else," Mr. Craig said. "Dr. Padrait and I have discussed the hospital's findings and her condition at length. At this point, there are really only two options."

"You mean once she's discharged?" Elizabeth asked.

"That's exactly what I mean. Since testing is nearly done, you'll need to make some decisions soon because your mother cannot leave until plans are in place to ensure her safety."

"Okay, so what should we do?" Jessica said.

"Your mother will require some sort of supervision from this point on. She will either need to be placed in a nursing home for twenty-four hour monitoring, or she will need caregivers coordinated to return home."

"There's no way she's going to a nursing home," Elizabeth said. "We can take care of her at home. That was our plan after taking her car away, if all of this hadn't happened."

"I understand," said Mr. Craig. "We have some referrals for home healthcare providers then, and you'll need to look into the cost and services offered." He shuffled through papers on his desk in search of the information.

"Hold on a sec, Lizzie," Teri said. "That may not be what we want. It would be easier for all of us if Mom was in a nursing home. I've got my own family to look after, ya know? And unlike you, Jess and I don't have loving husbands helping us out."

"We'd all have to pitch in and help out," Jessica said.

"Of course we would, but do we want to?" Teri said. "Can we handle it? Mom's out of her mind and won't listen to any of us, so how are we supposed to take care of her? Don't look at me like that, Elizabeth, I'm not only thinking of myself. I'm thinking about her, too."

Elizabeth rolled her eyes. "That'll be the day."

"You would still need to pay for outside help," Mr. Craig said to make the situation clear. "Even if you all take turns, your mother will require assistance from trained professionals. She'll probably need someone to check on her daily."

"Daily, really?" Elizabeth asked in surprise.

"Yes, I'm afraid so. She'll require medication and monitoring at all times if she's back in her home. I'm certain of it after talking to Dr. Padrait about her prognosis."

"Her funds are limited," Tom said. "I don't know if she can afford it."

"Yes, well, these are all issues you need to work out to determine the best course of action," Mr. Craig said and handed the stack of pamphlets he'd gathered to Jessica. "Start here to get some ideas, but begin right away, because your mother's need is immediate."

"Okay," Jessica said while flipping through a brochure.

"I should add that both Dr. Padrait and I feel a nursing home would be the best choice," Mr. Craig said, glancing in Elizabeth's direction.

"No!" Elizabeth said. "Absolutely not. She will *not* go to a nursing home! And Teri, stop looking so smug."

"What are you talking about? You're not even looking at me!"

"I can feel your smugness from the other side of the room."

"For God's sake, Lizzie, we have to consider it," said Teri. "We need to compare costs anyway—Mom is not made of money. You know that."

"Then we pitch in and share the cost!"

"Says the sister with the great job and a husband to help pay the mortgage."

"You're an ungrateful brat," said Elizabeth. "You were ungrateful as a teenager, and you're still ungrateful now—after all Mom has done for you. Always looking for the easy way out, aren't you?"

"And you're not being realistic about what's going on here!" Teri was on her feet with clenched fists.

"I know she'd be better off in her own home than in another nut house like this!"

"Come on, she was crazy before she got here! She's been crazy for years. She was crazy long before the Alzheimer's started."

"How dare you! You drove her crazy! She did more for you than any of us—she nearly killed herself just to get you through high school!"

"She didn't give me the one thing I really wanted. *You* hogged all that—none of us were good enough!"

"That's nonsense. She *never* gave up on you because she loved you. What about the time you went missing for days? What about the private school she had to pay for? Now look how easily you turn your back without even lifting a finger to help her."

"That's enough. Cut it out, you two," Tom said over the speaker.

"You're a fine one to talk, Tom," Teri said, leaning over to shout directly into the phone. "You disappeared years ago. You never had to deal with the craziness after Mom and Dad divorced. Now you think you can just sit in sunny Florida and act like you're the head of the family? Where the hell were you when we needed you?"

There was silence at the other end of the phone.

"Come on, Teri, sit down," said Jessica.

"Yeah, right," Teri said. "Cuz if Tom's not around, I should take orders from you. You may not have moved away, but you left us for your precious state job and your precious boyfriend and your precious babies. You left me alone with Mom and her darling little girl and their happy little club that excluded me. But *I'm* the ungrateful one because Mom did so much for me. Right, Lizzie?"

"You're some piece of work, you know that Teri?" said Elizabeth.

"Listen, listen," Mr. Craig said, waving his hands in the air. "Settle down. You need to understand a crisis like this always brings out the underlying resentments between family members. Sometimes it can be good. Sometimes getting things out in the open can bring people closer together."

"Yeah, I'm feeling really close to my brother and sisters right now," Teri said as she dropped back in her seat.

"Look, Teri, for what it's worth, I'm sorry I wasn't around when you needed me," Jessica said. "But I'm here now."

From the other end of the speaker phone came the sound of Tom clearing his throat. "And I wish I could be there now," he said. "I *did* leave to get away from the madness. When Mom and Dad got divorced, I offered to come home. She insisted she wanted me to stay away and make a life for myself." He cleared his throat again. "But to be honest, I knew she'd say that, and I was relieved when she did. I thought it gave me freedom from the mess our family had become. Not a day has gone by I haven't wondered whether it was wrong for me to have listened to her. All I can do is say I'm sorry for when I wasn't there, but I'm here now. I mean,

I'm not there, but I can be on a plane within an hour, anytime. And since Mom's been going downhill—let's just say being this far away has seemed less like freedom and more like exile."

There was a long pause. Teri had turned and was looking out the office window. Jessica still had a brochure open and was pretending to study it. Elizabeth was just staring off into space.

After a long minute Mr. Craig broke the silence. "Well, I'm glad some things have been said that apparently needed to be said. In the meantime, we haven't quite arrived at a conclusion yet. Dr. Padrait has recommended an occupational therapy evaluation for your mother."

"An occupational what?" Teri fell right back into mode. "I doubt she'll be looking for a job any time soon!"

"An occupational therapy evaluation, or OT evaluation, has nothing to do with employment," Mr. Craig said gently. "It's a test to assess a patient's ability to function in a home environment with household chores like cooking and cleaning. The results will indicate how your mother would respond in her home and help to determine how much assistance she'll need."

Jessica inhaled and exhaled deeply. "And when will this test be done?" she asked.

"Tomorrow. We'll know more after that, but until then you should get started checking options and costs. Look, I understand you have years of differences behind you. All families do, some more than others."

"Yeah," Teri said. "We'd be one of those in the 'more than others' category."

"Perhaps," Mr. Craig said. "But for now you need to do your best to put aside your differences and work together to help your mother. Can you do that?"

The room was silent for a long moment.

"I'm not quite sure how to take that," Mr. Craig said.

"Well, it seems that I'm with Elizabeth in wanting Mom to stay in her own home for as long as possible," Tom said.

"Thank you, Tom," Elizabeth said. "I knew I could count on you."

"Well, that's very sweet," Teri said, "and very easy for you to say, Tom, from a thousand miles away when you make a ton of money, have a great wife, and no kids."

"And what about me?" Elizabeth asked. "I'm here, and I have kids."

"You also have a husband and a good job," Teri said.

"Well, whose fault is that?" Elizabeth said. "You're the one who picked Eddie, not us."

"You don't know a thing about Eddie—leave him out of this."

"Could we keep our focus on your mother?" Mr. Craig asked.

"I vote for that," Tom said. "Jessica, you're the only one left. Where do you stand?"

Jessica hesitated, looking up at Mr. Craig and then down at the brochures in her lap. "I can see both sides," she said. "I think we should just wait until we hear the results of the OT evaluation and then decide."

"That's it, Jess," Teri said. "We can always count on Tom to be far away and you to take a firm stand."

"Oh, shut up," Elizabeth said. "Just accept it, Teri. Nobody agrees with you, as usu—"

"If I may," Mr. Craig said. "Jessica is right. What you need to do now is research your options so you're prepared, one way or the other, for the results of the OT evaluation. Can you agree on that much?"

"Yes," Elizabeth and Tom said in unison.

"Yes," Jessica added.

"Not like there's any real choice here, but yeah," Teri said.

In the end, the argument turned out to have been pointless. A few days later Dr. Padrait called a meeting to discuss the results of Janice's OT assessment. The three sisters assembled in a conference room within the psych ward with Tom, as usual, patched in by speakerphone. As the siblings sat waiting for the doctor to arrive, Elizabeth felt a wave of nausea. The tiny white room had spotless linoleum floors, bare walls, a metal table and folding chairs, buzzing fluorescent lights, and mini-blinds over a south-facing window. Between the August heat, the bright sunlight, and the smell of ammonia, Elizabeth felt the faint throb of a migraine coming on. Finally the doctor arrived, making small talk with Jessica and Teri while they made certain Tom was on the line.

"Okay, I think everyone's here now," she said. "Tom, can you hear me?"

"Loud and clear," Tom said.

"Let's get straight to it, then. We have the results of your mother's evaluation, and I'm honestly sorry to tell you she failed it miserably." Looking down at her chart, she continued. "Janice was asked to bake blueberry muffins from a pre-packaged mix and could not perform the task, even after forty-five minutes with help provided to all her questions. She was also asked to wash clothes and sweep the floor and was unable to carry out these tasks, becoming more agitated over time."

"Of course she was upset, she was in a strange place being asked to do unfamiliar things," Elizabeth said. "She doesn't cook anymore, we all know that. She buys ready-to-eat food, like fruit and lunch meat, or picks something up from the drive-thru."

"Yes, but regardless of the request, your mother could not remember what was asked of her or the instructions given to help her complete the objective," Dr. Padrait said firmly. "The evaluation also observed memory retention of less than one minute, and that's a dangerous condition."

"I'm certain in her own home she could sweep the floor, but here she's out of her element." Elizabeth was prepared to argue but wished someone else would jump in and back her up.

"I'm truly sorry to say it, Elizabeth, but your mother cannot live alone any longer because she is a danger to herself. What if she left the oven on overnight, or left a pot burning on the stove? There are too many perilous scenarios. She needs twenty-four hour supervision, whether that's in her own home or in a healthcare facility. That decision is yours."

"Your tests are unfair," Elizabeth said. "She's drugged and confused here. You think you can decide her fate by the results of bogus chores she doesn't perform anymore?" She waited for Tom to jump in on her side, but no sound came through the speakerphone.

"Look, I have parents too, and I know how hard this must be," Dr. Padrait said. At the moment Elizabeth didn't feel entirely certain Dr. Padrait's parents were human, but she kept her suspicions to herself.

"But you must accept this because your mother has dementia, and her condition will continue to worsen. There is no cure, and you need to protect her. That's the bottom line, and I'm very sorry."

"And if we refuse to follow your recommendation?" Elizabeth said with her chin held high.

"Then as her guardian you'll be liable and could be charged with elder abuse by the State of Illinois," the doctor said. "Let me make it clear, we're not making a suggestion any longer. It's a requirement that Janice has care at all times, a stipulation that will be closely monitored to ensure compliance."

Elizabeth felt powerless to respond. The tears were now spilling down her cheeks and she couldn't stop them. Embarrassed that she had lost control of her emotions, she got up and walked to the window. In the short span of their meeting, dark storm clouds had rolled in and a bolt of lightning suddenly lit up the sky. Thunder boomed, and the clouds opened up. The rain pounded the ground so fiercely it was no longer possible to make out the cars parked in the lot below.

Jessica and Teri discussed next steps with the psychiatrist while Elizabeth stood looking at the rain, unable to stop the tears streaming down her cheeks. Why was she the only one crying, she thought. How could her siblings so easily accept their mother's death sentence without a fight? After all, wasn't fighting what they all did best? Lost in thought, she found the downpour comforting. God was crying with her, she thought, grieving with her.

"Come on, Elizabeth, let's go see Mom," Jessica said once the doctor had left the room.

"I can't—I don't want her to see me like this." Elizabeth wiped her blotchy face. "You go ahead, I need some time alone."

"Okay," Jessica said. "You come along when you're ready."

Teri had already walked out without a word to her little sister. *I should know better than to let her see any sign of weakness,* Elizabeth thought as she left. *That's just not one of the options in her playbook, though no doubt she'll find a way to use it against me at some point.*

"Hello?" Tom said from the speakerphone. "Is anyone still there?" He heard only a faint buzzing in response. "Okay, well, if anyone's still listening, call me later and let me know how I can help. Bye."

Without an umbrella, Elizabeth decided to wander the hospital and wait out the storm. She came across the hospital's chapel and ducked into the darkness, thankful to find it empty. The room resembled a small church with only the most basic of necessities, including Bibles and hymnals placed in the nooks of five short, wooden benches. A center aisle separated the rows, and led to a table at the back, upon which sat a large wooden cross. She slid into the second pew and tried to draw peace from the serenity around her.

Opening her eyes a few minutes later, she spotted an artificial tree in the corner, twinkling in the darkness. A closer look showed it was hung with paper angels, and on each one a visitor had written a prayer for a loved one. "My sweet Bill is in your care now, Lord. Please welcome him home." "My daughter is such a good little girl. Please don't take her from me yet." "Dear God, I love my daddy. Please help him get well soon. Amen." Elizabeth was not alone in her pain, she thought, and nor was her mother the only one suffering. She reached for a pen to add her own appeal.

9
Murder By Numbers
1979

———— ⌘ ————

Because murder is like anything you take to
It's a habit-forming need for more and more
You can bump off every member of your family
And anybody else you find a bore

—Sting
Andy Summers

———— ⌘ ————

"Get out of the car," Janice said while twisted around to face Teri in the back seat. She had just pulled her Nova halfway up the driveway and opened the garage door.

"Huh, what do you mean?" said Teri, taken aback by her demand.

"Go on and take the groceries with you," said Janice, pointing to the garage. "We'll be along in a minute. I want to speak with Elizabeth alone."

"What about?" Teri said, hoping her sister was in trouble.

"Just go," said Janice with a sigh, too tired to argue.

Against her will, Teri peeled herself from the car and slunk inside, trying to glean any words before she was out of range. Janice waited for the door slam while Elizabeth fidgeted from the passenger seat, wondering what was up.

"I got a phone call from school today," Janice said as she turned to focus on Elizabeth.

"And?" said Elizabeth, searching her mother's face for a clue.

"Turns out you tested really high on your seventh grade assessment," Janice said with a look of pride. "So well, in fact, that they'd like to place you on the advanced math track next year during eighth grade—that means high school algebra."

"Oh." It wasn't much of a surprise. Math had always been her favorite and easiest subject. It was logical and made perfect sense. You learned the rule, applied it, and the numbers never failed. If only the rest of her life could be so simple.

"That's all you've got to say?" Janice was disappointed by Elizabeth's lack of enthusiasm. "You know, this isn't the first time I've been told you're brilliant."

"What?" Elizabeth said. "What do you mean?"

"When you were in kindergarten, Elizabeth, your school called us in for a meeting to discuss the results of IQ tests you'd taken. They told us you were off the charts in every area. They kept saying you were in the ninth stanine, and scores like that just didn't happen very often."

"Ninth stanine, what's that?"

"In fact, they said that only four percent of children nationwide would fall in that range," Janice said, ignoring the question. "They used the word gifted and recommended that we enroll you in a special school to keep you from being completely bored."

"But I never went anywhere special," said Elizabeth, bewildered that she was hearing about this now, so many years later.

"I know you didn't," Janice said. "Your father wouldn't allow it. He thought you'd grow up, get married, and have children. In his mind, putting you in an expensive program was a waste of money, and I couldn't convince him otherwise. He refused to listen or change his mind."

"I see," said Elizabeth. Her mother was getting angrier as she continued, like usual when her father was the topic.

"I took you to Mrs. Howard for lessons soon after that meeting. I wanted to give you something more, some sort of challenge, and music was the most your father would allow."

Elizabeth had never before wondered why she was the only one of her siblings to pursue a musical education. The family had an old Hammond spinet organ in the house for as long as she could remember. Janice bought it for a pittance from a friend eager to remove the dust-collecting instrument from her home. It was ancient but well maintained with polished wood in a gorgeous walnut finish. Elizabeth immediately took to the two-tiered keyboard with a bass pedal board, delighted to slide her fingers over the keys and flip the stops in a multitude of combinations to imitate all the instruments: brass, woodwinds, strings, flutes, and percussion. She fell in love with music thanks to that second-hand contraption and continued with private lessons until joining the grade school band.

Little did Janice know the effects those lessons would have on Elizabeth's soul. Music quickly burned into her brain and became her greatest source of happiness. The foundation of her fervor was built upon fundamentals and the classics, but she was most content playing contemporary tunes like "The Entertainer" by Scott Joplin, "Love Me Tender" by Elvis Presley, and "Yesterday" by Paul McCartney. She hid behind the melodies, allowing the notes to speak on her behalf more eloquently than she ever could on her own.

Elizabeth was soon obsessed with *American Top 40*, hosted by Casey Kasem and counting down hits on the Billboard Hot 100 singles chart. The radio show ran every Sunday afternoon for four hours, and she tuned in faithfully to find out which songs were moving up or falling off in popularity. Filling stacks of spiral notebooks with the rankings, she tracked the progress and inevitable decline of her favorites week by week. Something always pulled her away from the program though.

"Elizabeth, let's go," said Janice in a rush one Sunday afternoon.

"Not now, Mom, I'm busy!" Elizabeth said from her post during the broadcast, sprawled on the living room floor by the record cabinet.

"Oh, that silly show will survive without you," said Janice from the doorway. "I told you I wanted you to go with me today."

"Go where?" Nothing made Elizabeth madder than being pulled away from any portion of *American Top 40* because it left holes in her records.

"Duke's surprise birthday party, don't you remember? I've been working on it for weeks. Staff from headquarters are even coming up."

"You're throwing a bash for your boss—here in town?" said Elizabeth, not remembering a thing about it. "You're decked out like that for a birthday party? Even got your red dress and heels on."

"Well, I rented a banquet room at the hotel—hey, I'm not *that* dressed up! What difference does it make anyway?" said Janice.

"But I'll miss the top ten, Mom! Can't I just stay home, please?"

"Oh no, you don't! You need to wish Duke a happy birthday."

"Come on, Mom. He couldn't care less if I'm there or not. And I don't wanna wait another week to find out who hits number one."

"Turn that off this instant. You're going with me, and that's final!"

Thanks to the hours she could devote to Casey Kasem, Elizabeth turned into a walking encyclopedia of popular music. She could provide a song's Billboard rank, tell why the artist wrote

it, and recite lyrics nearly word for word. Music became her ref-
uge, a safe haven from reality, and consumed her waking thoughts.
In her spare time she pored over her growing collection of LPs
and cassettes.

"Elizabeth, are you listening?" Janice pulled her daughter back
to their discussion.

"Huh? Oh, yeah."

"Your test results only prove what I've known since you were
little. We moved here to this district because of you. We were told
this was the best public school in the area, and I wanted to make
sure you had the best education possible."

"We're here because of me?"

"I'm so proud of you, Elizabeth. I want you to work hard and
pursue every opportunity, so that one day you'll have more than
just this," Janice said with a wave of her hand across the front of
their ranch house.

Elizabeth stared out the windshield in silence, embarrassed by
the praise.

"I only wish I could help you along because now it's too late
for a special school." Janice stopped short, like she wanted to say
more but decided against it. Elizabeth already knew their financial
situation was grim; no one needed to explain that to her.

"Mom, it's fine—really," Elizabeth said. "I'll take the math
class, no problem." The thought of being the youngest student in
a class full of older kids was scary, so she banished the notion.
Elizabeth smiled at her mother, willing the discussion to be over as
she reached for the door handle.

"Okay, then," said Janice. "I won't mention anything to your
sister. I'll leave that up to you. Tell her or not—your choice."
Janice started the car up and pulled into the garage.

Elizabeth sank into the passenger seat to think. Telling Teri
about her achievements would be like dousing a wildfire with
gasoline. It would be insane to give her sister another reason to

hate her for the disparity between them. Entering the house, she decided to lock the secret away for safekeeping because she really was a smart girl.

On a blistering summer afternoon a few months after their math conversation, Janice and Elizabeth were in the car headed home when they saw Teri walking in the neighborhood alongside her friend Amy.

"Is that your sister?" Janice asked Elizabeth while squinting out the car windshield. Since they were all going in the same direction, Teri and Amy had no forewarning they'd been spotted.

"Hey, what are you girls doing out here? I thought you were supposed to be spending the night at Amy's house?" Janice barked out the window after reaching the two stragglers zigzagging down the sidewalk.

"Yeah, well, that didn't work out," Teri said with a snicker. The two girls looked at each other and grinned.

"You think this is funny, do you? And just where are you going?" Janice asked. "Never mind, get home right now! You can just kiss your social life goodbye, cause you'll be grounded again for this."

Janice cranked up the window and drove away.

"Now what?" Amy said in a panic.

"What a bitch," said Teri as she watched her mother's taillights fade in the distance. "She's never gonna cut me any slack."

"Teri, we *cannot* tell her the truth! You know that, right?"

"Would it hurt to fess up? Maybe she could help."

"No way," said Amy. "You think the beating I got this time was bad? If he knew I ratted him out to your mom, he might kill me." Fear, mixed with a heaping measure of shame, made her whole body tremble.

"Okay, okay, calm down," Teri said as she rested her hands on her friend's shoulders. "I won't tell. We'll figure something else out."

"I don't wanna ever go back there," Amy said as she broke down in tears.

Unemployed and drunk before supper, Amy's father had stumbled home to find her stealing from his liquor cabinet, unaware she had a guest in her bedroom. He had knocked her to the ground with one punch, then lost his footing and fell when he had tried to kick her. Taking advantage of his twisted ankle and slowed reflexes, she had grabbed a fifth of vodka and fled with her girlfriend.

Now Teri thought about her dilemma. Should she help her only friend or stay out of it to avoid more trouble? "I've got an idea," she said. "What the hell, let's do it!" She never did anything right anyway. According to her mother her grades were rotten, her girlfriends were trash, her boyfriends were losers, and she was a slacker who was never going to amount to anything. She'd never measure up to her freak-of-nature sister who shit twenty-four karat nuggets. Why not live up to her good-for-nothing reputation?

At home, Elizabeth knew it was time to disappear. She couldn't stand to be anywhere near Janice and Teri when they argued because her sister had become so foul-mouthed and rude. Headed for disaster, she dabbled in drugs, alcohol, sex, and bad-news older boyfriends as often as other girls her age changed clothes. She couldn't care less about her grades or school, and thrived on making their mother angrier with each new offense. She was a time bomb set to self-destruct, but for some reason there was no explosion.

"Mom, where is Teri?" said Elizabeth, leaving the safety of her room to check. The clock banged like a gong over the silence as her mother sat at the kitchen table with her hands folded in her lap.

"Your sister isn't here," Janice said with a hint of panic. "I've been waiting for her, but it's been over an hour."

"Want me to go look for her?"

"No, I don't think that would be wise since it's getting dark now." There was a long pause before Janice continued. "I may have to get the police involved if Teri doesn't come home soon."

Janice called the Smithburg Police Department sixty minutes later. Teri did not come home, but instead vanished with the setting sun. The area was searched late that evening without luck. Twenty-four hours later she was labeled a "missing person," more commonly known as a runaway.

How could her sister be so stupid, Elizabeth wondered. She wasn't overly concerned for Teri's safety and was more embarrassed about the police car that kept parking in their driveway, fearing her family would be the laughingstock of the town. While she was furious with Teri for what she'd done, she couldn't understand why her mother was beside herself with worry. Didn't she know Teri could fend for herself?

"Here, Mom, I made you a tuna sandwich." Elizabeth pushed the plate towards her mother, who was slumped over the kitchen counter the next afternoon when they still hadn't heard anything on Teri.

"What?" Janice said, lifting her head to reveal red, puffy eyes. "Oh, no, I don't want that."

Elizabeth had never seen her mother cry more, even after the divorce. Without any news Janice flirted with a nervous breakdown.

"You have to eat, Mom," said Elizabeth, unsure how to comfort her through the crisis. "I haven't seen you touch a thing since breakfast yesterday."

"I'm not hungry, I'm—" She shook her head. "Hey, was that the phone?"

"What—no, Mom, the phone did *not* just ring."

"Are you sure?" Janice dived for the receiver. "Hello? Hello?"

"Mom, no," Elizabeth said as she put the phone back on the hook. "Now you're hearing things!"

As the hours ticked away Janice and Elizabeth lost track of day and time, trapped in the void of unknowns. They hunkered down at home headquarters while bystanders passed through their revolving door—policemen, Jessica, Susan, and even Duke—all trying to be useful and offer hope. Madness set in, disguised as guilt, regret, and anger, with nothing to be done except wait.

"Mom, what are you doing?" asked Elizabeth when she found Janice sitting cross-legged on the carpet rifling through a shirt box of loose photographs. It was dark outside, the house too quiet with only the two of them.

"I can't find it!"

"Find what?"

"The police want a better shot of Teri, and I'm looking for her eighth grade school photo. If I ever had the time to put all these in albums . . . Why can't I find it?" She tossed a handful of pictures aside as she covered her face with her hands.

"I got this, Mom." Elizabeth knelt and felt her mother's back heave beneath her fingers. "I'll look for the photo."

"It's been two full days, and we don't even know if she's dead or alive out there . . . she's only fourteen years old!"

"Mom, you're exhausted. I haven't seen you lay down since Teri left. You've got to get some sleep. Come on, off to bed. I promise I'll get you if there's any news—anything at all."

"No, no, I don't want to miss—"

"You won't. But you'll need to think clearly once we do get word. There's nothing happening now, and it's getting late. I'll stay right by the phone until you wake."

"Are you sure?"

"Positive. Just a little shut eye will make all the difference, Mom."

"I don't know what I'd do without you, Elizabeth."

"You don't need to worry about that, Mom." Elizabeth pulled her mother up from the floor. "Now go."

After a fitful night's sleep Janice was back beside the phone early the next morning, the third day of Teri's disappearance.

"What's the latest?" asked Ron when she snatched it up on the first ring. "Any news?"

"No, nothing still," said Janice with a loud sigh. "So I don't want to tie the line up—"

"Oh no, you don't, wait just a minute. We need to talk."

"If you're gonna blame me again for this whole mess, I will not stand for—"

"Janice, listen, that's not why I called. I know Teri's been difficult the last few years, you're at your wit's end with her." Ron paused for a deep breath. "I want to help. Should I just come on down? I can be there in less than four hours."

"No, absolutely not!"

"How can I help then?"

"There's nothing to do, and I'm going crazy just waiting here. Having you hanging around certainly won't help matters one bit."

"She's my daughter too, you know?"

"Oh, really? You haven't had a thing to do with her the last five years, leaving me all the dirty work trying to handle her. But she's *your* daughter now . . . that she's missing . . . and who knows what's happened to her."

"Janice, stop, I'm sorry. I didn't mean to pick a fight and make you cry. For God's sake, what am I supposed to do?"

"Stay put right where you are. I'll call when we hear something."

"So you won't let me do anything?" Ron said as the line went dead.

Tom and Jessica searched for answers too. "So what's going on?" Tom asked his sister, reaching her at work. *No way I'm calling Mom again,* he thought. *She sounded hysterical the last time I talked to her.*

"Not a darn thing, that's what," said Jessica. "Hey, hold on a sec, will ya?" Tom heard the on-hold click and listened to elevator music for a minute. "Okay, now I can talk. I'm in the break room alone."

"They haven't found her yet?"

"Nope, not a trace. The cops say nobody saw or heard anything that night."

"That doesn't help," said Tom. "And Mom? How's she holding up?"

"Not good, as you'd expect. She's not sleeping or eating, you know, tearing herself apart over this. But Elizabeth is with her."

"She's not the only one broken up over what's happened. I'm feeling pretty lousy myself."

"Why's that?"

"Look, we both know Mom's been struggling with Teri awhile now, that's no secret."

"Yeah, so?"

"So maybe I should've gotten involved. Maybe Teri needs a man to sit her down and set her straight?"

"Um, that would be Dad's job, not yours."

"But he's not around, and besides, Mom likes to keep him in the dark about stuff, out of the loop. He probably had no idea how bad things had gotten, how uncontrollable Teri has become."

"So I guess we should've filled him in?" asked Jessica.

"Look, I'm praying this all turns out okay. Teri comes home, nobody gets hurt, end of crisis. But honestly, Mom's gonna have to deal with her, and she'll need help. Teri's not going to magically turn into an angel, know what I mean? She's crying out for attention."

"When did you get so smart anyway?"

"Well, I am almost twenty-five," said Tom. "I'd like to think I've learned a few things. I'm even ready to settle down."

"You mean?"

"Yeah, I'll probably pop the question to Audrey soon. We've been together since college and she did follow me down here to Florida after graduation for a reason."

"Good for you. I can't wait to get to know her better," said Jessica.

"At least her family is normal back in Indiana. Her parents have been married over thirty years, very down to earth."

"If that's the main reason for a proposal then she should run from you."

"Very funny. What about you and Vince?"

"A wedding? No thanks!" Jessica scrounged through the stale donuts on the table. "We're happy with our arrangement just the way it is."

"Hmmm, let's talk more about this later since you're working. We better stick to the problem."

"Right," said Jessica. "Well, to be honest, I haven't spent any time with Teri or Elizabeth since I started this job—and moved out. Maybe I could try to reach out to them a little more, figure out what's going on in that head of Teri's."

"And I should check in with Teri too, at least try to talk some sense into her, figure out why she's so pissed off all the time."

"It wouldn't hurt, that's for sure. But she's gotta come home first!"

Tom and Jessica weren't the only ones working on a plan to move forward.

Elizabeth lounged on her bed in her pajamas, her mother glued to the phone on the other side of the house. *No excuse in the world will ever make up for what Teri's done*, she thought. *Her rap sheet is a mile long—the gutter mouth, failing grades, cigarettes and pot, not to mention the threat of violence always a part of her act. None of that comes close to the hell of the last three days though. She's crossed the line, and I'll never forgive her. How could she put Mom through this misery?*

Teri's total disregard for their mother's struggles was a slap in the face. *If it's the last thing I do,* Elizabeth vowed to herself, *I will show Mom how grateful I am that she takes care of us. Unlike Teri, I will never, ever do anything to give my mother a moment of trouble or pain. I only want her to be proud, to hold her head high at the accomplishments of the children she has worked so hard to raise. Wait, that's the solution,* Elizabeth thought. *I'll become the perfect child Mom deserves since Teri isn't cut out for the job. No problem, it will be easy.*

—⟋⟍—

"Mom, it's Teri." She made the call from a pay phone after almost exactly seventy-two hours on the run.

"Teri! Where are you—are you okay?" said Janice with relief and anger all jumbled up in her response.

"Yes, Amy and I are fine," said Teri, huddled close to the phone booth. "We're in New Orleans, but we've got no money and haven't eaten since yesterday."

"Louisiana? How in the world did you get there?"

"We hitchhiked with a truck driver. I know, I know—don't say it," said Teri, braced for a thrashing as she started to cry.

"You did the right thing by calling, don't worry!"

"I'm so sorry, Mom," said Teri, not prepared for sympathy from her mother. "I know it was stupid."

"Let's not go there—not now." Janice's prayers had been answered, and she wasn't about to start yelling.

"Can I come home? I'm scared and it's getting dark. We need to get out of here."

"Tell me where you are and stay put. I'll have someone there in a flash."

The New Orleans Police Department arranged for Teri and Amy to be flown back to Illinois. Elizabeth refused to welcome her sister back from the vacation she'd taken at their mother's emotional and financial expense, forcing Janice to set her daughter straight on her intentions.

"Elizabeth, I do not want you to discuss this mess with Teri, do you hear me?" Janice said.

"What, are you kidding me? I want her to know what it's been like the last three days—the hell she's put you through," Elizabeth said.

"You'll do nothing of the sort. I'll handle this myself, and I don't want you interfering. She'll have enough to deal with from me, count on that. This is over as far as you're concerned."

Janice didn't waste time after pondering how best to get her wayward daughter back on track the whole time she was missing. After a home-cooked meal, a hot shower, and a good night's sleep, Teri had to face the consequences of her actions with a heart-to-heart behind closed doors. Luckily for Elizabeth talks in the Kraus family meant yelling matches, so she heard it all from her hiding spot around the corner.

"Nothing I've done has gotten through to you yet." Janice paced in front of Teri, who sat on the edge of her bed with her armed crossed. "And now you've pulled this stunt."

"Yeah, but you know—"

"Quiet, stop right there. I talk, you listen. Got it?"

"Fine."

"I've tried punishment, I've tried two different psychologists, I've pleaded until I was hoarse." Janice stopped to stare at Teri with her hands on her hips. "And still you are defiant, always in trouble, and act out in ways dangerous for you and unbearable for the rest of us."

Teri looked away and pouted, already tuning out. *Here it comes,* she thought, *another one of those lectures.*

"There's nothing left but drastic measures to consider. I'm going to take you out of your comfort zone and away from the bad influences you hang around. You're starting over, this time to get it right."

"Wait, what do you mean—"

"I've enrolled you in an all-girls Catholic high school in Springfield for your freshman year."

"You did what?" Teri's eyes bulged at hearing the last thing she expected.

"Yep, it's a done deal. You need more discipline, and to get

away from those distracting boys. This solution meets both require-
ments nicely."

"Oh, hell no!" Teri was on her feet waving her arms. "Girls-only school? Uniforms? Priests and nuns? Over my dead body!"

"Aha, that's funny seeing how I was afraid you might be dead only two days ago." Janice steadied the quiver in her voice, not wanting her daughter to sense weakness or doubt. "But you can cut the wisecracks because you have no choice in the matter."

Elizabeth covered her mouth to silence her gasp. *How ironic,* she thought. *Teri is nearly flunking out of school, only getting through because teachers don't want to deal with her another year. Now Mom wants to put a juvenile delinquent in a prestigious private school? How is that supposed to help her, really? She'll hate it and fall behind with the coursework. And I can't believe she's being handed the advantage that I was denied years ago. Go figure.*

"I have no idea how I'm going to pay for it either," Janice said as Teri flung herself across her bed facedown. "But I'll find a way. So get ready, things are gonna change around here."

Elizabeth snuck back to her room, trying to control her jealousy with logic. *Maybe this arrangement will work out even better for me,* she thought. *With Teri attending a different school, I won't be saddled with her reputation anymore. The fear in teachers' eyes after calling my last name during roll call on the first day might fade away as my sister is erased from memory, leaving me to shine at Smithburg High without being judged unfairly. I can solve this equation: two Kraus teenagers minus one troublemaker equals the idyllic education for one. Starting with the advanced math class, I'll stick to the plan.*

10

Love Is Stronger Than Justice

September 2000

Love is stronger than justice
Love is thicker than blood
Love, love, love is stronger than justice
Love is a big fat river in flood

—Sting

"You need to go *now*," Teri said through clenched teeth while Harold visited with Janice one evening in the psych ward. "I want to spend some time with Mom."

"Plenty of room here," said Harold as he glanced around the deserted activity room.

"Without you." Teri couldn't stand the sight of him since the Nebraska trip and blamed him entirely for the whole fiasco. Unfortunately, she couldn't avoid him because he spent all of his free time with her mother.

"It's getting late, dinner will be ready soon," said Janice.

"Get out, Gramps, it's my turn!"

"Well," Janice said, "you're in a hurry, aren't you?"

The hospital was not prepared for the argument that broke out between Harold and Teri, who were both too stubborn to back down. His devotion was equally matched by her volatile temper. Their quarrel was reduced to a popularity contest, and he had the upper hand because Janice preferred him over the family she considered to be the enemy.

"Elizabeth, it's Teri," she said, growling into the telephone one evening. "You'll never guess what Harold did tonight!"

"No, I don't want to hear this—stop."

"That man has some nerve," Teri said. "I was with Mom tonight. Everything was fine until Harold showed up and called her to his side, slapping his hand on his leg and repeating her name. It was pathetic! She ran to him like a dog obeying a command, leaving me standing there forgotten."

"I mean it, Teri, I do not want to discuss Harold!"

"You've got to do something *now*, Lizzie. He was out of line tonight, calling me crazy right in front of my kids!"

"I know what you want, and I'm not gonna do it." Elizabeth tried to keep her voice down while she pointed for her four-year-old to leave the room.

"The nurse kicked me out of the unit, saying I was the one who caused a scene! Can you believe that?"

"Teri, I will not block Harold from visiting, I've already told you that. He's the only thing Mom has left to look forward to, and I won't take it away from her."

"Think about me for a minute, will ya?"

"I'm thinking about our mother, *not* you. That's my point!"

"Harold is picking fights on purpose and making damn sure I can't spend any time alone with Mom," said Teri. "He attacked me tonight, and you're gonna do nothing?"

"That's right," Elizabeth said, refusing to bow to her demands. "This is your problem, not mine."

"He's *your* father-in-law!"

"Exactly! And unlike you, I will not be rude or pull rank. I'm not getting involved in this, no way." Elizabeth's husband had raised no objections out of respect for his father, and she felt obligated to do the same.

"Goddamn it! Figures you'd choose him over me!" Teri hung up on her sister, thinking *why can't she take my side just once?*

Elizabeth was stuck in the middle, but that was the least of her concerns. Unlike Teri, she'd been avoiding their mother but now needed to have a difficult discussion with her.

"So, this is how it's gonna be?" Janice asked from the privacy of her room in the psychiatric unit.

"Yes, it is," said Elizabeth. "Unfortunately things are out of our hands now, Mom."

"Out of your hands—right." Janice shuffled into the bathroom to gaze in the mirror.

"What are you doing?" Elizabeth peeked around the corner.

"Nothing," Janice said as she posed and gazed in the mirror from different angles.

"Do you have any questions about your diagnosis or what happens next?" Elizabeth held onto the doorframe and braced for her mother's response.

"I need a face lift!" Janice said as she continued looking at her reflection. She had changed the subject and moved on, already forgetting the topic. Conversation had become a luxury of the past.

Because Janice was physically fit, doctors had recommended an Alzheimer's special care unit to allow her space to move around freely while living with others suffering from similar impairments. A few calls eliminated the only two facilities that fit the bill in Springfield. The first maintained a two-year-plus waiting list for the highly demanded wing, and the second refused to accept

Medicaid patients. Jessica, Teri, and Elizabeth embarked on an exhaustive and discouraging tour of nursing homes within a reasonable driving distance from Springfield.

"Oh my God, I think I'm gonna be sick," said Teri. "This place reeks like piss and bad cooking."

"No way—we're not even staying for the tour," Jessica said. "Let's get outta here before anyone sees us."

They'd all seen the news stories on living conditions in seniors' housing. But this wasn't television, and Janice wasn't someone else's mother.

"I don't like how everyone's corralled in this center room like a herd of cattle," said Teri while they waited at another facility. "It's wall-to-wall blue hairs—there's hardly even room to walk around!"

"Wait, did you see that?" said Elizabeth as two residents started arguing over a seat on a sofa. "Those two are at each other's throats over there!"

"I'm gonna go find some help," said Teri as she headed for the nurse's station.

"Ladies, ladies, there's no reason to fight," said Jessica as she stepped in with arms raised to fend off blows.

"Well, there most certainly is," said a large woman seated on a tattered sofa. "I'm saving this spot for Eunice. And who are you anyway?"

"I want to sit down, Martha, so scoot on over," said the one still standing with her hands on her hips. "There's room for us both."

"I wouldn't sit next to you if —"

"Now, Martha—behave yourself," said an assistant who appeared with Teri. "You know you can't save seats. That's a rule, so let her sit down."

There were a million reasons to cross facilities off their list but few to help them pick one.

"Hi, we're considering this place for our mother," Jessica asked a visitor. "What do you think of it?"

"Oh, my husband's been here for about a year," said a well-dressed lady in the visiting room. "I'd rather he was at home, of course, but he's getting along okay."

"Have they taken good care of him?" asked Jessica.

"Well, I've been happy for the most part," she said with a glance around before lowering her voice. "Course, he did fall and break his hip several months after the surgery. Never understood how that happened, so he's been here a lot longer than what we planned."

The days of searching turned into weeks. "How'd it go today?" John asked one night over supper.

"Another nightmare," Elizabeth said. "I don't know how children live with themselves after putting their parents in some of these places. But the hospital is on our backs, so we have to choose something soon."

"Maybe those other children have as much trouble with it as you do, but even fewer choices," John said. "But I saw in the newspaper today that Good Samaritan Place in Litchfield is building a twenty-four bed Alzheimer's wing and still has some openings."

"Litchfield?" said Elizabeth. "That's only about forty-five miles south. Do you mind if I—"

"Go," John said. "Make the phones calls. I'll get the girls to bed."

"Bedtime with Daddy, yay," said Claire, turning to her little sister in the highchair. "That means *two* bedtime stories!"

"Dada!" Katie banged her sippy cup on her tray in approval.

"Shhhh," John said. "Stop giving my secrets away to Mommy."

Within days the three sisters had an appointment at Good Samaritan Place, starting with a tour. The special care unit was an addition to an existing building and offered the latest in comfort and technology. The single-story structure of red brick was completed on the outside while final touches were still being added to the interior. To keep wandering residents safe from harm, the design included locked doors with keypad access and an alarm system. For the mobility of the residents, the wing included a walking track around the main hall and a garden path amidst blooming shrubs. The facility looked like a hotel with its hospitality-style floor plan and centrally located nurse's station resembling a registration desk.

The director led the tour and answered all the family's questions, paying close attention to their concerns. Along the way, they received glowing reports from the residents and visitors they quizzed. While the original nursing home was not nearly as nice as the new dementia wing, it was well-maintained and included adequate living space for the residents. Most importantly, it looked clean, smelled good, and offered the continuum of care they were told Janice would need as her illness progressed.

On the spot the sisters agreed to place a deposit for one of the two private rooms. Although the singles were more expensive, Elizabeth hoped the privacy would soften the blow of the move for their mother. Calculating the cost, she realized it would deplete Janice's savings within four years. Would her mother still be living at Good Samaritan Place in four years? Elizabeth kept her thoughts and her calculations to herself. She didn't want her sisters to have any excuse to avoid giving their mother the very best.

As their plans for a nursing home came together, matters at the hospital fell apart. Harold was standing guard over Janice, having given himself the job to provide her with twenty-four hour care.

"That bastard is up there every waking moment," said Teri, fuming on Jessica's doorstep.

"You wanna come in first?" Jessica opened the door. *What now*, she thought while Teri's back was turned.

"Son of a bitch, I cannot get a second alone with Mom." Teri dropped on the couch. "I just came from Memorial and couldn't stay with Harold there. I wanted to smack that grin right off his face."

"He was there earlier today when I went too."

"Jess, we gotta do something. He acts like he's her husband, for God's sake, and they've only been seeing each other a few months!"

"Well, I guess he thinks someone needs to look out for her."

"That man is taking advantage of our mother, and he needs to be stopped! She is not in her right mind, so why does he think he can pursue her now?"

"Okay, listen, you gotta calm down," said Jessica. "Take a deep breath and relax."

"I will not! He's up to something, I'm sure of it!"

"Up to something? What do you mean by that?"

"I don't know—something bad," said Teri.

"What could he possibly do?" Jessica said. "Come on."

"Listen, I've been a troublemaker my whole life," said Teri. "And I can see it in his beady eyes, the way he laughs at me. He's up there plotting something at the hospital."

"Give it a rest, Teri," Jessica said. "He's harmless, really."

"Fine, don't believe me," said Teri as she stomped out the door. "Lizzie has you all brainwashed that Harold's a saint. But I'm telling you he is *not*."

Teri's intuition turned out to be right on target, and Harold broke his news soon after.

"That was my father on the phone," John said as he leaned against the family room wall for support.

"What now?" asked Elizabeth.

"I can't believe what I just heard," said John, shaking his head. He looked at his daughter curled on the couch.

"Claire, darling, why don't you go pick out your jammies and bedtime story?" said Elizabeth. "I'll be there in a few minutes."

"My father wants to marry your mother to keep her out of a nursing home," said John once he was certain Claire was out of earshot.

"What?" said Elizabeth. "No—you can't be serious?"

"He said he loves her and is trying to annul her first marriage to move forward with their wedding plans."

"Oh my God, Teri was right!" Elizabeth said. "She'll be insufferable about it, of course."

"I hardly think that's the main issue here."

"You're right, I'm sorry." *But she will be*, Elizabeth thought to herself.

"I'm so angry with my father, I can't see straight right now," said John, avoiding eye contact as he crumpled in a chair.

"How am I going to break this to my family?"

"Just what exactly is your mother up to?" John said.

"Excuse me?" Elizabeth said. "What exactly do you mean by that?"

"I just mean—well—somehow she's gotten to my father to make him want to—"

"Oh right, John! She just blurted out, 'Hey, I'm going crazy and won't be able to take care of myself much longer. How about you marry me and take on the job?'"

"I didn't mean it like—"

"My mother won't even admit she has a problem, so she certainly wouldn't be looking for a caregiver!" Elizabeth was on her feet in an instant and ready to storm off.

"Listen, hey, hey—" John reached out and pulled her close. "I'm so sorry. I didn't mean it, really. I just don't understand what's going on with Dad."

"Honestly, I don't know how much more of this I can take." Elizabeth pulled away in tears to go start the nighttime routine with their daughter.

Once Teri got wind of the marriage proposal, she renewed her crusade, fully expecting for Harold to be cut off for good.

"Listen, Tom, it's time to give that old codger the boot," said Teri one evening after her girls were in bed.

"I don't know what his deal is," said Tom, choosing his words carefully, "but he's all Mom's got right now and the least of our worries."

"He wants to marry her, but you don't think that's a problem?"

"Let's focus on the move coming up and forget about Harold, okay?"

"Are you kidding me? I saw this coming, I even warned you all! And you're still going to let him walk all over us?"

"I really don't think—"

"That's it, I'm done with this family," said Teri. "As long as Harold is around, I'm not visiting Mom or helping with anything—including her move to the nursing home and taking care of her house and stuff."

"Come on, Teri, there's no need to get so worked up."

"You're taking Harold's side over mine!"

"I am not. I'm just trying to get through this thing," said Tom. "Why do you have to be so dramatic and go overboard with everything?"

"Because no one ever listens to me, that's why!"

"That's not true—"

"Dramatic? I'm being dramatic. Fine."

Teri hung up. They could all just go to hell. She guzzled a beer in three gulps, then went to the fridge for another and settled back on the futon for numbness to sink in. She watched as shards of moonlight pierced the mini-blinds and retreated down the wall in stair steps.

I'm so sick and tired of being ignored, she thought as she swept her hair out of her face. *I have every right to be angry when they treat me like this over and over again. And now look what they've done to me.* She couldn't stop the tears that fell down her cheeks.

"Mama," said six-year-old Amanda from the darkness. "Are you crying?" She drew near and curled up next to her mother, putting her head on her lap.

"What are you doing up, sweetie?" Teri said as she wiped her cheeks. "It's late."

"I couldn't sleep," said Amanda, snuggling in deeper. "What's wrong, Mama?"

"I've had a hard day—with all that's going on with Grandma. That's all." Teri ran her fingers through her youngest daughter's hair, only a trace of red in the strawberry blonde locks. "I'm sorry if I woke you up."

"It's okay, I'll stay and cheer you up. I'm sorry you had a bad day."

"You're just the cure for my blues." Teri kissed her daughter's cheek and smelled her sweetness. "Cozy up here with me and let's see if we can both get some rest."

Teri listened to her daughter's breath as it slowed, but could not settle down herself. *Was I out of line with Tom,* she thought. *Is cutting the ties to my family the right thing to do? Or have I gone too far this time?*

—ᴓᴓ—

Meanwhile Harold, oblivious to the battles within his daughter-in-law's family, tried to shore up his case. "I'm here to ask for your help," he said to William Stevenson, Janice's former attorney, over a mound of paperwork. "I love Janice Kraus, and I'll be damned if I let those kids put her away in a nursing home."

"I see," said Mr. Stevenson with a poker face. "And how do you think I can help with that?"

"I want to marry her and take care of her myself," Harold said, his voice softening to reveal his devotion. "But guardianship is moving too quickly, and I need more time to work out the details."

"And *why* would Janice be better off with you?" Mr. Stevenson sized up the stranger, trying to figure him out. "I don't recall her *ever* mentioning you."

"We've grown close just this year, but I've known her for ages."

"How exactly?"

"I guess you could say I'm an old friend of the family since my son married Janice's daughter Elizabeth many years ago."

"So Elizabeth is your daughter-in-law—and you want to marry her mother? That makes you more of a relative than a friend, doesn't it?"

"A relative by marriage, I guess." Harold stopped short as his cheeks flushed. "Yes, I'll admit it's rather unusual."

"I see," said the lawyer as he paused to consider all the parties involved. "That would create an interesting branch on the family tree, don't you think?" He recalled how Janice gushed over Elizabeth. Maybe this guy was the real deal after all.

"I have her best interests in mind, unlike at least one of her daughters."

"You mean Teri."

"Yes. Wait—how'd you know that?"

"Janice has been my client for over twenty-five years," said Mr. Stevenson, leaning back in his chair. "Teri's come up frequently in that time."

"She's been causing trouble up at the hospital. They even kicked her out one night when she got out of line with me."

"Not surprising from what I've heard."

"Janice is not as sick as they all claim. She's as happy as can be when we're together," said Harold. "And I could save all her money by letting her live with me—nursing homes cost too much!"

"I'm listening." Money spoke louder than words to a man like William Stevenson.

"But I need the legal proceedings stalled to make it happen. Can you help with that?"

"Hmmmm," the attorney said as he weighed his options. "If I could, would you retain my services as her legal counsel?"

"You bet, and I'd hire you to be my lawyer too!"

"Then yes, I can throw a wrench or two into the plans. It would be easy enough. I'll draw up a contract for my services."

"Another month should do the trick," Harold said as he shook Mr. Stevenson's hand. They had a deal.

William Stevenson bombarded Alex Hartmann and the court with phone calls and letters, bringing into question the motives of the family and slowing the momentum to grant permanent guardianship. This gave Harold the time he needed. As a man of faith, he was seeking approval through his parish priest for a sacramental marriage to a divorced woman, a tricky undertaking in the Catholic Church.

⁓☙⁓

"Things are bad right now, aren't they?" said Tom one evening when he phoned to check in on Elizabeth. "You okay?"

"I'm just getting by one day at a time, you know?" said Elizabeth. "Really, I'm afraid to answer the phone. You're lucky I picked up tonight."

"Teri's still on your case?" Tom could hear the baby crying in the background.

"John, can you check on her please?" said Elizabeth. "Teri? I'm avoiding her calls because her demands are out of the question. It's the only way to keep my sanity."

"What about John? It's got to be hard on the two of you dealing with his father's interference."

"Yeah, well, things are getting a little tricky there, that's for sure." Elizabeth lowered her voice, unwilling to say more.

"Listen, Elizabeth, I'm sorry," said Tom. "I wish I could be there to take on some of this. I know it's hard, and you're in the thick of it with this mess—"

"No need to apologize—there's nothing you can do about it."

"Teri's pulled a lot of crap over the years. But, honestly, I've never been ashamed of her behavior before. It's inexcusable for her to bail on us right now."

"We've still got to get Mom moved—she's been in the hospital for two full weeks now. And there's so much more to do after that."

"It's awful to be so far removed from what's going on up there."

"Thank God I can count on Jessica, or I'd lose it completely."

"I'm the oldest. I should be able to help out more—"

"Did you hear what Mom said when Jessica asked her about Harold's proposal?" Elizabeth wasn't interested in hearing more of Tom unburdening his guilt.

"No, what?"

"She grilled Mom straightaway after getting wind of Harold's antics since she was already at the hospital," said Elizabeth. "She asked her point blank, 'Mom, have you agreed to marry Harold?'"

"And what was Mom's response?"

"Jessica said she laughed out loud and said, 'Well, of course not,' clueless about what he was up to. It proves Harold is acting on his own. Either he hasn't asked Mom to marry him yet, or he's asked and she doesn't remember."

"Hmmmm, so what happens next?" asked Tom.

"We ignore Harold and get ready to move Mom from the hospital, that's what," said Elizabeth. "He can't marry her since we've already been appointed her guardians. By court order she's not competent to make decisions any longer, and we'll never allow it."

"That's weird," said Tom to Jane when he hung up.

"What?" asked Jane, sitting down next to her husband.

"Elizabeth cut me off when I tried to apologize for not being able to help out more. She changed the subject completely."

"Your youngest sister is a doer, hon. She probably wants to focus on what needs to be handled instead of what is *not* happening, that's all."

"I just want her to know how I feel—that I appreciate all she's taking on."

"Hey, I know this is killing you, being so far removed and hearing everything after the fact." Jane gave her husband a peck on the cheek and a hug. "But you are offering support when and how you can, so don't beat yourself up, okay?"

"I think I'll fly home to help Elizabeth and Jessica get Mom set up in the nursing home. I can at least help out with that."

While Harold floundered in his efforts to marry Janice, the Kraus siblings relied on their lawyer to play legal hardball. Elizabeth was reading a copy of the letter that Alex Hartmann sent to William Stevenson for a second time when the phone rang.

"Have you seen the letter yet?" asked Jessica.

"Yep, brought it in with the mail tonight," Elizabeth said. "Ha, I can't wipe the grin off my face. Our lawyer is awesome."

"Isn't he? Love this line, 'The court has already appointed Janice's two daughters as guardians for all issues on her behalf. Even though the judgment is temporary, it is still binding until a permanent decision is approved.'"

"That's not even the best part," said Elizabeth. "Here's what makes it clear he has to back off. 'You have breached the attorney-client privilege of confidentiality by discussing the legal matters of your former client Janice Kraus with Harold Miller. If this misconduct continues, a complaint will be filed with the state disciplinary committee.'"

"Brilliant! If that doesn't shut Mr. Stevenson down, nothing will."

"He won't be interfering any longer."

"Oh wait, did you get a copy of Mr. Hartmann's bill too?" asked Jessica.

"Yes, I see it here."

"Ouch, that hurts. This explains why lawyers are so wealthy."

"He's worth every penny, Jess. I'll pay him, no problem."

Good Samaritan Place finally opened its locked doors wide for residents with a grand opening celebration. Janice was discharged from the hospital eighteen days after her admittance, but she departed a different person, no longer able to hide her illness from the casual observer.

"Thank goodness you're here for this, Tom," Jessica said as the three siblings drove their mother to her new home.

"Especially since Teri's abandoned us," said Elizabeth, failing to hide the bitterness in her voice.

"Okay, Mom, we're here," Tom said after pulling into the parking lot. "Let's go check it out." Janice had spent the last forty-five minutes gazing out the window, from time to time mumbling nonsense they tried to decipher.

"Here, let me get your door, Mom," Jessica said.

"Wha?" said Janice, looking around. "Where are we?"

"She's so loopy," Jessica said to her sister over her shoulder. "The hospital was worried about the transfer and doped her up pretty good."

"Remember, we talked about this," said Elizabeth as she took hold of her mother's hand and coaxed her to the door of the facility. "Come on, I'll show you around."

"Okay, but I can't stay long," said Janice as she shuffled inside. "It's getting late, and I have to work."

A friendly girl with a clipboard greeted them and pointed the way to Janice's private room three doors from the entrance. It smelled of fresh paint and new carpet, already decorated with her bedroom furniture and personal belongings to appear more like home. Her clothes hung in the roomy closet, ready to be worn.

"Okay, let's go," said Janice as she hurried for the door.

"Mom, wait," said Jessica as she grabbed an album on the bookshelf. "Let's sit and look at your photos."

"Well, I haven't got time for that now," said Janice with a snoot. "I have to get back. Harold's got dinner ready."

"In a little while," said Tom, trying to divert her attention. "Did you see your stereo and CDs here? Why don't you pick out something for us to listen to?"

"Where are we?" said Janice for a second time as she stepped out into the hall. "I want to—oh, excuse me." She backed up as an aide approached.

"Hi, I'm Sandy," said the petite blonde with a heart print on her scrubs. "And you must be Janice!"

"I have to go now, so goodbye." Janice skirted around her as Tom, Jessica, and Elizabeth exchanged worried glances.

"I've got this," Sandy said with assurance as she headed after her charge. "Let me show you around first, Janice. I've got some friends who've been waiting to meet you."

"You do?" said Janice as she stopped and rocked back and forth on her feet. "Who's that?"

"Come with me, and I'll introduce you." Sandy hooked her arm through Janice's, and they strolled like a couple of pals. She looked over her shoulder and smiled at the three siblings as they stood slack-jawed in the doorway.

"This seems like a nice hotel," said Janice as they reached the nurses' station in the center of the unit.

"I'm glad you think so," said Sandy as she patted her arm. "And we're so glad you'll be staying with us for a while."

"Stay?" said Janice as she sprung to attention and looked around again. "There must be some mistake. I can't afford this place!"

"Don't you worry about that," said Sandy. "I'm going to show you the dining room and introduce you to our other guests while your kids get the rest of your luggage."

The siblings were reassured by Sandy's skills, but worried she wouldn't be available to their mother every minute of the day. Sure enough, the change of schedule and scenery sent Janice into frenzied anxiety. She did not recognize her surroundings or understand why she had to stay in an unfamiliar place. Searching the corridors for a way to leave, she rattled the doors and tripped the alarms like a caged monkey. No explanation would pacify her, forcing nurses to increase her medication after consulting with doctors. Once glassy-eyed and sufficiently drugged, she surrendered to the monotony of nursing home life. Each new day dawned in a foreign land she had no desire to visit, jumpstarting her pacing and pleas to go home.

Luckily the nursing home had one saving grace that would help Janice transition into a new way of life. His name was Bruce, and he was relatively attractive by the lax standards in the wing. He was about her age and appeared to be in the same mid-stage of Alzheimer's progression. Most importantly he was a man, which was rare in a dementia unit. There was only one other gentleman in a far more advanced state of decline, apparent by his wheelchair and inability to talk or interact with others. This made Bruce bachelor number one to over twenty belles of a bygone era.

"What are you doing with that?" Janice asked as she shadowed her new target.

"I'm gonna eat it," said Bruce as he swiped a second cookie from the snack cart an aide had left unattended. "What about you?"

"Oh, thank you," said Janice with a giggle as she took his offering. "That looks good."

"I don't think we're supposed to take these, so we better skedaddle out of here!"

"Gotcha, I'm right behind you." They scampered around the corner to avoid getting caught red handed, devouring the loot to get rid of the evidence.

"Okay, good, she didn't see us," said Bruce, peeking back to check.

"Who?"

"That nasty woman in white over there. I try to steer clear of her—she never lets me eat anything."

"Maybe we should just get out of here then," Janice said coyly as she noticed the side exit down the hall. "What do you think?"

"Huh?" said Bruce as she headed for the door.

"Why is it locked?" Janice peered through the glass at a world now off limits and fumbled with the keypad on the wall, pressing buttons randomly. How did the darn thing work, and why did these contraptions have to be so complicated?

"I don't know," said Bruce, offering assistance by pushing on the security bar.

A shrill beeping made them scatter as the staff was alerted to their ploy. "Whoa—was that you, Harold?" said Janice while fleeing the scene of the crime.

"Those things are touchy," said Bruce as he headed in the opposite direction.

"Not again!" An aide came running to reset the alarm. "You two, stay away from the doors, will ya?"

Janice and Bruce became the inseparable mischief makers of the wing, roaming the halls in search of adventure while distracting each other from their bleak existence. Strangely enough, Bruce never corrected her when she called him "Harold" and replied regardless of the mistaken identity. He may not have minded, but the Kraus children found it a frightening sign that their names too would soon be lost to the tangles and plaques of her jumbled brain.

The real Harold turned up a few days after the siblings transferred Janice and figured out she had dumped him in favor of a more practical alternative. Though embarrassed to grasp how sick she really was, he continued to come and see her. As a precaution the Kraus children forbade him from taking her out of the nursing home. Staff was advised of the sticky situation and monitored his visits.

Harold realized he needed to make amends with his family for his behavior of the last nine months and invited his son over to clear the air. "So I really messed things up this time, huh?" Harold said with a sheepish grin. "I see now that Janice is much worse than I thought, and her illness made a fool out of me."

"I know it must be hard, Dad." John had never heard his father admit he was wrong about anything before. This vulnerability revealed a side he'd never seen of a lonely old man hoping for true love once again. After all the anger he'd kept pent up out of respect for his father, he could now feel only pity for what his dad had just been through.

"I'm not going to marry her. Obviously that was a mistake. I just didn't want her to end up like that—all alone."

"Neither did Elizabeth, and she and her family struggled with this decision for years, knowing what was coming. There was no other choice, and now her mother is in the best place to take care of her problems as things get worse."

"I know how I feel," said Harold, "so Elizabeth's heart must be broken too."

"At least things are finally settled. The doctors, social workers, and lawyers have all agreed to terms, so there's no need for a formal trial where Janice's kids would have to testify against her. Elizabeth was dreading that, but she and Jessica have now been named permanent co-guardians by the court."

"How can I make this right with Elizabeth? Will she ever forgive me?"

"Come on, Dad, you know her better than that," said John to relieve some of his father's load. "She knows your intentions were good and is grateful for the friendship you offered when her mother needed it most."

"Yeah, but—"

"But she did take a lot of heat, especially from Teri. Give her some time to heal, that's all she needs."

"What about Teri?" Harold spit out her name.

"That's a lost cause, I'm afraid," said John with a shrug. "You can't win there, so I'd let it be and leave her alone. Life goes on, and we don't want to miss it, do we?" John embraced his father for the first time in many years, and they sat back to rock on the glider without any further need for discussion.

Be Still My Beating Heart

2001–2003

Restore my broken dreams
Shattered like a falling glass
I'm not ready to be broken just yet
A lesson once learned is so hard to forget

—Sting

Janice and Bruce turned into the dynamic duo of the Alzheimer's unit, designated president and vice president of residential affairs thanks to their fast friendship. Patrolling the halls at all hours, they socialized with the others like old friends instead of strangers forced together by medical need. Jointly they served the subjects of their dementia kingdom through duties bestowed based on their areas of expertise.

"Hey, what time do we eat?" Bruce asked Sandy, who was headed to the laundry with dirty bedding, trying to avoid eye contact. With the appetite of a teenage boy, he took office as the meal monitor, a time consuming endeavor based on his memory deficit and the food schedule. The residents ate five meals each day, including breakfast, lunch, and dinner along with a morning and afternoon snack.

"Bruce, we'll have lunch at 12:30, okay? Today is meatloaf," Sandy said to the same question asked three times in the last half hour.

"Okay, 12:30? Let me see," Bruce said while checking his digital watch. "It's 11:27 now, so in about an hour?"

"Yes, Bruce, that's right," she said over her shoulder as she continued on her way.

"Okay then, did you all hear that?" Bruce said to anyone in the vicinity who bothered to listen. "We'll eat in about an hour! That's not so bad."

"Not bad at all," said Janice in dutiful echo.

"Now what's for lunch today?" Bruce asked himself five minutes later. Off he darted to grill another victim about the next meal with Janice on his heels like a faithful dog following its master.

"Hey, what's the problem here?" said Janice as she barged in on an argument in the TV room later that afternoon. Her wandering allowed her to keep tabs on everything around the unit, and she loved to be in the thick of the action as the social director.

"I told her to stop, and I mean it!" said Marge, towering over Missy, who was shivering in the corner.

"She's not hurting anyone," said Janice as she grabbed Missy's hand and pulled her out of harm's way. "Come with me, honey."

"Think you know it all, don't you?" said Marge as she released Missy and turned her attention to Janice.

"Just trying to help out, that's all," Janice said with a shrug as she walked away.

"You're nobody special, you know that?" Marge poked Janice on the back of the shoulder as a warning. "Just cause you got yourself a man, you think you're better than the rest of us."

"I beg your pardon?" Janice spun around to face Marge, who advanced and waved a finger of warning.

"You heard me, you ain't hot stuff around here. So take it somewhere else, okay?"

The women squared off in opposition, and Janice could feel hot breath as Marge moved in too close. Without hesitation she smacked her rival across the cheek in defense of her personal boundaries, which had been violated. The residents chattering nearby were silenced by the crack.

"How dare you, you little hussy! I'll show you—" Marge pinned Janice to the wall with a forearm across her throat.

"Help, help!" said Missy from a safe distance as Sandy sprinted to break up the fight.

Cindy, the head nurse of the Alzheimer's unit, was a no-nonsense kind of gal who kept her emotions in check like her closely-cropped gray hair. "You need to find a new doctor for Janice in this area," she said to Jessica during a visit one weekend. "Your mother continues to pick fights and cause problems, and she needs someone close to adjust her meds and monitor her behavior."

"I was hoping she'd settle down by now," said Jessica.

"I don't think that's going to happen," said Cindy, peering over her readers at the nurses' station. "I'm sorry, but she's been here for six months already. I'd recommend Dr. Wagner—he's local and knows the lay of the land around here."

Dr. Keith Wagner practiced internal medicine in Litchfield and took care of many of the dementia patients residing at Good Samaritan Place, some who had relied on his services for most of his twenty-year career. A burly outdoorsman who loved to hunt and fish, Dr. Wagner saw his patients from their rooms at the nursing home and was a familiar face roaming the wing. Even with his experience, he was unsure how to curb Janice's hyperactivity and aggression.

"Mom's fighting with the other ladies, hauling off and hitting them," said Jessica to Elizabeth during one of their weekly calls on pressing health issues in March of 2001.

"Still?" said Elizabeth, more with frustration than surprise. "Let me guess—Dr. Wagner has prescribed more drugs, right?"

"Yep, I approved the increase in her Risperdal dosage for that, but only because there aren't any other options," said Jessica with a shake of her head. "She gets even more agitated in the evening. Cindy explained it's called sundown syndrome and many Alzheimer's patients behave that way at night."

"Sundown syndrome?"

"Yes, to help with that Dr. Wagner recommended the anti-anxiety drug Ativan be given after dinner every evening."

"Another drug, great."

"That's not all of it either," Jessica continued with a sigh. "She's still pitching a fit at bath time, so she's being given tranquilizers beforehand so Sandy and Lilly can get the job done without Mom hurting them in the process."

"I don't like the fact that medication is the solution for every problem," said Elizabeth.

"Me either," said Jessica. "But if they can't control her, they might kick her out."

"Then we'd be back to square one, and we know there aren't any better facilities out there."

"Right. We don't have any other choice that I can see," said Jessica.

"I guess we'll just have to wait and watch then," said Elizabeth with a sigh of resignation. "Hopefully Mom will settle down, her health will stabilize, and we can wean her off all these awful drugs."

—◦◦◦—

"Your mother's having a heart attack, or so we think," said Cindy over the phone. "She's being taken by ambulance to the emergency room as we speak."

"What?" Elizabeth said. "She has Alzheimer's, not heart disease."

"Janice likely has both. She staggered out of her room this morning and collapsed in the hallway, hitting her arm against a table on the way down," Cindy said as she drew in a deep breath to continue. "She passed out twice while we tried to figure out what was going on."

"She's never mentioned any problems along those lines before—"

"It's not unusual since dementia patients aren't able to communicate what they think and feel."

Elizabeth rubbed her forehead. It was the first of May in 2002. Her mother had been settled into Good Samaritan Place for over a year and a half, and things were relatively good. She was not prepared to add another chronic condition to the list of her mother's problems. She hadn't even finished her first cup of coffee for the day.

"We couldn't get hold of Jessica, so we called you," the nurse said. "She'll need someone to call the shots—can you get to the hospital right away?"

"Yes, of course," Elizabeth said. Her sister handled the nursing home and healthcare issues best, not her. Where was Jessica anyway? "I'll leave right now and be there in forty-five minutes. Call me on my mobile if you need me."

During the drive Elizabeth speed dialed Jessica anywhere she might be found—work, home, cell—without luck. She reached Tom and filled him in with choppy sentences, promising an update when she knew more. She begged her brother to pass the news along to Teri so she could concentrate on driving safely. Who was she kidding anyway? She didn't want to deal with that drama queen at the moment.

As soon as she hung up, Elizabeth's phone rang and nearly scared her off the interstate into a cornfield. "This is Dr. Moore from the emergency room at St. Mary's Hospital. Am I speaking with Elizabeth Miller?"

"Yes, this is Elizabeth," she said in little more than a whisper, wishing she was someone else.

"I am treating Janice Kraus, and I need to know if you are responsible for making decisions on her behalf," said Dr. Moore.

"Yes, I am her court-appointed guardian along with my sister Jessica."

"She is having a heart attack here and now, and I need your consent to administer medication and provide the necessary care to save her life."

"Yes, of course—whatever you need to do," Elizabeth said as she stepped on the gas. "I'm on my way now and should be there within ten minutes."

"Fine, I'll update you when you arrive," Dr. Moore said.

As she dropped the phone, Elizabeth was hit by a wave of doubt. Had she made the right decision? She and her siblings had not discussed what should be allowed medically for Janice because there had been no crisis to this point. In an emergency she had responded with her heart. Now with her head she was second-guessing her decision.

Elizabeth's uncertainty evaporated the moment she saw her mother, wide-eyed and looking remarkably well for a sixty-eight-year-old Alzheimer's patient who had just suffered a heart attack. She inched past the machines surrounding her mother's bedside to take her hand.

"Everything's going to be fine," Elizabeth said.

Janice smiled, more in gratitude than comprehension. Two nurses stood nearby checking her vitals and dosing medication through an IV.

"Why do . . . have my . . . kenildotch?" Janice asked, words forming ever so slowly. Confusion clouded her face.

She must be terrified and overwhelmed by all these bright lights, beeping monitors, and the wires attached to her body, Elizabeth thought as she looked around. The ER hubbub wasn't helping her nerves much either.

"Can you turn off all that racket?" Elizabeth asked to no one in particular. "All that noise is scaring her."

"No," answered a technician without looking up from his contraption.

"Okay, so no special treatment for the mentally disabled here," Elizabeth noted to herself as she turned her attention back to the patient. "The doctors say you're responding well, Mom. As soon as you're stable, you'll be moved to Springfield for observation."

"Huh, it's not going hate to way off?" asked Janice. Looks exchanged around the room confirmed that no one understood the question.

"I know, don't worry, Mom," Elizabeth said, leaning in close to look in her eyes. "All you need to do is rest and let the doctors do their job."

Janice stabilized within a few hours and was transported to a better-equipped facility. During that time Elizabeth located Jessica, who had gone to Chicago on a business trip. After learning about their mother, she rented a car and raced home to Springfield. Meanwhile, Teri headed to St. John's Hospital and called a temporary truce with Elizabeth. The two sisters-at-odds perched on either side of Janice's bed and tried to put aside their differences, the bad blood between them evident through the silence. After consulting with Tom, they agreed to wait for Jessica before discussing how to proceed.

Although Janice improved, she remained confused and agitated, unaware that she needed medical attention no matter how often she was told. She fought to get out of bed and remove the IV, catheter, and monitoring apparatus affixed to her body. The staff grew weary of her attempts to escape and resorted to restraints to tie her arms and legs. While she had been granted a reprieve from the Alzheimer's wing by way of a heart attack, she remained a prisoner, shackled to a hospital bed against her will.

Jessica, Teri, Elizabeth, and Tom via speakerphone gathered in a room at the hospital as the sun sunk over the farmland.

"Okay, doctors are waiting for our orders, so let's figure this out," said Jessica.

"Seems like we've got Mom's life in our hands now," Tom said.

"We need to hammer out directives for her future care too," Elizabeth added. "This episode has made that painfully clear."

"The cardiologist thinks it's too risky to do a cardiac catheter right now to determine the damage to her heart because she won't stay still or cooperate," Jessica said. "He wants to continue monitoring her vitals and see how she responds to the new medications instead."

"Well, the bigger question is—do we really want to fix her heart?" said Teri. "Patch her up just to send her back to that nuthouse with those crazies?"

"Hold on a minute," Tom said. "Why not wait a while to see if Mom calms down enough to allow the procedure? Then we'd find out how serious the problem is before we make any rash decisions."

"I'm not sure—I just don't know," Jessica said as she bit her lip. "What do you think, Elizabeth?"

Recognizing she'd made a snap decision in a crucial moment on the phone with the ER doctor earlier that day, she thought carefully before saying, "I think we should leave her fate in God's hands. No extreme measures to save her life, and only medical treatment to avoid pain or discomfort."

Time stood still while the siblings sat with their heads bowed low, no one with the courage to look at the others.

"And the cardiac cath?" Tom asked at last.

"Invasive and unnecessary," said Elizabeth. "It really doesn't matter if the damage to her heart is great or small, because we shouldn't do anything about it. She's going to die, whether from heart disease or Alzheimer's." She wrapped her arms around herself to stop the shaking.

"I'd choose a heart attack any day," said Teri, realizing Elizabeth was on her side for once. "You all know I'm the last one in the family to admit when Little-Miss-Can't-Be-Wrong is right about anything, but I agree with her. Why would we fix Mom's heart just to let her brain rot away slowly?"

Jessica fidgeted in her chair. "What is it, Jess?" asked Elizabeth.

"I will agree to no surgery," she said slowly, "and I don't want to start an argument here—"

"Like that never happens," Teri said with a snort.

"But I think Mom should continue with the new blood pressure and heart medication prescribed to reduce the chance of another heart attack." Jessica sat up a little straighter, as if contributing her thoughts had taken a weight off her shoulders.

"Absolutely, I second that," said Tom.

"Fine with me," Elizabeth conceded. "Carry on with those preventative measures then."

"We still need to decide about CPR and stuff like that," Jessica said.

"No way!" Teri said.

"I think it's safe to say we all agree," said Tom. "If Mom stumbles out of her room or collapses again, we do *not* want CPR or any other procedures to save her."

"So we order a DNR?" Jessica asked. "I think we should all agree on this point. We do not want resuscitation under any circumstances. No life saving measures whatsoever—right?"

"As much as it horrifies me to say it," Elizabeth said, "I agree."

"Yes," Tom said.

"Me three, or I guess four," Teri said.

—⁀⁀—

The DNR directive turned out to be premature. Janice bounced back and returned to her Alzheimer's unit a week later without any memory of her trauma, the ER, or the hospital stay. Back on the beat shuffling the halls beside Bruce, she showed no signs of weakness.

After residing at Good Samaritan Place for nearly two years, Janice had grown accustomed to living with twenty-three similarly-disabled patients. While she accepted the insanity of the Alzheimer's environment, it always threw Elizabeth for a loop. Each trip ushered her into an alternate universe, like a disturbing episode of *The Twilight Zone*.

"Ho, ho, ho," said Bruce on one of Elizabeth's visits. He had taken to this strange greeting and repeated it throughout each day like some demented Santa on permanent holiday.

"Hey, Mom, there you are," Elizabeth said to stop her mother from wandering off with Kris Kringle. "I've been looking for you!"

"Aren't you even going to say hello to your father?" Janice said with a nod towards Bruce.

"Whoa—Bruce is not my father! You know that." Elizabeth scolded too quickly, forgetting that the truth held no meaning for dementia patients.

"Ho, ho, ho," said Bruce as he continued on his path to the nurse's station to check the next meal time.

"Harold, wait for me," Janice said as she headed off after him, forcing Elizabeth to grab her arm.

"Mom, I'd like to chat awhile," Elizabeth said as she guided her mother towards a couple of armchairs in the foyer. "Let's sit down."

Janice took a seat reluctantly, bouncing around on the cushion like a little kid while fidgeting with the upholstery. Paying no mind to her guest, she fixed her attention on Bruce, nearly out of sight down the corridor.

Elizabeth snapped her fingers to get her mother's attention. "So, how are you today, Mom?"

"Well, I'm perfectly fine, Betty, as you can see. I've been working really hard, and I need to get back to cleaning my house." Janice launched herself from the chair in search of the "ho-ho-hoing" down the hall.

Janice had plunged a dagger into Elizabeth's heart with their brief exchange. Her mother had just referred to her as Betty, but who exactly was that? Her thoughts were interrupted when a woman in her seventies, dressed in a housecoat and slippers, approached in need of assistance.

"I don't know what to do," Missy said as tears welled in her eyes. "I'm supposed to meet my mother at the theater but I've lost my car keys."

"Let's go check on that right now, Missy," said Elizabeth, leading her charge down the hall to the room occupied by an assembly glued to a *Lawrence Welk* repeat. As they walked she wondered why she found it so much easier to muster patience and compassion for the others instead of for her own mother.

Missy's relief at finding help vanished as quickly as her problem once she got wind of the drama unfolding in the TV room. Marge chewed out Edna for make-believe crimes, and witnesses on the scene jumped to defend the innocent victim. Elizabeth took advantage of the uproar to escape and explore her mother's state of mind further.

Janice roamed alongside Bruce at the far end of the wing. "Ho, ho, ho," Bruce said as Elizabeth took hold of her mother's hand.

"Ho, ho, ho yourself," said Elizabeth to play along. "I need to borrow Janice for a bit. Come on, Mom. I want to show you something."

"Alrighty, then," said Janice. "I'll be back later, Harold. Okay?"

"Mom, can you tell me how you and I are related?" said Elizabeth as they headed to Janice's room.

"Related? We're not related," Janice said as she let go of Elizabeth's hand.

Elizabeth stopped while her mother continued down the hall. Apparently the last child born was the first to be forgotten. Suddenly she felt she'd gladly trade all the advantages she'd enjoyed as the youngest if only her mother would forget one of her other children, preferably Teri, first.

By the time she caught up with her mother, Janice was flitting around her room. But something wasn't right. Taking a closer look, she realized her mother's elastic-waist pants were wet down the inseam all the way to her socks. *Great,* she thought, *what do I do now?*

"Mom, you've had an accident and need to get out of those wet clothes," said Elizabeth in a panic, betraying her frazzled nerves.

"Huh? Oh no, I'm fine. Really—I'm okay," Janice said and began dancing back and forth on her feet as Elizabeth tried to lead her to the bathroom. "No, I don't want to do that now!"

"Mom, how about you take those off, and I'll find you something dry to wear? That will feel much better."

Janice pulled away and busied herself moving random objects around from place to place, giving Elizabeth time to regain her composure and devise a new plan of attack. To her horror her mother sat down on the edge of the bed and soiled the covers, then darted up and off again. She was overcome by an urgency to push the issue before all the furnishings in the room were dirtied.

Armed with slacks and underwear from the dresser drawer, Elizabeth said, "You are changing right now, Mom!" Using both of her hands, she yanked Janice's wet pants and underwear down to her ankles with one violent jerk.

Dumbstruck in fear, Janice froze on the spot. She was still wearing Velcro tennis shoes, which presented a major obstacle to removing her pants while standing in an upright position. Elizabeth was afraid she might knock her mother over while attempting to take them off. As she cursed this lack of forethought, her mother took advantage of the oversight by pulling up the wet garments and making a break for it.

"My mother had an accident, and I can't get her to change her clothes," Elizabeth said to the nearest aide.

"Oh, no problem," Sandy said kindly. "Lilly, can you help me get Janice to her room? She's right over there."

Lilly went no farther than the snack cart. "See this, Janice? It's yours if you follow me." She walked to Janice's room, keeping the chocolate chip cookie just out of reach.

"That's a good girl," said Lilly waiting at the door.

How humiliating, Elizabeth thought. *Is there no end to the indignity of it all? I can't stop this illness; I can't take care of my mother; and I sure as hell don't want to watch the disturbing progression of dementia any longer.* She seized the opportunity to flee as her mother disappeared behind the door. In the parking lot outside, she let go and wept slumped over the steering wheel of her car.

Real life went on beyond the walls of Janice's Alzheimer's unit, but she didn't understand it because of her condition. She failed to greet the new millennium because her own calendar had already run out. She did not worry about the terrorist attacks against the United States on September 11, 2001, nor did she fret over Harold's decision to give up on their love affair.

He decided to move on and enjoy what little time he had left by marrying a widow from church only a year after Janice's nursing home placement.

Janice's ignorance of her health issues and the world around her carried her clueless into the next year with no further episodes. Her children watched and waited, certain she was running on borrowed time. And run she did, continuing her frenetic pace roaming the hallways day and night, rarely sitting long enough to eat a meal. She carried on like "normal" until she fell in the hallway clutching her chest one morning after refusing to eat her oatmeal.

Fifteen months after the first, this repeat performance played from a new script because the Kraus children were prepared.

"We think your mother's having another heart attack," Cindy informed Jessica over the phone like a broken record. "She went down just like last time."

"Oh dear, we knew this was coming, didn't we?" said Jessica.

"She's in bed, and we've got the situation under control."

"Keep her as comfortable as you can, but remember the DNR—no CPR and she doesn't go anywhere." Jessica felt like a coldblooded killer giving those cruel instructions.

Expecting to find their mother on her deathbed, Jessica, Teri, and Elizabeth rushed to her side and kept Tom in the loop by phone. Simple blood tests and an EKG performed at the nursing home confirmed a myocardial infarction. No further medical treatment was employed, and Janice remained unconscious for a full twenty-four hours while her children hunkered down in preparation for the worst. The chaplain offered prayers for the dying, and the siblings maintained a quiet vigil throughout the night. They were all stunned the next morning when their mother woke up and went about her business roaming and snacking as if nothing had happened.

12

King Of Pain

1980–1983

I have stood here before inside the pouring rain
With the world turning circles running 'round my brain
I guess I'm always hoping that you'll end this reign
But it's my destiny to be the king of pain

—Sting

"To what do I owe the pleasure of this visit?" Janice asked. She could count on one hand the times Jessica had come around since moving in with Vince last year.

"We need to talk," said Jessica, pulling out a stool and sitting at the kitchen counter.

"Okay then, out with it." Janice busied herself wiping down the counter without looking up. "I hope this isn't about money because I don't have a penny to spare."

"I'm pregnant, Mom." Jessica had practiced those three little words for months but they still sounded bad.

"Oh, Jessica—no! Are you sure?" The kitchen counter didn't seem as important anymore.

"Positive."

"Is that good-for-nothing grease monkey gonna marry you then? Huh?"

"Give it a rest, will ya?" Jessica said. "It's the eighties, for goodness sake. I don't need a ring on my finger to have a baby!"

"Well, I disagree," Janice said. "He needs to make an honest woman out of you!"

"Ha-ha, that's funny coming from you," Jessica said. "Since when has honesty been *your* priority?"

"We're not talking about me!" Janice's face flushed. "Watch your tongue."

Jessica glared at her mother but obeyed, gritting her teeth in silence.

"So you're planning to keep it?" Janice crossed her arms. "Even though you have no commitment from him?"

"Of course I'm going to keep it! How could you even suggest—"

"Just think about it, for you and the baby!" Janice said. She didn't want her grandchild growing up without a father, as she had. "What about your future? You'll be tied down with no way to—"

"My future?" Jessica hopped off the chair and turned sideways to show off her belly. "This is my future!" She was over six months along.

"But you're only nineteen, you could do so much more with your life," said Janice with a gasp. *How could I not have noticed this before*, she thought.

"No, you're wrong, Mom," Jessica said. "I've been a mother since I was fourteen, thanks to you. This is what I know how to do, and I don't need your permission." Janice opened her mouth to speak, but closed it again. There was nothing she could say.

Meanwhile Elizabeth, now a high school freshman, faced growing pains of her own—not in the form of a growing belly, but a full-grown bully. Kelly Hewill was an overweight girl with greasy hair pulled back in a ponytail. She wore the same plaid shirt and dirty jeans daily, and her face seemed fixed in a perpetual sneer. No one messed with Kelly Hewill. No one looked her directly in the eye. No one spoke to Kelly Hewill, though everyone had something to say about her. And for some reason people always referred to her by her full name.

"Hear what Kelly Hewill did to Shelly Oswald yesterday? Oh man, that had to hurt!"

"Maddie's sporting a shiner today behind those shades, and I'm sure Kelly Hewill planted that one!"

"I'll bet twenty dollars on Kelly Hewill. Ain't no way Tammy can win that catfight."

Elizabeth didn't spend a lot of time wondering why Kelly Hewill had chosen her as her new whipping boy. It could have been by chance since they shared the same fourth period P.E. class. Or it could have been because she was tall, thin, and not very strong. Elizabeth just hoped it wasn't that Kelly Hewill had guessed she was already being bullied at home.

Whatever the reason, Kelly Hewill loitered every day in the commons area waiting for Elizabeth to pass through on her way to P.E class, and she'd walk ten paces behind her. The walk across the courtyard was just long enough for Kelly Hewill to throw out two or three good taunts before they reached the gym, though always ensuring no one else was close enough to hear.

"I don't like the way you walk, girl," Kelly Hewill would say in her husky voice. "You better stop that swing, or I'll stop it for you."

"I wonder what accident you'll have today in gym?" she'd say. "Isn't it great how the teachers give us so much room to explore physical fitness on our own?"

Of all sports Elizabeth most feared dodgeball, the game forced upon the class whenever poor weather kept them indoors. A clumsy bookworm, Elizabeth lacked upper body strength and threw like a t-ball rookie, while Kelly Hewill was the star pitcher on the softball team.

She reveled in the sting of every fast ball that made direct contact with bare skin. While Elizabeth hated dodgeball, Kelly Hewill loved it; dodgeball games were among the few times that the permanent scowl on her face was replaced by a wide-toothed grin. Early in the school year Elizabeth learned that it was better to stand still, get knocked out of the game early, and have the rest of the period to nurse the welts that swelled upon her limbs than it was to prolong the misery by running to dodge the ball.

"I keep thinking it'll get old, but Kelly Hewill nailed me big time in dodgeball today," said Elizabeth to her friend over the phone one night. "She whooped it up while I limped off the floor."

"She's a monster," said Jill. "You'd think the teacher would do something, but I guess she's afraid too."

"No one's got the guts to stand up to her because nobody wants to be in my position." Elizabeth's voice quivered. "Ignoring her is not working—I can't get her to leave me alone."

"I wish I could help. But you're right, she scares everyone to death. I'd rather have my tonsils out than take her on."

"I'm so sick of being afraid all the time," Elizabeth said, trying not to cry. Jill didn't realize that Elizabeth was referring to life at home as well as at school.

"Hang in there. Remember, it's really only one period a day, on school days, and she'll probably find someone new to pick on by next year," she said. "I have to go. See you at school, bye."

As she hung up, Elizabeth realized her sister had been eavesdropping. "Kelly Hewill is bullying you?" Teri asked.

"Stop snooping on me," Elizabeth said as she brushed past her sister.

"How long's that been going on?" Teri followed her.

"Since the beginning of school," Elizabeth said.

"Wait—" Teri paused to count on her fingers. "For over three months? And you've done nothing about it, not even tell Mom? And I thought you were supposed to be smart!" She bent over in a fit of giggles.

"It's not funny, so cut it out! I'm smart enough not to fight her. And if I rat her out, she'd probably show up right here on the doorstep to finish me off!"

"The hell she would—over my dead body!" Teri said. The rage Elizabeth knew all too well flipped on as if by a light switch.

"I *do not* want to talk about this," Elizabeth said as she backed away.

"That Kelly Hewill ain't tough," Teri said as she grabbed Elizabeth's arm and forced her close to listen. "She ain't nothin' at all, acting all crazy and pushin' round a little freshman."

"Let go, Teri. You're hurting me!"

"How pathetic! If she had any guts at all, she'd pick on someone her own size." Teri released her and drifted off mumbling nonsense.

"Teri, forget about this! It's none of your business." She slammed her door shut. *Why can't all the nutcases just leave me alone*, she thought.

Teri dropped the subject of Kelly Hewill for several weeks until she showed up during the second quarter of a Smithburg High basketball game the weekend after Thanksgiving. Sitting out of place on the visitor's side of the gym, she scanned the crowd across the court. Her face lit up like the scoreboard when her eyes landed on her target. Spotting her and suspecting she was up to no good, Elizabeth followed her gaze up the bleachers to where Kelly Hewill was sulking in the corner with her burnout friends.

Oh my God, Elizabeth thought, visualizing the possibilities. *If Teri starts a fight and wins, Kelly Hewill will take it out on me at school, and Teri will feel more power over me at home. If she starts a fight and loses, Kelly Hewill will feel even more powerful at school, and Teri will take it out on me at home. Either way, this could not be good.*

The buzzer blared for half time, and the crowd surged to leave the gym. Kelly Hewill and her posse passed by Elizabeth in slow motion, heaving as a mass towards the concessions. As her gang turned right into the cafeteria, she continued alone down the hall. Meanwhile, Teri leapt from the visitor's side into the crowd, her Farrah Fawcett hair streaking behind her. She moved like one of *Charlie's Angels* on a mission, pursuing Kelly Hewill into the girls' restroom.

Fear stricken, Elizabeth stepped out into the parking lot and crouched between cars to cry. When she'd gulped enough of the night air to calm down, she went back to the game, now in progress. Scanning the stands, she saw that neither her sister nor Kelly Hewill had returned for the second half. As her heart rate slowed, she wondered what had gone down in the bathroom—and realized she didn't care who had been hurt. Either way she'd never forgive her sister for interfering. Didn't Teri make Elizabeth's life at home hellish enough without making it worse at school too?

"Good morning, Elizabeth," Janice said over the crackle of Rice Krispies the next morning. Teri was sitting beside her, elbows sprawled on the table and head bent low over a bowl of cereal. She did not look up.

Elizabeth said nothing as she sat down. She looked at her sister. There didn't seem to be a scratch, bruise, or ginger hair out of place.

"Cat got your tongue?" her mother said.

"Sorry, just a lot on my mind today," said Elizabeth as she pushed her chair back. "Think I'll skip breakfast."

"Oh no, honey, don't do that. You know what they say, it's the most important meal of the day." She laughed at her rhyme, in a good mood because her daughters weren't bickering. "Hey, I'm a poet, and I—"

"Don't you dare tell Mom," Teri hissed when Janice's back was turned.

After that everything changed at school. Kelly Hewill missed school for a week, without any gossip as to why. When she returned she was transferred out of fourth period P.E. class without explanation. Elizabeth spotted her in the halls, but she averted her eyes and kept a safe distance. It took a bully to know a bully, and Teri had proved herself a bigger bully than Kelly Hewill. Who was Elizabeth to disapprove of her sister's methods? She was too busy enjoying her freedom from oppression to think much about it.

What she did wonder about was why the sister who hated her so deeply would go out of her way to protect her. No matter how she looked at it, Elizabeth could come up with only two explanations. Either Teri was like an animal marking territory, or somewhere deep down inside Teri actually did love Elizabeth.

It was pretty hard to believe the latter, though, because at home everything carried on as it always had. Elizabeth clung to her mother, and her mother nurtured her in a way that alienated her from the rest of her siblings.

"Elizabeth got straight A's again this quarter, did you know that?" Janice asked Teri as she reviewed her dismal report card.

"Who cares?" Teri said, preparing for another lecture. "Things don't come as easily for me as that brainiac."

"She studies and applies herself while you make no effort at all," said Janice as she peered over her glasses. "And you're nearly flunking out of school that I'm paying a fortune to put you through."

"Yeah, well I never wanted to go to that damn hellhole," said Teri. "I'm sick of hearing how perfect Elizabeth is, and I *hate* that school, so feel free to pull me out any time you want!"

—⚬⚬⚬—

The same battle took place day after day and year after year. One day when Elizabeth was a sophomore and Teri a junior, Teri asked to borrow Janice's car. "Absolutely not!" Janice said. "After the grades you brought home, no privileges for you."

"It's not fair," Teri said. "You let Lizzie go out whenever she wants!"

"Elizabeth doesn't need my help to leave," Janice said. "She saved up and bought a car, but you just blow the money you've earned and have nothing to show for it."

Teri grew ever more resentful. Janice tried to keep her on the straight and narrow path through a constant deluge of criticism and punishment while allowing Elizabeth to do as she pleased without restrictions. In protest, Teri refused to follow any rules that applied only to her.

At the same time as she tortured her mother, she tormented her sister. Although Elizabeth had grown taller and stronger, she was still hard pressed to protect herself. When Jessica moved out Elizabeth had lost a referee, which allowed Teri to step up her game.

"Don't even think about using the bathroom now," Teri said one evening after dinner as Elizabeth headed that direction in her robe.

"I'm taking a shower," Elizabeth said.

"Oh no, you don't," said Teri. "I'm getting ready to go out, and I need it."

"Well, you'll just have to wait then," said Elizabeth as she reached for the handle. "I'll only be a few minutes."

"Get out of there, you fuckin' bitch." Teri lunged at Elizabeth, knocking her backwards into the door, which swung open and hit the bathtub with a thud. Teri clutched Elizabeth's neck and wedged her up against the creaking frame.

"Get off me!" Elizabeth said, pushing Teri away.

Teri hit the door jamb and howled. Her arm was ripped open by the hardware of the lock, and blood was gushing from a puncture above her elbow. Teri backed into the hall to assess the

damage, and Elizabeth slammed the door and locked it. "You can
bleed to death for all I care," she shouted through the door.

Janice drove Teri to the emergency room for stitches, chewing
her out all the way there and back, taking away her TV privileges
and threatening to ground her for life.

"How's that fair?" Teri protested. "I'm the one with stitches in
my arm and she gets off without so much as a warning?"

Janice paced the house all night, waiting for the girls to go
to sleep before phoning the one person whose opinion she valued
more than any other's.

"I can't handle Teri anymore," Janice said to Duke. "Nothing
seems to be working—the shrink, the groundings, taking
things away."

"Okay, so can she go live with her father for awhile?" Duke
asked. "Let him try for awhile and give you a break."

"No, I already checked," Janice said. "He's moved in with a girlfriend, and she rents a one-bedroom apartment—or so he says."

"How convenient for him," said Duke.

"Tonight only proved my worst fears," Janice said. "Elizabeth
is not safe with Teri around anymore."

"Then neither are you," said Duke. "I hate to say it—but
maybe it's time to commit her for evaluation."

"No, no," said Janice, crying. "I'd lose her forever. She'd never
forgive me, and it would destroy what good is left in her."

"You sure about that?" Duke asked. "In all the years I've known
you, I can't recall you ever saying one nice thing about Teri, ever."

"There's a decent human being buried somewhere under all
that anger," said Janice. "Really there is. Somehow I have to get her
through school and out on her own—just one more year."

"And if she snaps again and hurts you or Elizabeth?"

"What am I supposed to do? They're teenagers, and I cannot
babysit them all the time. I have to work to pay the bills."

"Isn't Elizabeth involved in a bunch of extracurricular activities at school?" said Duke.

"Yes." said Janice. "So many I can hardly keep up with it all."

"See if she can stay at school until you get off work," said Duke like he was directing his staff. "That way she doesn't spend any time at home with Teri."

"That might be possible," said Janice.

"If that won't work, have her join you at the office until you're done for the day."

"You'd let me do that?"

"I'm sure she wouldn't be a bother, she's a great kid."

"She'd sit and do her homework without a peep," Janice said. "I never have to worry about Elizabeth."

"Then keep her with you the rest of the time so you know she's safe. If you leave the house, she goes with you."

"I knew talking with you would help," said Janice as she wiped away her tears. "Thanks for listening, Duke."

"Hang in there," said Duke. "Let me know if you need anything else. Anything at all, Janice."

Though it had seemed like a good solution, Teri took it as a challenge, finding ways to bully her sister right under their mother's nose.

"Lizzzzzieee, pick up the fuckin' phone *now*," Teri would shout, slamming the receiver on the kitchen counter with a crack that must have been ear-splitting to Elizabeth's friend on the other end of the line.

"Hello," Elizabeth would say timidly, not sure what was about to come.

"Next time get the damn thing yourself," Teri would shout into Elizabeth's free ear.

"I would if I could," Elizabeth would say, holding her hand over the mouthpiece. "But you lunge for the phone the second it rings! How am I supposed to get there first?"

"Hey Elizabeth, are you there?" This time it was Jill listening in on the muffled spat.

"Yes, sorry," said Elizabeth with Teri still breathing down her neck.

"I'll be there to pick you up at six-thirty, okay?"

"Right, that's fine," Elizabeth said.

"Um—I'll wait out in the car, okay?"

Next, the battle of wills advanced to the garage. Elizabeth had worked part-time at the movie theater for two years to buy her car, a used Pinto with a red stripe down the sides. Parked next to Janice's sedan, Elizabeth's hatchback was solid proof of her hard work and determination. Teri wanted a car of her own, but more than that she wanted to punish her sister for being the sole recipient of their mother's affections. So when both cars were home Teri would slip out to the garage and open her mother's car door wide with a metallic bang into her sister's car. Within a few months the Pinto sported dents and scars the full length of the driver's side.

But Teri's biggest weapon was her looks. She had a fiery mane of hair and a personality to match, and when she wore skin-tight jeans and a skimpy tank top, total strangers would turn their heads to look.

"Four-eyed, tinsel-toothed, flat-chested freak!" Teri would sing to the tune of an old song from the sixties.

"Time for that one again, is it?" Elizabeth would say without looking up from where she was reading in the family room.

"Bookworm, frizzy-haired, freckled-face geek!" Teri would finish, slapping her thighs in amusement.

"What, are you like, five?" Elizabeth said. "Name calling is so childish, you know. Words will never hurt me."

"Four-eyed, tinsel-toothed, flat-chested freak!" Teri crooned again with a poke to Elizabeth's back.

"Get away from me and cut that out!" said Elizabeth as she

swatted at her sister. *Why do I let her get to me*, she'd think, hating her own weakness.

"Hey, what's going on out here?" Janice would say, jogging down the hall, summoned by the shouting.

"Nothing, Mom," Teri would say, leering at her sister before heading off to the kitchen. "I'm in the mood to sing but Elizabeth doesn't like it."

"Well, she's reading, so keep it down. Better yet, pick up a book yourself," Janice would say, surveying the scene. *Things seem to be under control here,* she'd think. *I guess Duke's plan is working.* And she'd return to whatever she'd been doing before she was interrupted.

Three masters ruled the Kraus household: one who dished out pain, one who sucked up pain, and one who could not stop the pain and eventually learned to ignore it. At home Elizabeth carried on by avoiding her sister and keeping her mouth shut, never confiding in anyone. Away from home she pretended to be the happy girl who had it all. She smiled more often than others, laughed louder than most, and excelled at every undertaking as she waited for the day she could escape. It would be years before she would understand that she was not as alone in her pain as she thought, that pain was possibly the greatest part of her family's legacy.

13

End Of The Game

2005–2006

———— ∞ ————

They chased us through brambles
They chased us through fields
They'd chase us forever
But the heart would not yield

And this river's still running
And time will come soon
Carried to the great ocean
By the drag of the moon

—Sting

———— ∞ ————

After residing at the Alzheimer's unit for nearly five years, Janice no longer knew who she was, what she was, when it was, where she was, or even why she was. Although she had lost possession of a past, present, or future, her family had no choice but to carry on with their lives.

At fifty-one Tom felt like he'd been given a second chance after being married to Jane for the last seven years. Her son Evan, from her first marriage, had moved nearby with his wife Vicky, and Tom was smitten with their two-year-old son Braden. Tom's ex-wife had never wanted children, and he had accepted her decision without a fuss, never knowing what he was missing. Curly headed and precocious, little Braden had opened his eyes to the wonders of being a grandparent, and now Tom looked forward to each and every weekend adventure with his family and grandson, whether that be sailing on his boat, swimming in his pool, playing at the park, or wandering the zoo.

Jessica doted on her two children to make up for the absence of their father Vince, who preferred to concentrate on his new wife and child. Megan was twenty-five now and rented a duplex in Smithburg after landing a good job with the state, just like her mother. She had given up on her college degree but not on her boyfriend Jack, whom she'd dated steadily for the last three years. Jessica saw Justin less frequently since he'd graduated and moved to Chicago, but she kept up with his big city antics over the phone and visited him often on weekends. She devoted her remaining spare time to her immaculate home, decorating the interior and tending to her yard and garden. Proud to be single and self-sufficient in her mid-forties, she was content living alone—her job, her house, her children—and she didn't plan to compromise or settle for less ever again.

Divorced for the last nine years, Teri focused on providing a stable environment for her kids as she turned forty; Ashley and Amanda were now sixteen and eleven, and their school activities kept her on the run. Eddie had taken pains to stay close to his girls, even though he lived seventy-five miles away. Teri's outlook towards her ex had softened, and she had decided to embrace their shared custody agreement. Arranging a visitation schedule they could both live with, she drove halfway to Peoria every other weekend to make sure the girls spent time with their father. While they were away she occasionally dated, but there was no one special in her life because it wasn't her highest priority.

Elizabeth turned her attention back to her nuclear family too, but from the top down, starting with her seventeen-year marriage. Her mother's illness and her father-in-law's involvement had placed a terrible strain on her relationship with John, the first real test they had faced. With vulnerabilities exposed, she worked to rebuild the closeness they shared in the early years before dementia. Divorce plagued the rest of her family like the flu, and she was determined not to catch the bug, for her sake and that of her girls. Claire and Katie were outgoing grade-schoolers taking piano lessons and playing soccer.

The four Kraus siblings forged ahead with their families while their mother continued to decline. They were stopped in their tracks only for her emergencies.

"Hi Jessica, it's Cindy," said the head nurse. "It's your mother. She's just had some sort of convulsion—she fell down, body shaking and foaming at the mouth, and her eyes rolled back in her head."

"Oh my God, is she okay?" said Jessica. "Has she pulled through it?"

"Her tremors lasted for several minutes, and we couldn't stop it. So we called for backup."

"And?" Jessica put her hand over her mouth to suppress the gasp.

"The paramedics assessed her condition and then moved her to the hospital when they felt it was safe—after the spasms stopped."

"Wait—why the hospital?" said Jessica. "What about her DNR?"

"We had no choice because of the violent nature of the seizure. We felt she needed more help than we could provide here. But don't worry, your wishes regarding her care were passed along, and she's in good hands."

"What an awful thing to happen the day after her birthday," said Jessica, more to herself than Cindy.

With a "do not resuscitate" directive in place, Janice had limited treatment options. The facility focused on pain management and monitored her vitals to ensure she was in no danger of another episode. With little to go on Dr. Moore speculated that she had suffered a stroke and seizure in combination. Realizing nothing further could be done, the same doctor who had saved her life after her first heart attack released her back to the nursing home.

Jessica, Teri, and Elizabeth hurried down to check their mother's condition for themselves; by this time she was resting in her room. After many uneventful hours passed with little conversation, the three arranged alternating shifts to sit by Janice's bedside while she remained unconscious. The sisters dared not speak aloud their fears because they weren't sure if their mother could hear them. Instead they whispered from the hallway as the hours turned to days.

"It's been two days—this waiting is unbearable. Is she ever gonna wake up?" Jessica asked Teri in the corridor while Elizabeth was on duty.

"And what damage are we gonna find if she does?" said Teri. "Jesus, what else will she have to deal with? Heart attacks, now a stroke and seizure. Why not invite cancer and diabetes along too? What the hell!"

"It's not like she was in great shape anymore, you know?" said Jessica. "She's really slowed down since that second heart attack."

Janice no longer roamed at all hours, but instead lounged around like the rest of the residents. When she strolled the unit, she soon lost interest due to a lack of endurance and motivation. She didn't remember where she wanted to go or why, eliminating her desire to patrol the halls.

"I know, and she really strapped on the food bag too," said Teri. Sedentary and always eating, Janice packed an extra twenty pounds onto her petite frame. She no longer knew her own food preferences or could tell if she was hungry or full, so she devoured everything within reach during each of the five daily meals. To accommodate her expanding girth, she wore elastic-waist sweatpants with adult diapers, necessary for some time because of the loss of control over her bodily functions.

"That one's hard to take—she was always so vain about her appearance, remember? Her hair, makeup, and clothes had to be perfect all the time," said Jessica. "In her right mind she'd be disgusted with the way she looks now."

"Yeah, but the worst is how she doesn't make sense anymore," said Teri. "Talking to her is like playing a game of charades you can never win."

Janice no longer uttered understandable words or phrases, although she did make quite a bit of noise still. Her speech sounded like a foreign language long on vowels and short on consonants, but complete with inflection, facial expressions, and body movements that sometimes helped to clarify what she was trying to say. Her children were aggravated to no longer be able to talk with her or understand what she wanted or felt.

"Well then, I guess things can't get much worse than they already are," said Jessica.

On watch beside her mother's bed, Elizabeth fretted over a different matter without letting on to her sisters. She wondered if she had somehow conjured this death threat by speculating about her mother's downfall on her birthday only days before. As far-fetched as that sounded, she couldn't help replaying the evidence in her mind.

"Happy birthday, Mom!" Elizabeth had greeted Janice with a peck on the cheek. Her mother had looked pale and smelled old—a musky odor that immediately brought her grandparents to mind. She had made arrangements to spend some time with Janice on her seventy-first birthday while her daughters attended school.

"Look what I brought for you on your special day." Elizabeth had caught her mother's attention by showing her the helium-filled balloon attached to a red curling ribbon. She had been sitting in the dining room with a bib tied around her neck, a rejected plate of food on the table.

"Waa ummm," Janice had said. Her eyes had widened as she focused on the festive balloon with "Happy Birthday" written upon it.

"Let me help you with your lunch, Mom," Elizabeth had said as she tied the balloon to the back of the chair. "You haven't touched your food yet, and it's not like you to refuse a meal."

"Oh, it's Janice's birthday today?" Lilly had asked as she delivered a cup of coffee to the next table, tipped off by the balloon.

"Yes, she's seventy-one," said Elizabeth. *Honestly, shouldn't the staff know that already*, she thought.

"Happy Birthday then, Jan! You're such a sweetheart," Lilly had said as she headed off to fill a request for hot chocolate.

"Ouch, this coffee's too hot," said Marge at the next table, always complaining about something.

Janice had given up on mealtime and stood, her food untouched and a bib still dangling around her neck. Elizabeth had untied the balloon and joined her mother for a turn around the wing, holding hands just like when she was a four-year-old afraid of the dark. She was still frightened, but for much different reasons.

"Waasorasi, moo faa ren?" Janice had asked Elizabeth after picking up a stray card and handing it over. The greeting had been addressed to Joyce with a cheerful message scrawled in flowery, purple script; it had been lifted from one of the other rooms. Thievery was commonplace and considered a minor offense because no one remembered what belonged to whom. Janice wore other people's clothes and shoes as often as her own, the owners' names revealed by the permanent marker on the garment labels.

Childcare centers employed this same identification system; there was no better way to keep track of personal items in a setting thick with sticky fingers.

"Yes, it's very nice," Elizabeth had said, recognizing the need to respond by the inflection in her mother's voice.

"Weero gamoo!" Janice had laughed as she took the note card back and turned it over in her hands for closer inspection.

"You're right, Mom."

Continuing to stroll towards her room, Janice had picked up an abandoned rag doll and clutched it to her chest with her free hand. She had taken up the strange habit of clinging to a toy or stuffed animal most of the time now. Once they reached the end of the line, Elizabeth had directed Janice inside and went to work checking the closet and drawers to see if her mother needed anything.

Janice's haze shielded her from the nosedive she took mentally, physically, and financially. Her meager savings had been depleted by the excessive cost of her specialized care; she was left penniless and dependent upon Medicaid. Once the government paid her bill, she was forced to give up her spacious and beautifully-appointed private room. She was reassigned to the older section reserved for the destitute.

Janice was still located in the Alzheimer's wing and gained a roommate just as dazed and confused. Small and dreary, their lodgings looked like a battered dorm room, minus the posters and hope for a bright future. Her queen-sized mattress and frame from home had to go, replaced by the low-to-the-ground medical bed, complete with electrical circuitry and movable bedrails. A built-in dresser and shabby wardrobe substituted for her antique dresser and closet. Her feet hit the cold linoleum squares every morning instead of plush carpet.

Janice had headed straight to her bed and tucked the doll under the covers. "Ohhhhhhh," she had said, fussing over the baby. She had adjusted the pillow and rearranged the sheet and blanket until they lay just right.

"Mom?" Elizabeth had said to get her attention.

"Ahhhhh." Janice had leaned down and kissed the doll on the cheek. Elizabeth had been reminded of her daughters playing house, innocent and full of wonder about a world they pretended to understand.

Elizabeth had slipped away and leaned against the wall outside Janice's door, tears blurring her sight of a resident's memory box across the way, stuffed full of keepsakes all but forgotten. Watching a grown woman reduced to infantile behavior, she had felt a helplessness that settled in her bones like the winter, with no way to stunt the bitter cold. She had connected the dots between her mother's conduct and that of her own children. Her daughters, only nine and six, were more astute.

How much longer would it take for Alzheimer's to claim her mother's life, Elizabeth had wondered as she left on her mother's birthday without saying goodbye.

Elizabeth interpreted her mother's attack the next day as a reply to her question; the answer was that Janice would live on with dementia. She regained consciousness three days after the stroke and seizure, shielding her eyes from a world she could no longer process. She responded favorably to the liquids given by Cindy and her vitals improved, but nothing remained of the woman except a body. The trauma stole the last fragments of her personality that previously lingered, flashing briefly as she went about her day. Even the most insignificant of traits—like the sound of her laughter, the pursing of her lips as she concentrated on a task, or the way she swept her hair from her forehead—had vanished for good.

Janice's eyes lost their spark, and she no longer tracked any type of movement; she looked straight through everyone and her face drooped in an unbearable expression of sadness. Weak and pale, she could no longer perform even the simplest of chores. She had been erased.

Janice remained bedridden for weeks and consumed only liquids, but slowly she mustered enough strength to venture out of her room with the assistance of Sandy and Lilly. Her homecoming was a bittersweet reunion with the other residents, who accepted the damaged version of her without question. In exchange for her life she had been forced to surrender mobility and speech. Pushed around in a wheelchair, she had to be propped back into an upright position on the hour because she slumped over in a crooked and unnatural pose.

Within a few months Janice regained her appetite and ate solid food again, although it needed to be mashed and fed to her. She spent the majority of her time sleeping and the remainder dependent on others to be bathed, dressed, groomed, and moved. Yet after a lifetime of scraping by, she still refused to surrender and carried on living.

Jessica, Teri, and Elizabeth tried to relay their mother's condition as gently as possible to their brother after the danger passed, but it was the things they didn't say that set off an alarm for Tom. As summer settled on the prairie, he cleared his work schedule and booked a flight to St. Louis, thankful to have missed the winter. After renting a sedan, he drove straight up I-55 to the nursing home to see his mother.

"Hi, I'm Tom Kraus, Janice's son," he said to Cindy at the nurses' station, looking around to take stock. He hadn't returned in five years since moving his mother from the hospital, but the place looked exactly the same, as if time stood still here. "Can you tell me where she is?"

"She just finished dinner, you'll find her down by the TV room," said Cindy, pointing down the main hall.

"Done eating already?" said Tom as he checked his watch to see it was half past five.

"Early birds round here. Lights out for most before eight."

What if I don't recognize my own mother, Tom thought as he walked amidst the residents glued to a "Murder, She Wrote" rerun. *I better focus on the women in wheelchairs.*

His anxiety passed when he found Janice pushed back against the wall, the farthest away from the television to avoid blocking the view. "There you are, Mom," he said with a sigh as he placed his hand on her shoulder. "It's so good to see you." She didn't flinch a muscle from her crumpled position, her arms splayed out lifeless on her lap.

"Let's go visit a bit," Tom said and wheeled her to the private visiting nook. He sat on the sofa facing her while she stared off over his left shoulder, paying no attention whatsoever. "Mom, it's Tom—look at me." He turned her face gently towards him, but she continued to gaze off with the corners of her mouth turned down in a permanent frown.

An hour's worth of prodding and pleading made no difference. Tom's mother did not acknowledge his presence, and he was grateful when Sandy pushed her away in preparation for bedtime.

She's gone, Tom thought. *And I'm too late.* He fled north in the rental to put some distance between himself and the horror of his discovery, taking comfort in the humming of the engine and the retreating lines of the highway behind him.

Tom parked the car on the cul-de-sac in front of his mother's old house in Smithburg, unsure why he had chosen this spot. He had never called this place home and only visited a handful of times in the last three decades. He felt disconnected as he eyed the overgrown hedges stretching towards the gutters, hiding secrets even now. His sisters had endured hardships he could not fathom behind those brick walls, of that he was certain. The bitterness of a painful childhood seeped from every conversation like blood from a wound that wouldn't heal.

"I failed you, Mom," Tom said aloud, "you and my sisters."

Trying to prove his love, he had remembered every Mother's Day with flowers and every birthday with an expensive gift. None of those gestures made up for the fact that he was gone, off working hard and playing even harder all those years. Instead of coming home to spend time with his mother, he had jetted around the world on vacations, sailed up and down the coast, and snorkeled the islands with his buddies. He was the oldest child and the only son who had deserted a gaggle of daughters honking and flapping their wings like geese trapped in the north. He ignored their complaints and sidestepped his responsibility as the man of the family after the divorce. He left behind his sisters to deal while he concentrated on his career and his hobbies, just as his mother had instructed.

"I ran away too." Tom continued the conversation with his conscience. *Like father, like son,* he thought in disgust as he buried his face in his hands. As dusk settled over the house, the cicadas wailed a mournful tune for the fireflies flashing messages through the darkness.

While time was against Janice and Tom, the last five years had been kinder to Jessica, Teri and Elizabeth. They overcame the trauma of their mother's diagnosis when it became their long term reality. Scars remained, but the resentment had lost its bite as they all moved on with their busy lives. Elizabeth stayed in touch with Jessica regularly to discuss Janice's care, but Elizabeth and Teri were now strangers by choice, brought together only by their mother's medical emergencies. This strained relationship made unexpected meetings uncomfortable.

"Oh hi," Teri said to Jessica after finding her among a flock of people crammed into the nursing home lobby for the resident Christmas party. She had spotted Elizabeth from across the room and ignored her sister, who sat up as rigid as the folding chair.

"I saved you a seat," said Jessica. Maybe she should have warned her sisters that they would all be attending this social gathering together? But it was too late for that now. She would sit in the middle, the buffer between them, like usual.

"Hi Mom," Teri said as she rubbed Janice's arm. She was slouched over in her wheelchair at the end of their makeshift row sporting a hideous red sweatshirt, an enormous snowflake glittering a holiday greeting to one and all. "Who dressed you today, an elf?"

"Here, it's time to sing," Jessica said as she tossed a book of Christmas carols.

"Okay, turn to page five, and let's start off with a favorite, shall we?" said the social director with a clap of her hands before playing the melody on her electronic keyboard.

"*Dashing through the snow—*" Jessica and Elizabeth jumped right in while Teri looked around in disgust at all the good cheer.

Together with the other families they pretended to be full of holiday spirit, reeking of peace on earth, goodwill towards men, and all that nonsense. The three sisters managed small talk between songs and focused on their mother, who ignored the racket and crowd of people. During awkward moments of silence the nursing home pet, a cocker spaniel named Cocoa for her coloring and sweet disposition, provided a welcome diversion.

"I know this isn't the best time, but it's the first time I've seen all of you kids here together," said Cindy, interrupting the celebration after all the residents unwrapped gifts. "Can we talk about your mother for a few minutes?"

"Sure, Cindy. What's up?" asked Jessica as they followed her a safe distance from the festivities.

"Well, Janice has continued to get worse since her seizure," Cindy said with a laundry list of problems on her mind. "We have to take care of everything for her now. She can't feed herself anymore and has to be moved around and repositioned all day. She's lost a great deal of weight, can no longer communicate, either with words or actions, and she seems to have lost her appetite."

"Yeah, we know all that already," said Teri. Did she think they were stupid or something, she thought.

Cindy winced and paused, wanting to break the news properly even though there really was no right way. "It is our assessment based on these tell-tale signs that Janice has reached the end stage of Alzheimer's," she said at last.

"Okay—end stage," Elizabeth said. "What does that mean exactly? Sorry, but does that change anything?"

"Yeah, what do we need to do?" Jessica said.

"Well, hospice needs to get involved now," Cindy said as she patted Jessica's shoulder. "I have the name of a person who can set up visits for your mother to provide more adequate care, and we feel at this point she needs it."

"Hospice?" said Teri. "Really?"

"They will talk to you about pain management," Cindy continued, "and other ways to keep her comfortable. Hospice can keep better tabs on her than we can."

"Are you saying she's dying?" Teri asked. "Cause if you are, that's a bummer of a party trick, don't you think?"

Cindy nodded with a pained expression. "Sorry about the timing. But trust me, you *do* want hospice care. It will help—in the end." She looked from one sister to the other, waiting for the news to sink in.

Cindy's recommendation was repeated by the hospice manager the next weekend. Her name was Shirley, and she droned on as she flipped through a portfolio retrieving paperwork. After giving the same speech for years, she had replaced her compassion with an irritating efficiency. She reviewed an exhaustive list of services and discussed the results of Janice's assessment. Jessica and Elizabeth wondered if she would ever shut up, but finally she asked if they had any further questions.

"Well, really there's only one thing you've failed to mention,"

Elizabeth said. "Based on your experience, how much time does our mother have left?"

"Your mother has lost a great deal of weight," Shirley said to a question she'd answered many times before. "And she doesn't want to eat. When that happens a patient usually has around one month left to live."

"Are you sure?" Elizabeth asked. She did appreciate the use of the word live instead of die, it was a nice touch. "I thought she had stabilized since the seizure. I honestly believed she was getting—"

"When will you begin?" said Jessica.

"Tuesday," Shirley said to Jessica before turning her attention back to Elizabeth. "And a month is just an estimate, by the way. We can never predict with any certainty, but you should prepare. The end is near, so tell friends to get their visits in soon, make arrangements for her passing, those kinds of things."

Thankful for something to do, Elizabeth followed directions and purchased a funeral package, chose a plot at the cemetery, and ordered a headstone to be ready for her mother's imminent demise. All the while the Kraus children panicked that each sunrise might be their mother's last. They continued to wait as the weeks turned to months while hospice watched Janice get better. Proving the prediction wrong, she continued to live in a hopeless state of nothingness as her desire for food returned and she put on a few pounds.

"Your mother is considered total care now, meaning she cannot do anything for herself any longer," Cindy said to Jessica and Elizabeth two months after their mother's miscalculated expiration date. Overworked and understaffed, she needed to get this unpleasant task off her plate.

"Total care, right," said Elizabeth, repeating the newest phrase like a vocabulary word she needed to memorize. "What you need to understand is that our mother is too ornery to die on cue."

"Yes, while that may be true, we can no longer provide Janice adequate care because her needs are too great," Cindy said with genuine regret. "We just don't have the manpower over here for total-care patients."

"What are you saying then?" Jessica asked.

"I hate to do it, really I do," said Cindy, shaking her head. "But we need to move her over to the other side to get the proper care."

"No way, not over there!"

"What? No, absolutely not!"

Jessica and Elizabeth objected as one voice; the term "other side" bounced off their wounded ears like profanity. Cindy was referring to the skilled nursing facility for patients in various stages of physical decline, those who required constant attention. They had chosen the Alzheimer's unit to keep Janice away from the medical wing, but now the nursing home was taking matters out of their hands. After five and a half years she would be moved again. Instead of mingling with the cognitively impaired, she would live like a leper among the physically infirm but mentally-intact residents, who would fear her as if she was contagious.

"Are you sure, Cindy?" Jessica said, shrugging her shoulders at Elizabeth.

"You require mobility to stay in the unit?" Elizabeth asked.

"Yes we do, but we will keep residents here who can maneuver around even a little bit in their wheelchairs. But your mother can't do that anymore. In fact, she doesn't move at all."

"There are no other options?" Elizabeth asked.

"No, I'm really sorry, but there aren't any other alternatives. We've put in a request for a room over there. And we'll move Janice as soon as one opens up."

"Okay," Jessica said.

"Listen, your mother has been here since we opened this unit," said Cindy. "We've all grown to love her, so I've waited as long as I could. I want you to know that."

"Thank you, Cindy," Jessica said, her voice cracked and raw.

"You've taken really good care of her, and we're grateful for all you've done."

Elizabeth found herself speechless because Jessica was the foundation for the family, always strong and silent while she and Teri gave in to their emotions. "Let us know when she'll be moved," Jessica said as she bit her bottom lip and wiped the tears from her cheeks, trying to avoid looking at her sister.

"It'll be a few weeks," Cindy said to finalize the transfer.

14

The Lazarus Heart

1983–1988

Birds on the roof of my mother's house
I've no stones that chase them away
Birds on the roof of my mother's house
Will sit on my roof someday
They fly at the window, they fly at the door
Where does she get the strength
To fight them anymore
She counts all her children
As a shield against the rain
Lifts her eyes to the sky like a flower to the rain

—Sting

I'm busting out," Teri said in a whisper as she squeezed into her third period desk.

"Whaddya mean?" said Lynette with a nod towards the teacher. "She's already seen you, it's too late to skip now!"

"Not just a day off, but a lifetime pass." Teri slammed her books down on the desktop, making up her mind on the spot.

"Bad day, huh?"

"Oh, you have no idea," said Teri. *There is no way in hell I'm putting up with this all-girls Catholic school for another year,* she thought. *I'm so tired of all the bullshit—the rules, the uniforms, the classes that are too hard, the stuck-up rich kids, and the holier-than-thou faculty. How could my mother ever expect me to fit in here, really? I've caused enough trouble over the last three years to know how to buy a one-way ticket out. Tormenting the freshmen or skipping a day here or there isn't going to cut it.*

"Turn to page 379, and let's get started," said Sister Mary Margaret the moment the bell stopped ringing. "We only have one week left to finish the syllabus, girls, so let's get going." The class let out a collective groan. She began writing on the chalkboard, but stopped when she heard a clicking sound out of place in the classroom.

"What was that?" she said as she turned to face a curtain of teenage girls with eyes wide and mouths agape, all staring at one person. "That almost sounded like a—"

"I'm not feeling the love for world history today, Sister," Teri said with a lit cigarette dangling from her mouth. She propped her feet up on the desk in front of her and took a long drag, then exhaled deeply. "I really don't give a damn what those Japs did during the war. It's boring as hell."

"Good heavens, Miss Kraus! What on earth are you doing?"

"What do you think?" Teri said. "It's pretty obvious!"

"Put that filthy thing out this instant! Do you hear me?" Sister Mary Margaret started down the aisle but stopped when Teri blew a haze of smoke in her direction.

"You think you can make me, you dried up old cunt?" Teri stood up and motioned for her to come closer with her finger. "Try me."

The student body sucked all the air out of the room with one collective gasp, the vacuum nearly shattering the windows.

"Well, young lady, I've never heard—"

"Yeah, well you should have by now, Sister. This place sucks! I have no intention of sitting around listening to this shit for one more second—"

"Now you listen. I will not tolerate your behavior or foul language a moment longer. You can just—"

"Oh, fuck off!" Teri said as she flipped the bird, trying her hardest to make a mental note of the contortions on the nun's face. She wanted to remember that expression forever.

"Tsk, tsk. Well, that's final then," the nun said and backed away. "You may report to the dean *now*." She opened the door and waited, her head held high.

"Gladly," Teri said as she grabbed her things. She turned and curtsied at the front of the room. "That's how you do it, girls."

"And put that vile thing out," Sister Mary Margaret called after her.

"Not a chance," said Teri as she tapped ashes on the floor and moseyed down the hall.

She was promptly expelled. With no other options she re-entered the public school system for her senior year.

Elizabeth was not affected by the move because Teri did not report directly to Smithburg High School. Diagnosed with dyslexia after her expulsion, she was placed in a special education program offered from a separate location in Springfield for the entire district. With a curriculum finally tailored to her needs, she settled down and granted her mother what she wanted most of all. She got her diploma in 1983 but refused to attend the graduation ceremony.

Teri held only one desire after high school—to get out of her mother's house. She entered the workforce as a secretary and moved after securing a steady paycheck. She struggled to make ends meet, living in one run-down apartment after another with a revolving door of questionable roommates tolerated only to split the bills. She didn't have a penny to her name but didn't care as long as she had her freedom.

Janice fretted over Elizabeth's future as she started her senior year of high school. Oblivious to the role she'd played in her older daughters' failures, Janice believed her youngest daughter simply had more potential than the other two. Elizabeth, she thought, would be more like Tom in her ability to escape the misfortune that had plagued the rest of the family.

Janice could foresee only one threat in Elizabeth's way. Enlisting the help of her oldest daughter, she plotted to ensure the success of her youngest.

Elizabeth heard the pounding above "Synchronicity II" blaring on her stereo. "What?" she said, annoyed at having to turn down the screaming guitar solo in progress.

"Can I come in?" said a familiar voice, but it wasn't her mother.

"Jessica? What are you doing here on a Saturday morning?" Elizabeth asked as she yanked the door open and peered past her sister's knees in search of her missing niece and nephew, only eleven months apart with the second as much an accident as the first. Jessica and Vince had finally caved to convention and married after she got pregnant again.

"What? Aren't I welcome out here anymore?"

"Yes, of course, but you never come around, that's all."

"Well, I'm a little bit busy these days—"

"So where are Megan and Justin then?"

"In the kitchen. Mom's pumping them full of sugar right now." Jessica plopped down on the mattress and eyed the band posters plastered over every inch of the walls. She looked exhausted, all rumpled and groggy with her hair begging for a brush. "How can you stand all these rockers staring at you?"

"What do you want?" Elizabeth asked.

"Huh?" said Jessica. "Can't I just have a regular con—"

"Cut the crap. You're here for a reason—out with it then."

"Well, okay. If you're gonna be like that."

"Uh huh." Elizabeth held her ground with eyes narrowed to slits.

"Ahhhh," Jessica said with a sigh. "Alright, here's the deal. Mom wants you to see a doctor to get on the pill."

"What?"

"That boy you've been seeing—"

"Yeah? Mark."

"That's the one," said Jessica. "She doesn't want you to get pregnant, that's all."

"Well, that's not gonna happen 'cause I'm not having sex with him!" Elizabeth said in a huff.

"You've dated for a while now, so it's a possibility. Teenage boys *cannot* be trusted, and Mom's worried."

"Oh, really? If she's so concerned, then why doesn't she talk to me about it herself?"

"You know Mom," Jessica said. "She's too embarrassed to talk about this kind of stuff. Hell, she never talked to me about any of this, and look how that ended up. Probably why she asked me to bring it up, now that I think about it."

"So she's sending you to do her dirty work?" said Elizabeth. *Jessica's right though*, she thought to herself. Their mother came from a generation of women tight-lipped on the topics of menstruation, sex, and birth control. She never gave any of them a heads up about their changing bodies, let alone the birds and the bees. She had left them to their own devices to figure it out. Everything they learned about puberty was delivered through baffling films in a health class full of petrified middle-schoolers, gleaned from locker room gossip, or discovered by trial and error.

"I guess, but whatever." Jessica pulled a slip of paper from her pocket and handed it to Elizabeth. "Here, it's my gynecologist. Make an appointment, it's no big deal."

"Did you hear me?" Elizabeth said. "Mark and I are *not* sleeping together! I'm not stupid!"

Jessica paused. *Right,* she thought, *I get the real reason Mom asked me to do this. She wanted me to be a living, breathing example of stupidity to get the point across. Too bad Mom never cared enough about my future the way she does about Elizabeth's—or Tom's or Teri's, for that matter.* "Just do it," she said at last. "You'll need to sooner or later anyway, plus you'll like how it makes your periods shorter and your cycle regular. Trust me."

"Trust?" Elizabeth slammed the door as her sister left to collect her hyperactive kids. *I trust only myself,* she thought, and then cranked the volume higher on her stereo.

Elizabeth went on to graduate at the top of her class the next spring. She planned to attend a university far from home and pursue a career in the field of technology. It was 1984, and anyone with a pulse could see the revolution looming thanks to the personal computer. She intended to ride that digital wave into the sunset of prosperity, leaving her broken family in her wake.

"Mark," she'd said to her boyfriend when he whined about the possibility of a long-distance relationship, "do you really think I'm going to throw away all the scholarship offers I've received just so I can drown here with the rest of my family?"

"Won't you consider staying here with me?" he'd asked.

"No way, I'm outta here. We'll both be better off apart," Elizabeth had said but thought to herself, *who needs this grief anyway? Good riddance.*

Meanwhile, Teri continued to struggle in a low paying job and grew weary of crazy roommates and relentless debt collectors. Her meal ticket turned up late one night when she met Eddie in a local bar, drumming like a Neil Peart wannabe in a Rush cover band. The two started living together within weeks. Eddie held a day job working for an insurance agency and provided the stability that

Teri needed, or at least a steady paycheck, so Janice didn't object for long to their living arrangements.

They were married in 1986 before sharing four seasons of the year together. Although Janice was delighted her daughter wouldn't be moving back home, the wedding brought out the worst in her when the Kraus family converged for the event.

"Teri and Eddie, I'd like to introduce you to Ruth," said Ron at the reception, held at a hole-in-the-wall banquet facility on the south side. The bride and groom were making the rounds with their guests after the buffet dinner of fried chicken, mashed potatoes, and green beans.

"Nice to meet you," said Eddie.

"Hi, Ruth," said Teri with a hug. "Thanks for coming. I hope you got enough to eat."

"Yes, thanks," said Ruth. "Your dress is lovely."

At a nearby table Janice listened to every word and strained to keep the corners of her lips upturned. "Isn't it great your father brought his live-in along for all of us to meet?" she asked Jessica through gritted teeth.

"Well, they've been living together forever, Mom," said Jessica. She was sitting beside Vince watching Megan and Justin roaming the dance floor like maniacs. Megan twirled her junior bridesmaid skirt, and Justin had already pulled his clip-on tie off. "It's not like they're hiding their relationship or anything. What'd you expect?"

"I expected him to think about his daughter instead of himself," Janice said.

"Teri doesn't mind that Ruth's here," said Jessica. "Come on, Mom—"

"Oh, never mind," Janice said loud enough for everyone to hear. "I'm going to the restroom."

"Oh my, was it something I said?" Ruth asked Ron after Janice stormed off.

"Trust me, there's nothing you could say or do that would ever make her happy," said Ron. "Let's go get a drink at the bar, Tom's over there."

"Might as well make the best of it, I guess," said Ruth.

"I warned you, remember? You still wanted to come."

"I know, I know, you don't have to remind me. I figured it was time to get to know your kids. But maybe I was wrong."

"Too late to second guess now."

"What's her problem anyway?" said Ruth. "You and I hadn't even met yet when you two split up."

"She's mad at everyone, that's what," said Ron as they headed across the room. "Hey, Tom, have you met Ruth yet?"

"Yes, hello again," said Tom. "Can I buy you two a drink?"

"Absolutely, so kind of you to offer since the drinks are free tonight," said Ron as he and Ruth lit up cigarettes.

Tom was distracted as he searched across the room for Audrey. They had been married over four years now, but none of his family had been able to attend his wedding because of the location and cost. It had been a small but lavish affair, nothing but the best for Audrey on her big day. She had insisted on a spring wedding in Florida, complete with exotic flowers, a gourmet five-course meal, and a dress all the way from New York. He would have been fine with a ceremony from a barn in Illinois so his family could have been there, which would have made more sense since her relatives were from Indiana.

As he watched, his wife scowled as she raised her water glass high to inspect it. *She's going to just sit there instead of getting up and mingling with my family*, Tom thought. "Excuse me, Dad, I need to take Audrey her drink. I'll catch up with you in a little bit."

"Hey, Jess," Elizabeth said, weaving through the tables to find her sister. "It's almost time for cake. Can you come help me serve?"

"Yeah, sure," Jessica said as she stood and straightened her uncomfortable dress. "This fabric is not flattering at all. Hey, Vince, keep an eye on the kids, okay?"

"No problem," said Vince, "as long as I can see them from
the bar."

"Mom just headed to the bathroom for a meltdown," Jessica
said with a sigh.

"Let me guess," said Elizabeth as they neared the dessert
table. "Ruth?"

"Yep. That and Dad."

"Well, she'll just have to deal like the rest of us, won't she?" said
Elizabeth. "Now—how exactly should we cut this thing anyway?"

Janice didn't handle the situation well; instead she circled
the bathroom, getting angrier by the step. *Why should I have to
share my daughter's most important day with a man who wasn't even
around for the last twelve years of her life,* she thought. *How dare he
pop up at the last second and pretend like he had anything to do with
bringing her up! I'll be damned if I stick around and watch him take
credit, celebrating like he's been a part of Teri's life all along.*

Just like that Janice convinced herself to leave and disappeared
from the festivities without a word to any of her family.

"Where have you been, Mom?" Tom asked Janice when she
turned up at home hours after the reception was over. "We were
looking for you everywhere!"

"What?" Janice said as she scanned the mail in the foyer. "I
just needed some fresh air and time alone."

"Mom, people were asking for you all night," Tom said. "All
the friends and co-workers you invited were waiting to talk with
you, especially your brother who came all the way from Nebraska.
How could you just leave without telling anyone?"

"Well, too bad," Janice said, flinging the envelopes across the
table. "I'm sure I wasn't missed that much anyway, and I couldn't
stand watching your father for one more minute."

"You could have told us you were leaving, Mom!"

"He has some nerve, having a good ole time tonight. It's all
just one big bash for him, drinkin' and smokin'."

"But it was a party—"

"And Ruth, did you see her?" Janice waved her arms wildly. "Running around and bossing the staff like she was in charge. I couldn't stand it and had to leave before I did or said something I'd regret."

"Where did you go then?"

"Just driving around, that's all. No place special—just giving myself space to cool off."

"It's not okay, Mom," Tom said. "It was childish to take off without thinking about your guests. And besides, we were worried about you, disappearing like that without a word." *She's certainly done worse things*, Tom thought to himself. Still, he was really ticked off at how inconsiderate his mother had been tonight.

"I couldn't help it, Tom. I just couldn't." Janice's voice trailed off as she headed for bed, ending the evening on a bitter note.

—⚬⚬⚬—

In June of 1987, nine months after Teri's wedding, Elizabeth announced her own engagement to John, her college steady of the last two years. He was three years older and had just graduated with his MBA. A gentleman who loved his mother and appreciated his family, John won Janice's approval straight away.

As Elizabeth discussed wedding plans with her mother one summer afternoon, Jessica shared the news that she was divorcing Vince. "I guess he turned out to be one of those guys I warned you about, Liz," she said.

"Sorry, Jess," said Elizabeth, looking up from her bridal magazine.

"Just like your father with his wandering eye," said Janice. "Can't say I'm surprised."

"Mom, the kids and I are gonna need a place to stay until I figure things out—save some money, you know."

Janice sighed. "Just when I was finally going to have the house to myself," she said. "Fine, you can move in, but not until after

Elizabeth's wedding. We have so much work to do if we're going to
make your sister feel like Princess Diana!"

Predictable, thought Jessica. *I don't remember her making such a fuss over my wedding, and she didn't even stay at Teri's reception, but Elizabeth's has to be of royal proportions. Look at her flashing that smile, thinking it's actually going to work out that way. So naïve. She doesn't realize weddings in this family are more like something out of Grimm's Fairy Tales.*

After a yearlong engagement Elizabeth's nightmare commenced the following June of 1988. Jessica had finalized her divorce, getting full custody of her kids, and was packed and ready to move back in with her mother. Teri had adjusted as a housewife and had stopped using birth control, hoping to get pregnant soon. Tom had traveled back alone after Audrey claimed a work conflict would prevent her from making the trip.

A few hours before the wedding rehearsal Janice stomped into her daughter's room with her ultimatum. "Elizabeth, I cannot and will not attend the dinner tonight if your father insists on bringing that girlfriend of his."

"What are you talking about?" said Elizabeth as she yanked the tube of mascara away before poking her eye out. "Of course he's bringing Ruth! I invited her myself. Why would you bring this up now when we're heading to the church for practice?"

"I won't stand for it. She cannot come if I'm going to be there, and that's final." Janice turned away, the decision settled in her mind, leaving Elizabeth to deal on her own.

"Dad, you're not gonna believe this, but Mom refuses to go to the rehearsal and dinner tonight if Ruth is there," Elizabeth said over the phone.

"What?" Ron said. "Oh, you've got to be kidding me!"

"I'm dead serious, Dad, and I don't have time for this crap. Not now!"

"Hey, I'm not the problem here," said Ron.

"Jessica said she'd love for Ruth to join her for dinner tonight," said Elizabeth with a sigh. "Can she do that instead, please?"

"Absolutely not—no way!" Ron said. "If Ruth can't come, then I'm not coming either. You go ahead and tell your mother that!"

By this point Elizabeth was livid with both her parents for their infantile behavior; it was inexcusable to put her in the middle of their fight on the night before her wedding. She responded like any other bride-to-be and panicked. She went straight to her fiancé, who was staying at his parents' house until the ceremony, for advice on how to handle her mother and father. "Can you believe them?" she asked.

"Well, actually—" said John.

"How could they do this to me? They're going to wreck our wedding!"

"I'm sorry they're being so difficult, but nobody's going to spoil anything unless you let them, Elizabeth."

"But John, they are so far out of line with—"

"Settle down and listen." John wrapped his arms around her and pulled her close. "Don't let them drag you down on their level, and don't make this your problem. Simple solution—tell them we're getting married no matter what they do and leave it at that."

Elizabeth rested her head on John's shoulder. "Thanks," she said at last after taking a deep breath. "I needed to hear the voice of reason."

Janice and Ron received the same tempered monologue. "This is not my problem, and I will not let either one of you hijack my wedding," Elizabeth said over the phone while holding tight to John's hand. "You and any guest you would like to bring still have an invitation. Come or don't come, it's your decision. But you do not have the right to forbid others from attending, and I will no longer respond to your ridiculous demands. I will be married tomorrow whether you show up or not!"

In the end Janice, Ron, and Ruth turned up. Elizabeth snubbed

them all night and focused on a brighter future within her grasp.
John and his family sensed the friction and tried to compensate, showering her with support and affection. All the while she worried about the poor impression her family left on John's relatives. Trying to pacify her parents had been a mistake because that was impossible.

Elizabeth married John on a sunny summer afternoon without a cloud in the sky, just weeks after graduating from college. According to her wishes her parents both walked down the aisle to give her away, one on each side with neither speaking to the other. The members of the Kraus family were uncomfortable gathering together for the photos taken after the ceremony, and the bride hurried the photographer along to be done with the torture. The newlyweds greeted all the well-wishers at their reception, and before long it was time to head out for their honeymoon. Janice found their departure to be the perfect moment to share her suffering over her ex-husband, whispered in confidence as Elizabeth gave her a goodbye hug. "You're the last wedding—thank goodness I'll never have to deal with him again," she said.

Not really the parting words I'll cherish forever, Elizabeth thought to herself, although she dared not speak her mind. *So much for happily ever after. I feel so cheated.* "Bye, Mom."

Elizabeth was grateful to be moving to Kansas City, thereby putting some distance between herself and her family. Her mother's comment suggested that she didn't have a firm grasp on the future, which would be full of grandchildren and more family gatherings like baptisms, birthdays, graduations, and eventually weddings. If Ron was the source of all Janice's anguish, then there were miles of misery left to travel over the mother road, like Route 66 heading westward out of the Heartland.

15

When We Dance

2007

⚬⚬⚬

If I could break down these walls
And shout my name at heaven's gate
I'd take these hands
And I'd destroy the dark machineries of fate
Cathedrals are broken
Heaven's no longer above
And hellfire's a promise away
I'd still be saying
I'm still in love

—Sting

⚬⚬⚬

"Number 82?" the lady in a hairnet behind the counter called out on the first warm Saturday morning in April of 2007.

"That's me. Oh…excuse me…coming through," said Elizabeth as she made her way to the front of the crowd and placed her numbered stub on the glass. "I'll take four chocolate Long Johns, two of those cake sprinkles, and a large coffee with cream, please." Spring had arrived at last, and Elizabeth wanted to surprise her girls with their favorite breakfast to celebrate.

"Is that you, Elizabeth?" said a woman's voice from the back of the line.

Elizabeth handed over a ten-dollar bill and turned to scan the faces behind her, then saw a hand waving above the heads before she recognized her mother's best friend. "Oh, Susan, hello there. What a surprise to see you, it's been years!"

"But you look exactly the same," said Susan, "I'd recognize you anywhere."

"Hey, I'll go grab a table and wait," Elizabeth said as she shoved change in her pocket. "Come find me in the back after you get your donuts, okay? It's crazy here this morning—pardon me."

"So what brings you to Springfield?" Elizabeth asked when Susan joined her at an old booth with split vinyl cushions. "It's so good to run into you."

"Charlie and I are visiting our son and his family over school break," said Susan. "And those two boys of his are crazy about donuts, so I decided to splurge this morning."

"That's exactly what grandparents are supposed to do. So how is Charlie, and how are you? Let's see, you've been retired to Florida for a while now."

"Six years, we love it and are doing great. Best thing we ever did was to move down there close to Laurie. Her daughter Maddie—I've sent you pictures of her with our Christmas cards—she's an absolute joy. She's four now, and I babysit while Laurie works part time."

"Sweet, I bet Laurie appreciates that," said Elizabeth.

"Is Tom still in Florida?"

"Yes, Tom remarried almost ten years ago to a lovely woman,

and he's still over on the east coast. His wife's grandson is about the same age as your granddaughter, and he's crazy about that boy."

"How nice for him." Susan opened her box and reached for a donut. "Maybe I'll have just one. What about your sisters? It's been ages since I called Jessica—it's so hard to stay in touch, you know?"

"She's doing well on her own, and her kids too. Megan just got married last month, happy as can be and her husband Jack is a great guy. Of course, Jess is hoping for some grandkids soon."

"I can't believe Megan's old enough to get married!" Susan took another bite of her old fashioned. "Mmmm, I don't miss much about Illinois, but I sure miss Mel-O-Cream."

"I know, they are pretty tasty. Let's see, Justin's a swinging single in Chicago, an up-and-coming advertising executive now. He works all the time though and doesn't make it home much."

"I'm so glad to hear they're doing well," said Susan. "Do I dare ask about Teri?"

"She's hanging in there, just working and taking things day by day. Ashley will be going to the community college here in the fall. Amanda's in junior high."

"Janice would be relieved to know Teri and her kids are getting along okay."

Startled by the mention of her mother, Elizabeth took a sip of her coffee, not knowing where to start or what to say.

"So how is she—your mother?" Susan grabbed a napkin to clean up her crumbs. "I'll be here for a week. I could drive down and visit her if you think—"

"I wouldn't do that if I were you," said Elizabeth.

"I used to call her you know, at that place in Litchfield."

"No, I didn't know that."

"It didn't last long," said Susan. "She never wanted to talk. She'd set the phone down and walk away, so I gave up. I'm sorry about that."

"Don't be, we've all shared that frustration, not being able to talk to her anymore. It's just … to be honest …"

Susan reached out for Elizabeth's hand on the table. "I know it's heartbreaking."

"She's gone, Susan. Completely gone. She wouldn't know you, or respond, or even look at you. You should remember her the way she used to be, when you two laughed and joked around and were the best of pals."

"Remember the surprise sixtieth birthday party I threw her at my house?"

"Ha, sure do," said Elizabeth. "You got her good, she had no idea that was coming! What a great night that was. I have such fond memories of you two."

"We made a sport out of shopping," said Susan, "that's for sure."

"Shoe shopping, as I recall."

"Your mom had more shoes than anyone has a right to own. She was always in search of the perfect pair."

"And what about that trip you two took to Hawaii?" said Elizabeth. "I bet you've got lots of great stories about your adventures there."

"Yeah…well…" Susan glanced at her watch. "I hate to say it, but it's getting late, Elizabeth. I really should get back."

"Of course, don't let me keep you." They walked out together and hugged in the parking lot. "So good to see you, Susan. Enjoy those grandkids, and let's stay in touch, okay?"

The next morning Elizabeth phoned her sister. "Happy Easter, Jessica."

"Oh, same to you, thanks," Jessica said. "What are you up to today?"

"We're heading out to John's sister's house for dinner later, like usual. Right now the girls are on a sugar high, scarfing everything in their Easter baskets."

"I remember when my kids did that too, though it was a

long time ago," said Jessica. "Megan and Jack are coming over here later to eat. I was hoping Justin would make it home too, but he couldn't."

"That's too bad," said Elizabeth as she remembered something she wanted to tell her sister. "Hey, you'll never guess who I ran into yesterday at the donut shop."

"Who?"

"Susan! She's in town visiting her son and his family."

"Oh, how is Susan? We haven't talked in—gosh, I guess it's been several years now."

"She looks great and loves living in Florida. She's happy as can be babysitting Laurie's daughter. You know, doing the grandparent thing."

"That's nice. I could handle some of that myself!"

"Give Megan time, for goodness sake, she just got married! Don't be so pushy."

"Just wait, you'll get the bug once your girls get older."

"Seeing Susan made me think about her and Mom again," said Elizabeth. "Remember when they had their falling out and wouldn't even speak to each other?"

"Yes, I remember."

"I always wondered what happened between those two, about what caused the split," Elizabeth said. "It was odd. Mom would never explain their fight, and it went on for a couple of years. She'd change the subject or flat out refuse to discuss it."

"Lucky for us they made up," said Jessica. "Susan was such a good friend to Mom those last four years when she started getting sick. She filled us in on problems Mom was having that we wouldn't have known about otherwise."

"I know, Susan was a godsend, looking out for Mom the way she did," said Elizabeth. "But what did happen between those two anyway?"

"You mean when they wouldn't have anything to do with each other?"

"Yeah, I never got a straight answer out of Mom."

"You really wanna know?" Jessica asked.

"Well of course I do," Elizabeth said. "Otherwise I wouldn't have asked."

"They had a blow up on their trip to Hawaii."

"Oh, that was Mom's dream vacation," Elizabeth said as she recalled the details. "When was that—'91 or '92?"

"That sounds about right."

"I didn't realize they stopped hanging out after they got back. Now that I think about it, Mom never talked about that trip much."

"Because they got into it in paradise," Jessica said as if it was the end of the story.

"But what happened?"

"Mom invited Duke to join them without Susan's permission," Jessica said.

"What?" Elizabeth said. "You mean her boss?"

"Yeah, Duke showed up a few days after they arrived without any warning," said Jessica. "After that Mom spent all her evenings with Duke while Susan refused to join them because she was so angry."

"No wonder Susan was so upset!" said Elizabeth. "They saved for ages and spent a load of money on that trip. How could Mom do that to her?"

"Susan was furious and never would have agreed to go if she had known Duke would be there. Mom never told her anything, and he just turned up unannounced."

"Why—why didn't you tell me before now?"

"Susan told me in confidence," said Jessica.

"You should have told me years ago," Elizabeth said.

Jessica heard her sister's voice breaking. "I'm sorry, Elizabeth. I just thought—"

"Never mind, I gotta go."

Elizabeth put the phone down without waiting to hear her sister say goodbye. All her life she'd idolized her mother as a woman who had a deep faith in God and could do no wrong. Now her sister was telling her—no, it couldn't be true. If there had been something going on between Duke and her mother, she would have known. She wanted to get in her car and drive to Litchfield that minute to confront her mother. *Not much point in that,* she thought. *I don't really know that woman anymore. Did I ever?*

Looking for answers, Elizabeth went to the family room and started taking photo albums down from the bookshelf. Somewhere in one of these albums there must be something that would tell her the truth. A photo of her college graduation caught her eye, and she remembered the ceremony.

"Elizabeth, be sure to send Duke one of your announcements," Janice had said. "He'll want one."

"Are you sure, Mom? I don't want your boss to think he has to send me any money."

When she came to her wedding photos she remembered finalizing the guest list with her mother and Janice had said, "You must invite Duke to your wedding."

She'd protested, "Mom, he lives in Belleville, he won't come."

"It doesn't matter whether he does or not," Janice had said. "I just want to make sure he gets an invitation, that's all."

Elizabeth began to wonder if they'd been lovers from the very beginning. Going further back she stumbled upon one of Janice, Duke and her all posing with arms intertwined at a banquet hall, tables formally set for a meal behind them. It had been taken at the company's annual convention, and Janice had invited Elizabeth to stop by during happy hour to "say hello to Duke while he's in town."

"Won't he have more important things to do at the convention than say hello to one of his secretary's children?" Elizabeth had asked.

"Oh, he takes an interest in all his employees," Janice had said.

Flipping pages, Elizabeth settled on a print of Janice sitting at the dining room table during a visit to Elizabeth and John's apartment in Kansas City, which brought to mind the strangest request her mother had ever made regarding Duke.

"Elizabeth, I need you to look for used cars for sale in the area for Duke," Janice had said out of the blue one afternoon. "Duke's always wanted a Mercedes, and he's decided it's now or never since the scare with his heart attack."

"What?" Elizabeth had said with a laugh, caught off guard. "Mom, I don't know a thing about cars!"

"I told Duke you could just check around and do the legwork for him."

"No way, Mom. I am not vehicle shopping for Duke, and that's final!"

"But I already told him you would."

"Sorry, but you should've checked with me first," Elizabeth had said as she tried to understand. "Why would you expect me to roam the city in my Corolla scoping out a Mercedes Benz for your boss?"

"Can't you make the time to help him out?" Janice had said.

"He can do that himself. Better yet, he can hire someone who actually knows something about cars to do it for him." Elizabeth had refused the task, and her mother had sulked about it for weeks afterwards.

Janice beamed in another photograph with her own new automobile. She'd bought it after receiving a promotion in the early '90s when the company expanded its services. Along with Duke she'd been appointed to the board of directors and received a substantial pay raise. Her new job duties had included trips to the southern office for days at a time, prompting the need for more reliable transportation. Looking back, it made perfect sense why she enjoyed those business trips so much and focused all her time and energy on her job.

Elizabeth collapsed in a heap, convinced of Janice's guilt by the testimony in pictures strewn across the carpet. *If I was that blind to my mother's flaws,* Elizabeth wondered, *what else have I not seen? Have I really been as much a victim of the divorce as I've always thought? What about Tom's claim that Mom insisted he stay away? Have I been blaming Tom for things that weren't his fault?*

Elizabeth realized that in the past few years as Janice had deteriorated, she and Jessica had grown closer as sisters. Elizabeth had more or less forgiven her for abandoning the family and exposing her to Teri's relentless bullying. *Was I wrong about Jessica, too,* she wondered. *Oh my God—have I been wrong about Teri all this time?* Elizabeth felt like her brain was going to explode. She couldn't think anymore.

She recalled Teri's brutal bullying all too well, and she'd always assumed that Teri was the source of the whole family's dysfunction. Teri, who just couldn't clean up her act no matter how much anyone did for her. But was their mother, the mother who had always doted on Elizabeth, the real reason that Teri could never pull herself together?

Flipping further through photo albums, Elizabeth remembered times when they'd been really small. Teri had tried hard to do things to please their mother, but she had never been interested. But if Elizabeth did anything, praise always followed. *I've been wrong the whole time,* she thought. *I've blindly accepted the world according to Janice Kraus, and hurt so many people—including my father.* She didn't know how much more of this she could take and sat on the floor in a daze.

"Hey, hon, if you're off the phone could you help me—" John said as he bounded down the stairs. "Whoa—what's going on here? You looking for something?"

"Yes," said Elizabeth, looking up to reveal her splotchy face, "my mother's innocence."

"Okay then, did you find it?" John walked over and sat down.

"You won't believe it." Elizabeth began to sob and covered her face.

"Try me."

"Mom . . . and Duke . . . were lovers . . . for . . . years. Jessica let it slip today, and I wondered if I could see it on her face looking back."

"Oh."

"You aren't surprised?" Elizabeth looked up and saw acceptance.

"No, I can't say that I am really."

"Why?"

"I always wondered about him," said John. "Like a used car salesman pushing a lemon, you know? He rubbed me the wrong way."

"Not you too?" said Elizabeth. "My friends always asked about my mother. 'Does your Mom have a boyfriend? Will she ever get married?' I always answered those questions the way I saw it—she was too hurt to ever allow anyone to betray her again."

"I don't think you're far off base there. She did choose a lifestyle that prevented her from ever remarrying."

"I am such a fool, John! She was carrying on with Duke right under my nose the whole time—probably from the beginning when she started working for him! If she lied about that, what else was she dishonest about?"

"Sorry, Elizabeth," said John as he rubbed her back. "But it doesn't matter anymore, does it?"

"It's important to me! I wrote my father off because he cheated on my mother!"

John remained silent.

"Don't you see? What she did was so much worse because it went on for years and years, and Duke was married with kids. How could she condemn my father and then turn around and do the exact same thing?"

"Come on, Elizabeth. It's not our place to answer that kind of question."

"She hid their relationship all those years because she knew I wouldn't approve. And it's too late for me to demand the truth. Not now when she's so sick."

"What good would that do, honestly? We all make bad decisions—make mistakes. She's made them, and you've made them because of her. So what? The only thing that matters now is taking care of her because she's ill. She needs you."

"You're right, but I feel like I've lost her all over again." Elizabeth hung her head and wept, mourning for minutes before finally speaking up. "You suspected her and Duke—why didn't you ever say anything?"

"Because she's your mother, Liz. And I know you love her."

"Uh-huh," said Elizabeth. "I get it, kinda like we never questioned what was going on with your dad and my mom?"

"Yes, exactly," John said as he shoved photo albums out of the way and pulled his wife close as her eyes filled with tears.

"My family—they all knew. Why? Why didn't they level with me?"

"Probably for the same reason I didn't."

"I feel so stupid," said Elizabeth with shame, unfamiliar with the sentiment. "How can I face them now?"

"Well, you're not the first in your family to do something foolish," said John as he lifted her chin to look directly in her eyes. "And you won't be the last either. So you're in good company."

⁓༄⁓

"Sorry to bother you, Tom," Jessica said to preface her late-night call. "But there's a problem."

"What's wrong now?" said Tom, muting the television to prepare for the worst.

"Elizabeth just figured out what was really going on between

Mom and Duke all those years—" Jessica paused when she couldn't find the words to continue.

"Oh my, she's a bit behind, isn't she?" said Tom with a chuckle. "Sorry, I know it's not funny, but what's the big deal?"

"She had no idea—none—and fell to pieces. You know that scene in *Bambi* when his mother dies?"

"Yeah," said Tom.

"It felt like that—heartbreaking! I killed the mother she knew and loved. She was so upset that she hung up on me!"

"I can see how it'd be a shock. It took me years to stomach it, and thankfully the distance between me and Mom made it easier."

"None of us have ever discussed this before. It's—awkward," said Jessica, reluctant to mention it even now.

"Yeah, I know. Maybe we thought by not bringing it up that it would just go away?"

"Listen, I'm really worried she's gonna bail on us," said Jessica, getting to the real reason for her call. "You know, refuse to pay Mom's bills and manage her finances."

"Oh no, there's no way she'd ever walk out on us like Teri."

"You sure?"

"Think about it, Jess. Elizabeth's the baby. She's been spoiled her whole life, so she has a blind spot where Mom is concerned, that's all. Just give her some space, and she'll come around."

"I hope you're right," Jessica said.

"Even if I'm wrong you don't have to worry. I'd figure out how to handle the money from down here if I had to."

"You mean it?"

"We're in this together, Jess—until the end."

16
Fortress Around Your Heart

2008

⸻ ∞ ⸻

And if I've built this fortress around your heart
Encircled you in trenches and barbed wire
Then let me build a bridge
For I cannot fill the chasm
And let me set the battlements on fire

—Sting

⸻ ∞ ⸻

"**R**uth passed away yesterday," Jessica told Elizabeth over the phone on a snowy Sunday afternoon in February of 2008.

"Oh, I'm so sorry to hear it," said Elizabeth. "Just a minute, Jess. What is it that can't wait until I'm finished with this call, Katie?"

"Can I go play in the snow now, please? I'm getting hot." Katie fidgeted while waiting for her mother's inspection: coat, snow pants, boots, hat, scarf; only her hands were left uncovered.

"Go get some waterproof mittens from the front closet, then you can head out."

"Thanks, Mom!"

"Sorry about that," said Elizabeth to her sister. "Katie's been waiting for a big snowfall to build a fort—now's her chance with over eight inches on the ground. So how's Dad holding up with Ruth's death?"

"Not great, he's a mess."

"That's understandable, they were together a long time."

"Over thirty years," said Jessica. "Teri and I are driving up to Chicago tomorrow, roads will be cleared by then. Dad thinks the funeral will be on Wednesday, so we'll be up there probably until Thursday. You wanna go with us?"

Jessica wouldn't have dared update Elizabeth on anything to do with their father in the past, but things had changed since she'd discovered her mother's affair. Over the last year she'd been trying to re-establish ties with her family. She'd let Jessica know she was interested in their father by asking for his address and phone number in Chicago. Starting with little gestures, nothing big, she sent holiday cards with brief messages and even burned CDs of her favorite Christmas songs to share with her siblings and father. The gift felt like a small victory when Teri, of all people, called to thank her after listening to the music.

All of Elizabeth's siblings had maintained some sort of relationship with their father as adults, except for her. She had found distancing herself from him to be easy after her wedding to John; she didn't need anything from her dad and he was miles away. Her mother had been so pleased that she didn't think twice about cutting him out of her life. Finding her way back proved to be much more difficult.

"Three whole days? I can't possibly be gone that long with the girls and work," said Elizabeth, grabbing the easiest excuse to hide

the real reason for her hesitation. She just didn't know where to
start with her dad.

"Okay, I'll email you the funeral details when I get them," said
Jessica. "I already talked to Tom, and he's flying up Tuesday night.
You're welcome to join us, we'll all be there."

"I'll need to check my schedule—and talk with John. I'll
let you know. Thanks for passing along the news." *I should go,*
Elizabeth thought as she hung up. *Attending the funeral would be a
great way to show my father I still care, and I've been trying to figure
out how to do that anyway.*

By the morning of the funeral, she still hadn't made up her
mind. "I just don't know if I can handle it after all this time," she
said to her husband over breakfast.

"There's no snow in the forecast, Elizabeth," said John, looking up from the newspaper. "And you'd have no problem taking
the day off work. Why don't you just go? What are you so worried about?"

"I'm scared he won't want me there," said Elizabeth. "I never
made any attempt to get to know Ruth. What if he kicks me out
in his grief?"

"All I know is you'll never regret going, even if there is a
scene," said John, "but you'll definitely regret *not* going, because
you'd never know what would have happened."

"That's true—"

"I can get the girls to school and pick them up, no problem."

Elizabeth looked at the kitchen clock. *The funeral is at noon,*
she thought, *so I still have time to make it.* "Okay, I should go."

She made the three-hour drive north without telling her family she was coming and wrestled with what to say to her father over
every mile. With Jessica's directions she located the funeral home
right away and arrived with ten minutes to spare. Paralyzed with
fear as she parked, she sat frozen to her car seat like the piles of
snow that dotted the edges of the neatly plowed lot. She could not

convince herself to move no matter how good the intentions that had brought her this far.

At twelve forty-five Elizabeth was still debating in her car when people filed out the doorway, wiping at their downcast eyes with tissues or blowing their noses. Along with the mourners she started up her car and followed the procession to the cemetery only four blocks away, cursing herself for failing to show her face at the funeral.

Not far off the main road into the cemetery, a lawn tent stood over artificial grass for the graveside service, six folding chairs placed nearest the stark brown earth upturned on the snow. Headstones poked from the drifts all around, a blanket of white hiding the stories of those laid to rest. Immediate family claimed their seats up front—Ruth's sister and Ron first, followed by Tom, Jessica, and Teri. Remaining loved ones and friends crowded in to stand behind the family, stomping snow from their boots. Elizabeth followed the flow and ducked into the back, pulling her hat lower on her downturned head.

Mindful of the weather, the minister made only a few remarks before offering a prayer. Ron then stepped forward and placed his hand on the coffin for only a moment before giving the caretaker the go-ahead to lower the casket. As he turned for his seat, Ron studied those standing beneath the tent, grateful to everyone who had braved the cold. Just as his eyes came to rest upon Elizabeth in the back row, she looked up to meet his gaze and nodded her head.

The minister released the crowd at that moment, and Ron was surrounded by condolences and hugs. Elizabeth wasted no time making her way back to her car and left the cemetery both panicked and relieved that her father had seen her.

⁓∘⊙∘⁓

Jessica found the opportunity to pass along more news about their father when she treated Elizabeth to a birthday lunch the next month. "Dad's moving to Springfield," she said after they had ordered from their favorite Mexican restaurant. "He's already found a place and should be here before summer."

"Really?" said Elizabeth with a sip of her margarita. "Wow, that hits the spot. What about his house in the suburbs?"

"He cleaned it out and put it on the market," said Jessica. "Without Ruth there's nothing left to keep him in Chicago. He decided it was time to move closer to his own family now that she's gone."

"Huh, that's really odd."

Jessica swallowed her chips and salsa. "How so?"

"He's going to be living in the same city as his three daughters for the first time since the divorce—and that was thirty-two years ago."

"Never thought of it that way, but you're right. It's going to be quite an adjustment for him."

He's not the only one who'll need to adjust, thought Elizabeth. *I need to figure out how to handle this myself. I can't even start a conversation with my own father, how pathetic is that? And he's almost eighty now, meaning he's probably too set in his ways to change. Unless I do something we'll continue at odds until time runs out—strangers who just happen to live three minutes apart instead of three hours.*

As fall approached Elizabeth started hearing her sisters mention their father more frequently. Then she ran into him unexpectedly at a Halloween party Jessica threw to show off her two-month old grandson, Megan's newborn son Logan. Elizabeth realized she needed to take action when their encounter proved painfully awkward. For everyone's sake she needed to find a way to ease the tension between her and her father.

Elizabeth decided to host a holiday gathering between Christmas and the New Year to welcome their father back home. She buried herself in the details and invited her siblings and all of their families. With nail-biting anxiety she extended a special request to her father by email, in hopes he would accept the apology buried within the message. Her sisters accepted at once, and her brother phoned his regrets.

"I'm sorry I can't make it, Elizabeth," said Tom. "I'm flying out the next morning for Japan to meet with our investors, and they don't like delays."

"I figured it was a long shot, but I crossed my fingers that you might manage it somehow."

"Wish Jane and I could be there, really do," said Tom. "I think it's great you're reaching out to Dad this way, getting to know him better."

"Better? I don't know him at all, except for the horrible things Mom told me about him all those years."

"I have some great memories of him—vacations we took, playing ball in the backyard, helping with my homework."

"He split when I was eight, Tom, and he was missing in action for years before that. You may have happy-go-lucky *Father Knows Best* memories from your childhood, but my upbringing went more like *One Day at a Time*—no man around the house."

"Okay, I get it. Want me to call him—give him a nudge in the right direction maybe?"

"Suit yourself—guess it couldn't hurt though."

"Will do then. Let me know how it goes, okay?"

As the holiday approached Elizabeth was consumed with worry waiting for the guest of honor to respond to her invitation.

"Hello?" she said after grabbing the phone, certain it was her husband to pass along a warning about the weather, but she already knew about the ice storm. Three days before Christmas she was sprawled on the floor amidst mounds of presents and wrapping paper.

"This is your father calling," Ron said.

"Oh—hi there—what a surprise," Elizabeth said. She hadn't spoken to her father in an eternity, yet his voice still sounded familiar.

"It is indeed," said Ron in agreement, followed by a long pause.
Elizabeth had no one to blame but herself for the words she could not speak.

"Listen, I'm calling about your dinner invitation," Ron said to fill up the dead space of Elizabeth's shock. "I won't be able to make it."

"Oh, I see. Well, okay, thanks for —ummmm, I appreciate it—yeah then, sorry you won't—I mean, can't come." What made her think her father would jump at her offer? It was too little, too late, and she was an idiot to have hoped it would work.

"I'm sorry, Elizabeth, I just can't do it, although I'm happy you wanted to include me in your plans," Ron said. "But fifteen years is far too long, and I can't just come waltzing into your house pretending like everything's fine."

"I know, I understand. I just thought since you've moved back home that maybe we should try—"

"Try to get along?" said Ron.

"Yes, get along, exactly," Elizabeth said. *Fifteen years,* she thought, *has it really been that long?* She must have blocked the passage of time to soothe her guilty conscience. His explanation was perfectly valid, and for that reason incredibly irritating.

"Well, if you're serious, then you and I should get together to talk—alone. We need to meet face to face," Ron said.

"How about next week then?"

Ron sighed. *Can I do this now,* he thought. *All I want is to be left alone to get past the holidays, but it just won't come quick enough. Without Ruth there's nothing merry about this time of year.* "Okay," he said.

"All right, great," Elizabeth said.

"Just call me next week about it," Ron said. "Goodbye."

"Wait, are you angry with me?" Elizabeth said, wondering why he was ending their conversation so abruptly.

"Angry? Yeah, well, I guess you could say fifteen years has left me with a need to clear the air, which is why we need to talk."

"I'm sorry, Dad." Elizabeth's voice cracked with regret. She hated the way she sounded, pathetic and guilty. "I'm sorry for my indifference and for doing nothing to repair the damage that's been done."

"You certainly aren't the only one, Elizabeth. I'm as angry at myself as I am at you. We're both responsible for what's happened, and neither one of us is perfect. We both share the blame, and we're both headstrong. It runs in the family, remember?"

"I'd like to work on us, okay?" Elizabeth said.

"Listen, you're my daughter and I love you, but we need to straighten things out between us. We'll have to work on our relationship if you really want it, okay? We'll see how things go from there."

"Okay, I will, for sure."

"Merry Christmas to you and your family. See you next week."

Elizabeth's composure crumbled as she grappled over the exchange of less than five minutes. The bravery she had mustered to reach out to her father had been matched by his courage to make contact with her. After what she'd done, she didn't feel worthy of her father's love.

As it turned out Elizabeth's party never happened.

"Elizabeth, I'm sicker than a dog," said Teri two days before the dinner.

"Oh no, what's wrong?" said Elizabeth over the phone as she eyed the calendar in her kitchen.

"I've been up puking all night, and I've got a fever."

"Geez, that doesn't sound good."

"Listen, I don't wanna spread any germs. I'm not gonna make it, and I wanted to let you know as soon as possible."

"Okay, thanks. I sure hope you're feeling better soon."

Megan added Logan to the list of the infirm several hours later. "Sorry, Elizabeth, but this is his first fever. We need to stay home."

"I understand, poor baby. Another time, okay?"

Jessica called to check in soon after. "Well, timing is everything, isn't it?"

"Oh no, you're not feeling well either?" Elizabeth asked.

"No, no, I'm fine. I just meant everyone dropping like flies right now."

"I know, it's really a bummer."

"I can still come if you want. We can have our own mini-celebration."

"Would you mind too much if I postponed, Jess?" Elizabeth tried to hide the disappointment in her voice.

"Absolutely not, that's fine." Jessica felt bad for her sister. Here she was trying to do something nice and get the family together, and everyone was backing out.

Elizabeth was left with mixed feelings. She had planned and prepped for this homecoming with great hopes, and she couldn't help but question the rash of illness. Was everyone really sick, or had they changed their minds about coming to her party? Her rational mind told her not to fret, but her bruised ego worried that it might be too late to make amends. This setback strengthened her resolve to find out for sure.

Elizabeth turned her attention back to her father and arranged a date to meet as he had requested. Thankfully she didn't have long to wait for their historic luncheon. She arrived at the Chinese restaurant dressed in her warmest coat on a frigid day with the high temperature in the single digits. Like the scarf wrapped around her neck she was bundled in nerves, and the cold weather only made matters worse.

"Hi, hope you haven't been waiting long," Elizabeth said as she slid into the booth opposite her father. She busied herself taking off her gloves and parka to avoid eye contact.

"No, I just got here a few minutes ago," Ron said matter-of-factly, but he had already been served hot tea.

"That looks good. It's freezing out there!"

"Here, let me pour you some."

"Thank you." Elizabeth sipped tea, hoping to find strength at the bottom of her cup. With no such luck, she was forced to look up at her father across the table. Where should she begin after fifteen years?

"Well, I've decided to keep our first meeting easy," Ron said.

"Okay, sounds good," Elizabeth said as she glanced around. Suddenly she felt ill at ease because of the way her father's voice carried like a megaphone. He must be losing his hearing, and she was embarrassed to think of the diners nearby eavesdropping.

"I'd really like to hear about you—your job, the kids, stuff like that. But first I need to decide what I want."

"I'll have the moo shu pork, it's delicious."

"Moo shu? What's that?"

"Um, it's kinda like a Chinese burrito, I guess." Elizabeth couldn't help but stare at her father as he grilled the waitress before ordering. She hadn't seen him up close in ages, and it was obvious by looking at him that his health had been compromised by emphysema, inevitable after smoking since he was fifteen. Just like she remembered, his eyes were still a deep blue, and she admired his curiosity and composure. He must have noticed the changes in her appearance as well, since she had matured from a newlywed to a soccer mom during the length of their separation.

Ron and Elizabeth covered a variety of topics, ranging from the bleak weather to the disparity between living in Chicago and Springfield. His intelligence had not diminished in the slightest, a striking contrast to Janice. As the table was cleared Elizabeth knew it was time to say what had been postponed for too long.

"Thanks for agreeing to see me, Dad," Elizabeth said. "I know it's hard—for both of us. I've got a lot to make up for, but I have to start somewhere."

"Yeah, I know, but I'm not very good at this sort of thing."

"I was wrong about you," Elizabeth said, launching into the apology she'd rehearsed a thousand times in her head. "It's no excuse, but I was just a miserable kid swayed by Mom's bitterness."

"It's not your fault, Elizabeth. You were the secret weapon in her arsenal—the blow that hurt the most."

"I didn't understand what was really going on—"

"Oh, and you think you do now?" said Ron, his eyebrows raised in question.

"I know that it was wrong to blame you for everything, especially after finding out what was going on with Mom and Duke."

"Ah, okay, so you do know." He leaned back and nodded his head.

"You don't seem surprised in the least, so obviously you knew too?" She lowered her voice and pushed a glass around the table. He waited to speak until she looked up at him.

"I did—almost from the beginning."

"How?" Elizabeth said. "How did you know?"

"The lockbox." Ron said calmly.

"The lockbox? What about it?"

"Your mother and I had a lockbox for important documents."

"I remember it," said Elizabeth. "She showed it to me in case I might need to get into it—if something ever happened to her."

"The combination was my birthday."

"10-18-30, she made sure I knew that."

"When our divorce was final, she gave me the key to the house one day while you girls were in school—I was given two hours to get all my stuff out."

"You still had personal things in the house?"

"A stamp collection, old books, just things taking up space. Nothing important really."

"So?"

"I found the lockbox while I was there," Ron said. "I'm not

proud to admit I was snooping, okay? I opened it when I shouldn't have, but I wanted to know what she was up to."

"Okay, that would have been around 1976. What did you find?" Elizabeth leaned in close to hear.

"There was a letter she had written to Duke in there."

"What did it say?"

"I won't go into detail. Trust me, it would be too embarrassing for us both. But it was clear they were—um—involved. She had written to tell him exactly how she felt about him—to share her dream for a life together."

"But that was over thirty years ago!" Elizabeth ran her fingers through her hair while she thought.

"It was a love letter," Ron said. "They were carrying on all along."

"But you never said a word! Never stood up for yourself, never let on! She blamed you all those years, talked bad about you. Why didn't you defend yourself and set the record straight?"

"Why?" he said with a soft laugh, mulling over his answer carefully. "Well, I guess it was because I knew you kids needed her, and I wasn't around to look after you."

"So you took the bullet—for her?" Elizabeth couldn't believe what she was hearing. Her perception of her family had been so screwed up—the victims and the villains could not be sorted into black and white but were instead a study in gray.

"If that's the way you wanna look at it, then yes." He shrugged his shoulders. "But I don't see it that way. What difference does it make anyway?"

"It means everything to me." Elizabeth turned to look out the window and wrapped her arms around herself to stop the shaking. "Don't you see? I'm so sorry, and I don't know what else to—"

"Forget it. Let's just leave it behind us, okay?"

"Dad," Elizabeth's lip quivered.

"No, it's okay," Ron said as he held his hands up to stop

her tears. "What's done is done. And we're all guilty, one way or another. No need for more apologies."

"But—"

"We're square, you hear me? Let's not dwell on the past when we can fix the future instead."

"Just like that?" Elizabeth dabbed the corners of her eyes with a napkin.

"How about we do lunch again when it's warmer, say in March?" Ron said after paying the bill. "The cold weather makes it hard for me to breathe, so I'd rather wait for spring."

"I'd like that," Elizabeth said, the edges of her lips turned up slightly. "Next time you call me."

17

The Hounds Of Winter

March–May 2009

―――――― ∞ ――――――

A season for joy
A season for sorrow
Where she's gone
I will surely, surely follow

I still see her face
As beautiful as day
It's easy to remember
Remember my love that way

—Sting

―――――― ∞ ――――――

E lizabeth arrived at the nursing home as the residents finished their midday meal and spotted her mother at the table in the corner. "Good afternoon, ladies," she said, resting her hands on the back of her mother's chair. "I'm Janice's daughter, and it's nice to see you all again."

"Oh, aren't you pretty," said Missy with a gap-toothed grin. Marge scowled and bent low over her plate while Edna pretended not to hear.

"Why, thank you, how kind," Elizabeth said as she kissed her mother's cheek. "Hi, Mom, it's good to see you." She didn't feel the need to announce her mother's seventy-fifth birthday to this hen house since they were unlikely to break into song.

"Hi, I'm Amber," said the aide feeding Janice by baby spoon.

"Oh hello, I'm Elizabeth. Looks like she's eating decent today. Can I take that job off your hands?"

"Sure, I'll go help Nancy, thanks," said Amber before rushing off.

Elizabeth sat in Amber's seat, studied the plate of mush and took a whiff, guessing at the menu by the colors—brown, white, and green. As she alternated between what she assumed to be roast beef, mashed potatoes, and peas, she assessed her mother's condition. She still looked the same, maybe a bit thinner.

Like usual when not flat on her back in bed, Janice was propped up in her geriatric chair, the equivalent of a La-Z-Boy on wheels. Her movements were monitored by the safety alarm pinned to her right shoulder, and she wore a bib to catch the gruel that dribbled past her jaw. Dependent on others for her meals, she swallowed birdlike portions, as if eating required absolute focus.

Janice sat twisted like a pretzel: arms wrapped around her midsection, legs pulled up to her side, fingers clenched into fists. This fetal position was possible because the footrest of her chair was extended. For no apparent reason, her left arm shot up high in the air, like a student requesting permission to ask a question. No inquiry passed her lips, however, because she had not spoken a word in four years, since the stroke and seizure.

Applying gentle downward pressure, Elizabeth attempted to lower Janice's arm but failed. "One good thing about all this, Mom," she said, "no one would ever recognize you now."

Janice looked nothing like the beauty who had walked through the nursing home door nine years ago, the aging process sped up like a time-lapse video in that time. For starters, her wardrobe demanded function over fashion. To allow for easy dressing and laundering she wore sweatpants and button-up tops over an undershirt and diaper. Her neatly cuffed socks were bright white because her shoeless feet never touched the ground; she had not walked in four years either.

Her wiry head of white hair was cropped short like a man's and always looked like she'd just rolled out of bed. As her illness progressed her weight had fluctuated wildly and her wrinkled skin finally surrendered in confusion, hanging off her limbs in defeat. Age spots dotted her hands and arms, mingling with bruises that appeared without explanation. Her pale complexion gave away her confinement indoors, and her muscles drooped from lack of use.

No other part of Janice's body bore the attack more than her teeth. She developed a nasty habit of grinding them, and many were cracked, chipped, or broken off, several to the depth of her gums. Her precarious state prevented sedation for proper treatment, so the problem went from bad to worse over the years. Because she could not communicate it was impossible to tell how much pain she was in. She clamped up and refused to let anyone poke around inside her mouth or even brush her teeth, leaving her with bad breath that could knock a person off their feet.

Elizabeth stopped her inspection when Janice clenched her jaw shut, indicating lunch was over. After wiping the spittle from her face, she wheeled her mother past the nurse's station to the family room.

"Okay, Mom, let's get straight to work then." Elizabeth enjoyed this part of their visits most of all. She pulled out her supplies and brushed Janice's hair in a misguided attempt to make it lie flat. Next she cut and filed her mother's jagged fingernails, then finished up by slathering Vaseline on her chapped lips and massaging lotion on her skin.

"Sure wish you could tell me if you like this or not."

Dementia has stolen everything from my mother in the last thirteen years, Elizabeth thought—*her personality, job, freedom, home, money, memory, mind, dignity, happiness, and finally her health. She has only one defense left: her extraordinary will to live. This last trace of her fighting spirit must be what continues to keep her alive.*

Somewhere along the way Elizabeth allowed herself to accept her mother's fate by letting go of the things she could not change. She found the strength to cast off the selfish desires that spoiled every visit. She stopped watching for a smile of recognition and waiting for her name to be spoken one last time. Without expectations she was freed to enjoy what little time was left and the simple pleasures that remained with Janice, like holding her hand, painting her nails, reading to her, or wheeling her outside to feel the sunshine on her face.

Elizabeth rolled her mother back for her afternoon nap, wondering how many more birthdays she could possibly endure. Winter crept in and curled up at the foot of the bed, content to wait out the waning days of the season. Sensing a chill in the air, she felt the need to call her brother for some reason.

"Hey, Tom, did I catch you at a bad time?" asked Elizabeth.

"I'm at work, but it's okay. What's up?"

"Well, I'm here with Mom and wondered if you wanted to wish her a happy birthday? She's seventy-five today."

"Shit, I forgot her birthday," Tom said. "I've never done that before."

"No problem, just talk to her now," said Elizabeth.

"Okay, sure."

"Here, Mom, it's Tom," said Elizabeth as she held the phone to Janice's ear, then leaned in close. "Go ahead, Tom."

"Hi, Mom, happy birthday! I hope the sun brings warmer

weather to you soon. I'm thinking of you and love you." Janice
didn't twitch a muscle. Without a response, Tom saw no reason to
carry on.

"Great, thanks," said Elizabeth when she heard nothing.
"Hopefully that registered someplace, although I didn't see it here."

"So, how's she doing anyway?"

"The same, I guess." To be honest, all Elizabeth's visits were
alike now, and she hesitated to describe the abyss that had become
the norm. There was nothing more to report.

―⁓⁓―

"I'm sorry to break the news this way," said Cindy over the phone
one day in May, "but we believe the end is near for Janice based on
the signs over the last week."

"What? Are you sure?" Jessica asked as she spilled coffee all
over the newspaper spread across the table.

"She's taken only liquids by straw the last eight days," said
the nurse. "I already told you she wouldn't open her mouth for
solid food."

"Yes, I remember."

"But this morning Janice would not wake up, no matter what
we tried. She's panting now, and she's lost twenty pounds in the
last three weeks."

"Oh dear, that's not good, is it?"

"I'm afraid not, Jessica. With the DNR in place, we're monitoring her and keeping her comfortable, but there's nothing more
we can do for her."

Janice's nosedive could be traced back to the grinding of her
teeth, which caused an incisor to crack in half the month before.
Dr. Wagner had ordered a dental assessment after the CNAs
reported the grimaces she made while eating and drinking. She
lost her appetite soon after, likely caused by a toothache.

"Janice's teeth are rotting away, luckily without any sign of infection at this point," a local dentist said after an exam made possible by a sedative. "But the one causing the pain needs to be pulled."

"I was afraid of that," Jessica said, hoping to avoid the scenario. "We tried to have dental work done years ago, and she reacted so badly that we've been afraid to do anything since."

"How exactly?"

"She got so upset with the poking around inside her mouth—thrashing about and wailing," said Jessica as she flung her head and arms around for emphasis. "We were afraid she was going to have a heart attack, it was that scary."

"I see," the dentist said as he rubbed his chin.

"Since she wasn't in pain at the time, leaving things alone seemed like the best option."

"I've dealt with dementia patients before, and I'm certain I can handle things this time around to avoid any trauma."

"Are you sure?" Jessica winced at the memory of the episode, but there was no other option to help Janice eat.

"Absolutely, let's get the extraction scheduled."

The procedure was performed without incident using a local anesthetic after another sedative, which knocked Janice completely out. After coming around she seemed unaware that anything unpleasant had happened.

The chronic pain, along with the drugs and oral surgery, took a greater toll than first believed. Janice ate less of her all-pureed food as the days passed, forcing extra fluids. These nutrient-rich shakes soon replaced solids altogether as she would drink only through a straw. The liquid diet triggered weight loss faster than a celebrity detox plan, and soon the staff dosed medicine as a last resort to boost her appetite.

The notice set off a four-alarm fire over the phone lines. "Hey, Cindy just called to say they think Mom's dying." Jessica blurted the news before her sister mustered a greeting.

"We've heard that before," said Elizabeth. "Hospice gave her one month to live over three years ago. Look how that turned out."

"I know, but this seems serious. She won't eat or get up, and she's dropped a ton of weight in the last month."

"How much?"

"They said twenty pounds."

"What? Oh, that's a lot." Elizabeth stopped flipping through the pile of mail. "You tell Teri yet?"

"No, she's next on my list."

"I'll let Tom know then," said Elizabeth. "I'm tied up this morning, but I'll check on her this afternoon."

"Okay, I'm heading up in a bit. I'll call you later."

Elizabeth delivered the report to her brother. "They claim she's dying, Tom, so this appears to be serious." Living far away, he needed to understand the prognosis to plan his next move.

"Oh no," said Tom. "Well, what do you think?"

"I'm not convinced at this point, and you know Mom. She may have some surprises left for us. She won't roll over and play dead just because someone gives the order, that's for sure."

Janice had rebounded before, so recovery still seemed possible. After walking into room 113 to judge for herself, Elizabeth changed her mind. At first she thought her eyes were playing tricks. Janice lay on an air mattress to prevent bedsores, and her leg looked about the size of an arm poking from beneath a sheet. Her skeletal frame betrayed just how serious her condition had become in a short period of time.

"Oh my God," said Elizabeth as she sank into a chair and wrapped her arms around herself. "She didn't look anything like that a month ago."

"I know, it's crazy," Jessica said as they perched beside the bed.

"How's she doing, Jess?"

"Nothing has changed. She won't respond or open her eyes."

Jessica and Elizabeth discussed only the basics they dared speak aloud, and then took turns wetting Janice's chapped lips by dipping a sponge on a stick in a glass of water. The efforts backfired as she clenched her jaw whenever moisture touched her mouth. Over the next few days her eyes and cheeks sank farther into her skull, and Teri joined her sisters on guard beside their mother's bed. Four days after Janice stopped eating, Tom cleared his calendar and flew home to spend what little time was left with his mother.

Since the four siblings rarely touched ground in the same state, Elizabeth decided to host a meal and bring everyone together under her roof at last. This dinner would mark the first time her father attended a gathering in her home. The timing seemed right since Janice remained stable, even though she had not touched food or water in the last eight days.

The reunion was interrupted before strawberry pie when Jessica's phone rang, and she left the table to answer. "This is Jessica," she said from the safety of the family room. "What is it?"

"It's Cindy, and I think you better get here. It's time."

"What's going on?"

"Janice's breathing has changed, and her legs have started to turn blue."

"I see—"

"I'm sorry, hon, but these are the things that happen when the end is near. There's no need to rush, so please be safe. But we've gone from days to hours left now."

"My whole family is here—every one of us."

"Is there anyone else we should call then?"

"No, you just rounded us all up." Jessica felt eyes boring into her and tried to squelch the panic that threatened to buckle her knees. "We're on the way, thanks."

"Strange," Tom said as the diners scrambled to clear the table. "I wonder if Mom planned this departure time."

"What do you mean?" asked Teri as she grabbed for dishes.

"Well, I mentioned we'd be here tonight when I visited with Mom earlier."

"So you think she waited for us all to be together?" said Elizabeth, glancing from sibling to sibling. "Leave this stuff, let's get going."

Everyone scattered for the unknown to come. Ron made his excuses and slipped out to let his children wrestle with their emotions alone, not wanting to impose on their grief. With no clue what came next or how long it might take, the Kraus siblings changed their clothes for more suitable attire, packed their overnight bags, and arranged backup plans with spouses before regrouping at Good Samaritan Place.

Jessica arrived first for the status report from Cindy. Elizabeth followed next and tried to calm her fears outside the door to her mother's room, only to fall apart the moment she entered. "How can she still be alive, Jessica?" she asked her sister in a whimper.

Before them a shell of a woman vanished into thin air, nothing more than bony joints poking out from beneath a blanket. Her cheeks had sunken farther into her skull, her hair was smashed against her head, and her vacant eyes stared off into the nothingness that consumed her.

"I don't know," Jessica said without looking up. She could not meet her sister's gaze, so she bowed her head and clung to her mother's hand.

"What's with the Darth Vader racket?" asked Elizabeth.

Janice strained to breathe and droned a disturbing sequence of sounds. Each quick gulp forced a low groan, followed by a clatter of congestion with the release. The effort to maintain this gasping—inhale moan and exhale clang—sapped the last of her strength.

"The aide called it the death rattle—it's common at this point. Her lungs are filling up with fluid."

"Okay, then. Is she in pain?" Elizabeth brushed back her mother's matted hair and kissed her forehead.

"The nurse said it sounds worse than it feels."

"Like she'd know. Look at her, Jessica. She's exhausted, dehydrated, and disappearing before our eyes. We have to do something!"

"Well, morphine was already suggested," said Jessica as she shifted back in her seat and crossed her arms.

"But?"

"But they said it could speed things up—bring the end quicker because her breathing would be suppressed by the drug."

"You've got a problem with that?" Elizabeth's eyebrows rose in question despite her best effort to remain nonjudgmental.

"Well, I—just don't want to be the one—" Jessica squirmed under the scrutiny.

"You do understand this is hell on earth for her now, right? Would you want to struggle like this?"

"No, of course not. But it's a crappy decision to make for your mother."

"Fine, then I'll make it. If that was me I'd want the show over as soon as possible—for my kids' sake." Elizabeth was unsure about every other decision they had made on their mother's behalf in the last nine years, but this time she was certain.

"Oh, all right then, have it your way." Jessica dashed off to pass along the request before she changed her mind.

Cindy returned with Jessica, and the narcotic was given in liquid form by mouth without need for an injection. Tom and Teri showed up soon after and were warned that time was running out.

"I don't know about you guys," said Tom, "but I'd like some time to speak with Mom—privately."

"Good idea," said Jessica. "Me too."

"Okay, I'll wait outside then." Teri wandered off down the corridor past the darkened doorways of the slumbering residents with Jessica close behind.

"Go ahead. You go first, Tom," said Elizabeth before following her sisters out of the room. On her solitary stroll she thought, *what exactly is the last thing I want to say to my mother?*

Tom started his apology when they were alone. "I'm sorry, Mom, for not sticking around when you needed me most—after the divorce and when you got sick."

Janice's eyelids did not move, but Tom turned off the light to lessen her strain just in case. "But I'm here now, and I love you . . . so very much." He wept by cover of night.

"I don't want you to go," Jessica said when it was her turn. "It's like losing a part of me, and I don't know who I'll be without you. Even like this, as you are here, you still make me who I am today. And I'm so grateful, Mom." A quarter moon traipsed across the sky, content to cast a waning beam on her body draped over her mother's bed.

"Timing's a bitch, isn't it, Mom?" said Teri. "I finally figured out . . . how much you mean to me . . . after all these years. And just when I get my act together . . .bam, you get snatched away. But you must know—I've always loved you." June bugs pelted the window screen in reply, and Teri watched the beetles flit off in search of light elsewhere.

"You can let go now, Mom," Elizabeth said in confidence, like they shared a secret none of the others could guess.

Janice tilted her head in Elizabeth's direction and fluttered her eyelashes. Startled by the reaction, she bent down to examine her mother's face up close. Was she actually listening? Elizabeth shivered at a northern breeze that dared to intrude and then rubbed the goose bumps that dotted her arms.

"Thanks to you, and all you've done, we're all fine. There's nothing to worry about any more. You did your best, and your work here is done. I love you, Mom, and it's time now, okay?"

Elizabeth adjusted the blanket and pressed her lips to her mother's hand, but she shed no tears. She had prayed for this moment for years, begged for the end even. Death was the only way out.

Confessions were called to a close when Janice's breathing slowed and the death rattle disappeared. Tom, Jessica, Teri, and Elizabeth settled in around her bed, rotating positions to give everyone the chance to hold her hands. Instead of closing tight, her eyes opened wide without alarm or remorse for a life already stripped away.

Everyone followed Janice's gasps, willing her to carry on by copying her breathing. Endearments were offered up as the time between each intake extended to an agonizing length.

"I love you, Mom," Teri said as the end seemed near.

"Go now," said Elizabeth under her breath with one hand on her mother and the other resting on Teri's shoulder.

Unable to continue at the dwindling pace, the Kraus siblings had all drawn in air when Janice stopped breathing and surrendered to Alzheimer's disease. They remained motionless around her for some time, holding onto her body in silent prayer.

—ເວວວ—

"I'm home." Elizabeth woke her husband later as she crawled into bed and kissed his cheek. "Mom died around 11:30 tonight."

"Oh, I'm so sorry, honey," said John as he rolled over and pulled her close.

"No, I'm glad it's over—glad she's not suffering any more. I'm okay, really."

"You sure?"

"Yes, go back to sleep. We'll talk more tomorrow."

Elizabeth wrapped relief around herself like a comforter and drifted off with mixed emotions that conjured the solace her heart demanded.

In Elizabeth's dreams Janice followed tire tracks on foot down a dirt road towards a farmhouse rising from the fields. Newly sprouted plants surrounded her and swayed in the breeze, the rows extended miles in every direction towards the horizon. The crop coaxed her onward and led the way to a homestead set against a brilliant blue sky. Her pace quickened to a jog as she neared, and recognition lit her face. The anticipation burst into a peak of adrenaline, and she found herself winded, unable to call out the names of the loved ones she ached to see again.

As Janice dashed up the steps of the porch, the screen door creaked open. An older man and a younger woman hurried outside to greet her. She heard a familiar bang as the door closed behind them. Tears wet her cheeks as she rushed towards her mother Helen. They embraced in a hug that erased the past and promised of a great future.

Janice felt all the pain she had lugged along her entire life begin to drain away. Releasing her mother, she was wrapped in the arms of her grandfather.

"We've waited so long for this day," said Helen as her hands came to rest on Janice's shoulders. "And now you're here."

"Together at last," George said with a pat on her back, "just as it should be."

Janice was beside herself with joy at this reunion. Happiness flooded every corner of her spirit as she realized she would never again leave her mother and grandfather. Now they would be together for eternity, the only thing she ever wanted or needed, although she had not realized it until this moment. She sensed that they had secrets to share, but there was no need to explain. She had faith they would guide her onward and remain by her side.

"There are others waiting to see you too, darling," Helen said as she squeezed Janice's hand and led her to the rickety door. "We cannot make them wait any longer."

Around them the cornstalks, just beginning to grow once again, would ripen and wither forever in the sweet Nebraska fields because Janice was finally home.

18

Why Should I Cry For You?

May 22, 2009

Dark angels follow me
Over a godless sea
Mountains of endless falling
For all my days remaining
What would be true?

—Sting

"I thought I was prepared for this." Tom addressed less than twenty friends and family gathered in Smithburg for Janice's funeral. "Thing is—" he said as he looked from his sisters to their spouses and children, "my speech isn't going to work for this group . . . it doesn't fit."

"You okay?" Jessica mouthed to her brother from the front row. Beside her, Teri and Elizabeth shot a questioning glance at each other.

"Yes, I'm fine," said Tom as he leaned his elbows on the

podium. "We're all family here, with a few exceptions. Susan and Cindy, thank you both for coming today, it means a lot."

Both ladies nodded in reply.

"Mom's been away for a long time, so I understand why her former friends and co-workers wouldn't come. They all moved on with their lives." Tom lowered his head and sighed deeply. "The rest of us here, we all know how Mom's story ended."

"Uh oh, we've got a problem here," said Elizabeth. "He's really struggling."

"What do we do now?" asked Jessica.

"Don't look at me," Teri whispered. "Is he crying?"

Reverend Wentworth approached the podium and placed a hand on Tom's shoulder. "Should I continue, Tom?"

"No, please." Tom looked up with watery eyes. "There are things I need to say—give me a minute to get my thoughts together."

"That's fine," said the minister. "We're in no hurry here. Just let me know if you want me to take over."

Jane ached for her husband's grief and prayed he'd find the strength to continue. Sitting between Justin and Jack, Megan reached for her husband's hand. Ashley and Amanda slouched in their chairs next to Eddie, who had come in support of his children and ex-wife. John wrapped his arms around Claire and Katie, who fidgeted on either side of him in their uncomfortable dresses. Walt leaned back and crossed his arms, the only relative from Nebraska. Everyone waited in silence as Tom collected himself.

"I guess . . . what I want to tell you is . . . I'm sorry," said Tom at last. "It's hard to stand up here as a spokesperson for the family when I haven't been around much for the last thirty years, that's all. Yet I offered to give the eulogy . . . rather pretentious of me . . . under the circumstances."

Elizabeth was on her feet when Tom's voice cracked with regret. *This won't do at all,* she thought. *He needs help.*

"Let me try to explain," Elizabeth said as she slipped her arm around her brother's waist and faced her family. "As the oldest, Tom tends to blame himself for things, making him feel the need to apologize." She turned to her brother, "But it's not necessary, Tom."

"I just want to—"

"No, I got this. Please listen." Tom gave up and sat back down in the front row while the congregation turned their attention to Elizabeth. She searched their faces for someone, but just as she suspected, Ron was not among them. Although she had spotted her father in the parking lot earlier, he had chosen not to come inside.

"I have a confession," Elizabeth said with a heavy sigh. "I used to blame Tom too. In fact, I blamed all of my siblings …and our father… for our screwed up family."

"Where exactly is she going with this?" asked Teri.

"Shhhh, be quiet," said Jessica.

"But Mom's illness—so agonizing and drawn out—has taught me a lot in the last thirteen years. And here's the thing—there's no point in blaming anyone. Not you or you, or even you, Teri."

"What? Really?" said Teri.

"We all know Janice had a troubled life, from her childhood to her final years and everything in between. She did the best she could, in spite of the hardships she faced, for herself and for her children."

Elizabeth saw heads nod in agreement, and it gave her the nerve to continue.

"Those difficulties made her the person she was, and she passed on what she learned to each of us, in different ways I'll admit. By example she showed us how to be strong in the face of adversity. She proved that love was enough to keep us together— even when everything fell apart, and she taught us to laugh loud and long whenever we had the chance. And for the things most precious to us, she taught us how to fight back. We're especially good at that, right?"

A round of laughter made Elizabeth pause and smile.

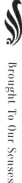

"She was as stubborn as they come. But I've come to realize this defining trait was her final gift to us. She stubbornly clung to life, refusing to give up for so many years, even when we prayed and begged for God to release her from her suffering. By lingering for so long . . . and through so much . . . she gave us the time we needed . . . to come to terms with our own lives, and more importantly to accept each other, faults and all."

Elizabeth shut her eyes to stop the tears that wet her cheeks and held up her hand as she paused, determined to finish. "Mom waited until she was sure we'd all be okay . . . and then she let go. So I just want to say 'Thanks, Mom' for being so pigheaded. Because I needed that time to realize how much my family means to me . . . Mom knew it, and I know it . . . we're all going to be all right. And I love you all."

Tom was at Elizabeth's side before she uttered her last words, and Jessica and Teri followed close behind. They pulled each other in tight for a group hug, crying and celebrating in a huddle of emotion completely out of character for the family. From an eight-by-ten portrait on a table front and center, Janice smiled at the spectacle.

Reverend Wentworth guided the Kraus children back to their seats as the nose blowing and sniffles subsided. "That was no easy task," he said when he returned to the podium. "I couldn't give my own mother's eulogy, and I speak for a living. Thanks to both Tom and Elizabeth for that touching tribute to Janice. I don't think there's any way I can top that, but I'll try my best to wrap things up."

―⁂―

Janice's children, grandchildren, and friends assembled at the gravesite during a lull in the showers that had fallen on and off all day. "Look, Grandma's stone already has her name and birthday on it," Katie said as she pointed to the monument beneath a sapling. Only the date of death was missing.

"I know, I had it set here years ago when I picked this spot," said Elizabeth. "From this hillside you can see the corn for miles and miles. I knew Mom would approve of the view."

A small hole surrounded by piles of black earth reminded everyone of the purpose for their gathering. Tom stepped forward in the wet grass since Elizabeth had released the minister from further duties.

"Our Father who art in heaven, hallowed be thy name . . ." In unison, their voices joined together and held off the downpour.

Elizabeth lost track of the prayer when she spotted a solitary figure leaning against a massive oak tree down the hill. Even from the shadows she recognized Ron, who stood with head bowed and hands folded to pay his last respects from a safe distance. *How about that,* she thought. *I guess we'll be able to count on Dad from now on.*

After finishing "The Lord's Prayer," Tom nodded and the elderly groundskeeper hobbled forward with Janice's remains. He dropped the urn in the hole, which triggered a loud plop in response.

"Well, Mom always did love to swim," Teri said, delivering her punch line with perfect timing. A fit of giggles defied the graveyard gloom.

"Oh, that's too funny!" Elizabeth laughed as she planted a kiss on her sister's cheek.

"Remember how Mom made us all take lessons when we were little?" Teri said.

"How could I forget?" Elizabeth said before turning serious. "And by the way, I did ask Harold not to come today. He just didn't listen to me." The others watched the caretaker shovel dirt into the hole.

"Well, I guess he's no different than the rest of us," Teri said, failing to keep a straight face. "Nobody likes a know-it-all."

"Or a bully," Elizabeth said, watching for her sister's reaction.

"You're right, like usual," Teri groaned, looking around at their family. "How does anyone put up with us then?"

"They have to—because we're family," Elizabeth said with a shrug.

"Hmmm, thank goodness for that." Teri moved to embrace her sister but couldn't bring herself to do it and instead pushed Elizabeth away playfully.

The raindrops waited only long enough for the hole to be filled, ushering everyone's departure. Meanwhile, rays of sunshine pierced clear sections of blue sky.

"Come on over to my house," Jessica hollered as everyone dashed to their cars.

As she left the cemetery Elizabeth thought, *I wonder if Mom would have been pleased with the service?* Her reflections were interrupted when she looked out the window and caught sight of a breathtaking rainbow. She could make out each distinct color of the spectrum spread across the northern skyline. Her voice caught in her throat, and she could find no words to speak. *Could it be a figment of my imagination, some coping mechanism conjured by my subconscious mind?*

"Mom, Dad, look!" Claire said as she pointed.

"Oh, wow, that's a big one, how pretty!" said Katie. "Do you see it, Mom?"

"The rainbow connection?" Elizabeth smiled at John as he drove. The phenomenon couldn't have been more obvious unless accompanied by a choir of angels singing "Hallelujah" in divine harmony.

19

I Was Brought To My Senses

September 2009

If nature's red in tooth and claw
Like winter's freeze and summer's thaw
The wounds she gave me
Were the wounds that would heal me

—Sting

"Tom Kraus?" said the nurse from the door to the waiting room.

"Oh, hey, I just got called back for my appointment," Tom said to his wife as he stood up. "I'll let you know as soon as I'm done here, okay?"

"We've got a schedule to keep, watch the time," said Jane. "Friday flights are always booked solid."

"I will, promise. Goodbye." Tom silenced his cell phone as he followed the nurse beyond the examination rooms to a private office in the back. She ushered him in with a smile and shut the door as she left.

Dr. Sorenson closed the single file on his desk. "Please have a seat, Tom," he said as he took off his readers.

"Thanks," said Tom. "I know you're a busy man, so let's not beat around the bush. What are the results of all those tests?"

"First, I want to point out once again that—"

"Never mind all that, the waiting has been torture," said Tom as his hand shot in the air. "You've poked and prodded, scanned and tested, collected samples, and reviewed lab work. What's the verdict?"

"You're not guilty," said the physician, his face set like a bone in a cast.

"Huh? What does that mean?"

"It's good news, Tom," said Dr. Sorenson, breaking into a grin at last. "I've found nothing that would suggest the onset of dementia."

"But—are you sure?" Tom asked. "After all the problems I told you about?"

Tom had sought out a medical opinion when his internal alarm had sounded like a winter storm warning. The lost wallet and misplaced car keys were easy enough to explain away. Even the overlooked dental appointment seemed like no big deal. Calling colleagues by the wrong name had raised some questions however, and he admitted those lapses had occurred a number of times in meetings or while crossing paths in the workplace. The trivial flurries he had brushed off began to accumulate into a snowfall of incidents, and suddenly he feared for a blizzard.

"Look, I understand your concern with the family history and all," said the doctor. "But right now nothing indicates a cognitive impairment of any kind. The issues you describe can all be chalked up to normal aging."

I find it hard to believe the "senior moments" theory, Tom thought. *My behavior of late reminds me of the reports I used to get* *about my mother. And I'm fifty-five, the same age she first started showing the telltale signs of Alzheimer's.* "The mental test?" he asked. "What did you call that one?"

"The mini-mental state exam," said Dr. Sorenson. "Your score was in the acceptable range—twenty-nine out of thirty."

"Wait, I missed one on that? You gotta be kidding me."

"It's normal, few people get a perfect score."

"And the CT scan?"

"No evidence of problems there."

"Well, that's a relief anyway."

"Are you under any stress at work, Tom? That might explain what's going on here."

"Of course I am, we're trying to launch a new product on schedule," said Tom. "But that's not unusual, I deal with deadlines and setbacks all the time."

Out of embarrassment Tom hesitated to bring up the flight to Tokyo that he'd missed last month. His boss had blown a fuse because he'd never before done anything so stupid. He couldn't understand how he had bungled the departure time and showed up two hours late. "I forgot" did not cut it when a million dollar deal was on the line. The blunder was the reason he had sought out professional help.

"You need to eliminate as much pressure as possible. It can really mess you up."

"I'm not sure there's much—"

"Take a vacation, learn to meditate, relax over the weekend." Dr. Sorenson interrupted to stop the excuses. "There are plenty of things you can do."

"Okay, I'll try," said Tom as he noted the diplomas hanging on the walls and medical tomes on the shelves. "As a matter of fact, I'm leaving town for a little R&R after we get done here."

"Great, that's a good start then," said Dr. Sorenson. "Listen, we've established a cognitive baseline with these tests, and you're fine, trust me."

"I can't help it with—you know—with what happened to my mother."

"Look, I've been your doctor a long time, right?"

"Over twenty years now," Tom said with a nod.

"I know you, okay? And I'm telling you to stop worrying and live your life." Dr. Sorenson stood and opened the door. "We can follow up on this again next year—compare future results to the ones we've just confirmed. Until then, you've got to relax."

"Okay, thank you, Doc," said Tom with his arm extended for a handshake. He waited until he reached his car to phone Jane. "Good news. The doctor told me everything's just fine."

"See, honey, I told you it wasn't anything to worry about. So I'll meet you at the airport like we planned?"

"Yep, I've got my suitcase with me, and I'm ready to go celebrate in a different time zone. See you in a half hour."

—⚬⚬⚬—

"Megan, I don't think this jacket is big enough for Logan," said Jessica as she helped ready her grandson to leave. "He's grown so much, you may have to buy him a bigger size."

Megan dropped the diaper bag on the couch and eased up the zipper on the fleece hoodie. "Hmmm, it'll work for tonight when it gets colder, but you're right. He's definitely going through a growth spurt since his first birthday."

"You're such a big, strong boy, aren't you?" said Jessica as she tickled Logan to make him giggle.

"Dada, Dada," said Logan, bouncing his Velcro sneakers off the sofa cushions when he saw his father approach.

"Can I take this to the car with the food?" Jack asked as he picked up the diaper bag on his way to the garage.

"Thanks, babe, that would be great," said Megan. "We're almost ready to go."

Jessica reached for her phone when it vibrated in her pocket. "Hi, Justin, we're just getting ready to head out. Where are you?"

"Chicago traffic was awful, but I just passed Lincoln, so I should be there in about a half hour," said Justin on the road from his convertible.

"Great, we'll meet you there then. Drive safe!"

"You sure it's a good idea for me to come along to this?" asked Becca from Justin's two-seater after he hung up.

"Absolutely, don't worry Becca." Justin rested his hand on her thigh. "My mom loves you—can't stop talking about you every time I call her."

"But breaking our big news tonight?" she asked while twisting the diamond solitaire on her finger.

"It's going to be the perfect place for our announcement, trust me."

Teri was headed in the same direction with her daughters. "Ashley, I'm so glad you could make it home this weekend. You've been away four whole weeks. Sounds like you needed a break to me."

"Geez, Mom, I'm a junior now. College is supposed to be hard," said Ashley with a laugh from the passenger seat. "But I love it, and my classes are awesome now that they're in my major. I've learned so much on my clinical rounds, you wouldn't believe it."

"I want to hear all about it. And I'm so proud of you, honey, for going into nursing. Your grandmother would be proud too."

"Oh, Mom," said Amanda from the back seat. "Stop with the warm and fuzzy lovey-dovey talk. Yuck."

"Just wait, Amanda. You'll be off to college before you know it, and I'll be gushing about you too!"

"I'm only a sophomore, Mom. But wherever I end up, I gotta play soccer," said Amanda. "That's all I want."

"I know, you killed it at the game last weekend. You should've seen her, Ash. Two goals in the second half, and she's playing varsity this year!"

"You got a game this weekend, Amanda?" Ashley asked over her shoulder.

"Yep, tomorrow morning at ten against our arch rival. It's payback time for that last loss if I have anything to say about it!"

"Maybe I'll catch that with Mom since I don't head back till Sunday. You can show me your moves."

"Deal!"

"Oh good, your father will be at that game too," said Teri as she looked up to see Amanda beaming in the rearview mirror.

—⁂—

Elizabeth surveyed her backyard from the doorstep with her hands on her hips. "How does it look to you, John? I want everything to be just right."

"Wow, fantastic," John said from the garden. "You've done a great job. This place will light up the night when the sun goes down."

Elizabeth had worked for weeks to transform their patio for the party. She had wrapped a pergola of climbing vines in twinkling lights overhead and scattered hanging baskets of red flowers and ferns around the cushioned wicker furniture. Glasses, plates and utensils glimmered against the late day sun from a long table in the grass laden with fifteen informal place settings. Antique candle lanterns were lit as centerpieces to ward off the day's end. Tiki torches lined the perimeter of the terrace, and piano music drifted from the back window.

"Mom, are there enough drinks in this tub?" Katie asked as she shoved water bottles down deep in the ice. "Yikes, that's cold!"

"Yes, I think that should do. Thank you, darling."

"What about the snack bowls, Mom?" said Claire. "I've got one right here, and a couple over on those tables."

"Hmmmm, what do you think, Dad?" Elizabeth walked towards the double glider where her father sat supervising the last minute details.

"I think it's perfect, Elizabeth," said Ron as he swung back and forth slowly. "You've really outdone yourself, which is saying a lot."

"I'll check on the lasagna and direct everyone outside," said John as he headed for the kitchen. "It's time for our guests to arrive."

"I think we're ready," said Elizabeth with a sigh.

John leaned out the screen door a few minutes later, a funny look fixed on his face. "Elizabeth, sorry, could you come inside for just a minute?"

"What's wrong?" While hurrying past the butcher block island loaded with baskets of garlic bread, Elizabeth caught her breath along with the unmistakable stench of a problem. "I don't like the sound of your voice, and what's that smell?"

"The lasagna is ruined."

"What? Are you kidding me?" She eyed the covered dish he held out with oven mitts as proof. "Surely some of it can be salvaged? I like the cheese burned a little bit anyway."

"Nope, both pans a total loss, see?" John pulled back the aluminum foil to reveal a miniature model of Death Valley, blackened beyond rescue.

"Oh, for heaven's sake." Elizabeth poked at the charred remains with a fork as she realized her mistake. "I forgot to set the timer!"

"We'll have a yard full of hungry people soon. Now what?"

Elizabeth closed her eyes and raised her fingers to her lips, as if in prayer. "Figures I'd screw this one up, doesn't it?"

"Well—Elizabeth?" John checked the digital clock on the stove.

"Oh my, we're gonna have to wing it here." She covered her

mouth to stifle a groan that quickly turned to a chuckle before a full attack of laughter. "Ah ha . . . pizza is Italian, right?"

"I guess you could call it that," said John.

"Let's order Gabatoni's then—they'll have it ready in a jiffy. Problem solved."

"Okay, that'll work. Good thinking, hon," John said as he went to search for his phone. "I'll make the call."

"Right, thanks. I need to get back outside."

"Oh, here you are," said Jessica to Elizabeth as she and her family came through the gate to the backyard. "Here's the salad ready to serve. You couldn't have ordered better weather to eat out here."

"Hi, Grandpa," said Megan as she sat Logan down on his lap. "How about a swing with your great-grandson?"

"I can't think of anything I'd like more," said Ron as he pulled Logan close. "Nice to see you again, Jack."

"Hi everyone," said Tom as he and Jane were led out by John. "We made it on time!"

"Oh, Elizabeth," said Jane as she clapped her hands together at the scene. "Look what you've done back here. It's gorgeous!"

"It is pretty cool," Tom said as he snagged a beer from the tub and took the open seat on the glider. "Hi, Dad, looks like you've got a special friend there."

"Why am I always last?" asked Teri when she arrived minutes later. "You can't start without me and my girls." Ashley and Amanda rolled their eyes, grabbed sodas from the ice, and settled on the cushions nearest the munchies.

"Justin's not here yet," said Jessica. "He's running a little late."

"Did I hear my name?" Justin said as he covered his mother's eyes from behind her back. "Surprise, I've brought along someone I know you'll be glad to see again."

Jessica swatted Justin's hands away as she spun around. "Well, Becca, hello. I had no idea you were coming!"

"Yes, well, we wanted to—"

"Listen up," said Elizabeth. "We're all here now, so let's gather around the table before things get out of hand. I'd like to start the evening off right."

"Oh, okay then, it can wait." Justin shrugged at Becca.

Claire and Katie hurried to help everyone find their assigned seats, and the family assembled on the lawn just as the setting sun painted the horizon in shades of orange and pink. Elizabeth stood at the center of the table, where the framed photograph of Janice from the funeral had been placed and surrounded by red roses.

"I'd like to offer a toast to our mother," Elizabeth said, raising her glass. "Over the years she nearly drove each and every one of us nuts. And in the end her life got pretty crazy. Along the way there were times when I was sure she'd pushed all of us permanently apart. But her stubborn will to keep going, no matter what, and our efforts to take care of her is what finally brought us to our senses. Without her we wouldn't all be here today, and for that I am so grateful. Here's to Janice."

"To Janice," they all repeated as wine and water glasses clinked together around the table. "Hear, hear!"

Request For Readers

Thank you for reading my novel. If you enjoyed the story, please take a minute to leave an honest review wherever you buy and discuss books online, like <u>Amazon</u>, <u>Barnes & Noble</u>, and <u>Goodreads</u>. The best support an author can receive is enthusiastic, word-of-mouth recommendations from satisfied readers.

Your opinion and feedback matter to me, so feel free to reach out and send me an email to BroughtToOurSenses@gmail.com. I'd love to know what you think about the book.

Thanks again,
Kathleen

ACKNOWLEDGEMENTS

THIS NOVEL IS a dream come true; I've wanted to write since I was a bespectacled bookworm devouring every children's series in my grade school's collection and Lincoln Library, classics like *Nancy Drew* and *Little House on the Prairie*. I could not have written *Brought To Our Senses* without the help of many others. I am grateful for the encouragement offered by so many incredible people in my life, and I am blessed by those I have come to know while working on this story.

First and foremost, I need to thank my mother. Her strength and courage in the face of Alzheimer's disease helped me to find my voice and a story to tell. Thanks to my husband and children for their love and support as I toiled for many years on this project. My daughters are the reason I strive to raise awareness about Alzheimer's disease. My greatest desire is for a cure to be found so their generation will never experience the devastation of dementia. Thanks also to my creative muse Sting, whose music and songwriting I've admired since the post-punk era. I find inspiration to follow my heart and tackle new endeavors after watching the calculated risks he's taken over the years to grow as a musician and artist.

Thanks to my beta readers for the time they devoted to reading the numerous drafts of my story and for their excellent feedback: Jill Robinson, Ann Jirmasek, Greg Kyrouac, Jeanne Campbell, Tina Arnold, Karel Homrig, Jill Kinnett, Brenda Cawley, Eliza Maxwell, Gretchen Hodges, Nada Holland, Jean Lee, and Dr. Daniel C. Potts.

I am grateful to the talented and creative professionals who helped craft the final version of this novel. Thanks to the editors who polished my novel for publication: developmental editing by Lynne Melcombe Communications and line editing by Mary Yakovets. Thanks to Damonza for the fantastic book cover and interior design and Scott McCullar for other graphic elements. A final thanks to Brenda Bucher for her photography services.

ABOUT THE AUTHOR

KATHLEEN H. WHEELER is a child of divorce and Alzheimer's disease called to tell a tale. She writes stories that sing because she cannot, and her work has been featured in *Chicken Soup for the Soul*, newspaper, trade, and academic publications. A graduate of the University of Illinois, she has worked as a marketing communications professional for ad agencies and corporations since Nike first coined the slogan "Just Do It." Wheeler is a self-professed music enthusiast and lifelong fan of a British musician known by a one-syllable nickname. Along with her husband and two children, she calls the Land of Lincoln home. Learn more at AuthorKathleenHWheeler.com and subscribe to her mailing list for updates at AuthorKathleenHWheeler.com/subscribe.

Made in the USA
Lexington, KY
25 September 2017